Books by Shirleen Davies

Historical Western Romance Series

MacLarens of Fire Mountain

Tougher than the Rest, Book One
Faster than the Rest, Book Two
Harder than the Rest, Book Three
Stronger than the Rest, Book Four
Deadlier than the Rest, Book Five
Wilder than the Rest, Book Six

Redemption Mountain

Redemption's Edge, Book One
Wildfire Creek, Book Two
Sunrise Ridge, Book Three
Dixie Moon, Book Four
Survivor Pass, Book Five
Promise Trail, Book Six
Deep River, Book Seven, Releasing 2017

MacLarens of Boundary Mountain

Colin's Quest, Book One,
Brodie's Gamble, Book Two
Quinn's Honor, Book Three

<u>*Contemporary Romance Series*</u>

MacLarens of Fire Mountain

Second Summer, Book One
Hard Landing, Book Two
One More Day, Book Three
All Your Nights, Book Four
Always Love You, Book Five
Hearts Don't Lie, Book Six
No Getting Over You, Book Seven
'Til the Sun Comes Up, Book Eight, Releasing
2017

Peregrine Bay

Reclaiming Love, Book One
Our Kind of Love, Book Two

The best way to stay in touch is to subscribe to my newsletter. Go to www.shirleendavies.com and subscribe in the box at the top of the right column that asks for your email. You'll be notified of new books before they are released, have chances to win great prizes, and receive other subscriber-only specials.

Kindle Readers: Sign up to follow me on http://www.amazon.com/author/shirleendavies to be notified of new releases as they become available. It's the Follow button just under my photo on the left side.

Quinn's Honor

MacLarens of Boundary Mountain

Historical Western Romance Series

SHIRLEEN DAVIES

Book Three in the MacLarens of Boundary Mountain

Historical Western Romance Series

I care about quality, so if you find something in error, please contact me via email at shirleen@shirleendavies.com

Description

Quinn's Honor, Book Three, MacLarens of Boundary Mountain Historical Western Romance Series

"Every book of Shirleen's never fails to draw me in and make it impossible to put down until I devour it!"

Quinn MacLaren has one true love…Circle M, the family ranch. He makes it a habit of working hard and playing harder, spending time with experienced women who know he wants nothing more than their company. He buries the love he feels for one woman deep inside, knowing he'll never be the man she needs.

Emma Pearce is a true ranch woman, working long hours to help keep the family ranch thriving. Feisty, funny, and reliable, she's the girl all the single young men want—after they've sewn their wild oats. Few know Emma has her heart set on one man. A man who may never grow up enough to walk away from his wild ways and settle down.

When tragedy strikes, Quinn's right where he doesn't want to be—as temporary foreman of the Pearce ranch. Stepping in to fill Big Jim Pearce's shoes isn't easy. Neither is keeping his feelings for Emma hidden and his hands to himself. Honor-bound to do what is right, Quinn meets the challenge, losing Emma's friendship in the process.

Adding to Quinn's worries, something sinister is working its way through the thriving town of Conviction. Unforeseen forces are at work. Debt builds, families lose their ranches, and newcomers threaten to divide not only the land, but the people—including the Pearce family.

As events unfold, Quinn faces the difficult challenge of keeping his feelings for Emma hidden and his honor intact. Doing what he believes is right couldn't feel more wrong.

After all, what's a man without honor?

Quinn's Honor, book three in the MacLarens of Boundary Mountain historical western romance series, is a full-length novel with an HEA and no cliffhanger.

Visit my website for a list of characters for each series.
http://www.shirleendavies.com/character-list.html

Acknowledgements

Many thanks to my editor, Kim Young, proofreader, Alicia Carmical, and all of my beta readers. Your insights and suggestions are greatly appreciated.

As always, many thanks to my wonderful cover designer, Kim Killion, and Joseph Murray who is superb at formatting my books for print and electronic versions.

Quinn's Honor

Prologue

Conviction, California
December 1864

"Tell me I'm dreaming." Quinn MacLaren sipped the punch his cousin, Blaine, had spiked with whiskey, watching two young women walk into the church Christmas social.

Blaine chuckled as he tipped his glass up and took a sip, his gaze catching sight of the two dark-haired ladies. "You mean there are women in Conviction you *haven't* met?"

"I think you need to be more specific, Blaine. Quinn doesn't waste his time with innocents. I believe his tastes go to older women. Those he doesn't have to train." Caleb Stewart, a man the MacLarens considered family, glanced around, noticing several ladies he had yet to meet. "I, on the other hand…"

Quinn placed a hand on his heart, feigning hurt at his friend's comment. "Ach, you make me sound as if I have no feelings for the women I spend time with, Caleb."

"You do?" Blaine asked, raising his eyebrows.

"Of course I have feelings for the lasses." He took another swallow, his gaze following another young woman as she and her family entered the room. She'd twisted her light blonde hair into an intricate knot, a few wisps escaping to fan her cheeks. Her bright blue eyes scanned the room, jerking to a stop when she spotted him. Quinn inwardly groaned when she licked her lips, a brilliant smile flashing before she turned away.

"Who has caught your interest?" Blaine followed Quinn's gaze, seeing Emma Pearce talking to his brother and sister-in-law, Colin and Sarah MacLaren. "I know it's not Emma, so who did you see?"

Quinn finished his drink, ignoring the question, asking one of his own. "Has anyone seen Brodie?"

"At the jail. I don't think he plans on coming over." Blaine's expression sobered. Their cousin and sheriff of Conviction, Brodie MacLaren, hadn't been the same since his fiancée, Maggie King, left him behind to return to Texas with her family. "It may take the lad a while to get over her."

"Then it's our duty to help him." Without waiting for a response, Quinn took one last look in Emma's direction, then headed for the door.

The townsfolk adored her, and most lads wanted to court her. It had been that way since he'd first met Emma. She attracted people the way honey drew flies. Vivacious with a wonderful sense of humor and a ready smile, she won people over with little effort. The same way she'd won his heart years ago. A fact he'd never shared with anyone.

Caleb didn't know how right he was in saying Quinn preferred older ladies with experience. Working hard and playing harder suited him just fine. He had no intention of settling down with one woman, and no business showing any interest in a sweet innocent such as Emma. Too bad the desire he felt for her never diminished, no matter how many years passed since he'd first been attracted to her as they sat side-by-side in school.

"Quinn MacLaren. You weren't planning to leave without saying hello to us, were you?" Emma's mother, Gertie Pearce, touched Quinn's arm before she slipped her hand through the arm of her husband, Big Jim.

Quinn's face softened. Gertie and Big Jim were good people, hardworking and generous, and the MacLarens' closest neighbors to the north.

"Never, Mrs. Pearce." Quinn shook Big Jim's hand, his gaze catching Emma's before he shifted his attention back to her father. "Colin tells me you bought a new bull."

"It was Emma's idea."

Quinn's gaze snapped to her. "That a fact?"

"Sure is. She's got it in her head we can produce better stock with him than the bull we've had for years." Big Jim shot an indulgent smile at his daughter.

"As good as any of the MacLaren cattle. Right, Papa?" Her blue eyes sparkled, her smile so bright, Quinn thought he'd be struck blind by the intensity.

"Now, Emma, I don't know about that. We'll give it a good try, though." Big Jim's chuckle died on his lips when three men walked into the room. Even though the gathering took place in a church, all wore guns, their hats pushed low on their heads, clothes caked with dirt. "Do you know those men, Quinn?"

Turning, he saw the men split up, pushing past people as they made their way around the room. On instinct, Quinn stepped in front of Emma, his hand moving toward his hip, remembering his gunbelt hung in the entry hall.

"No, sir, I don't." Shifting, he set his intense gaze on Emma. "I want you to take your mother and walk outside."

Emma's eyes narrowed. "But—"

"He's right, Emma." Big Jim looked at his wife. "Take her outside, Gertie. I'll come get you when I know what's happening."

Gertie took Emma's arm. "Let's do what your father says."

The glare Emma sent Quinn would have amused him if his gut wasn't telling him danger stood twenty feet away in the form of a stranger whose hard gaze roamed the room. A movement of the man's hand toward his gunbelt had Quinn shoving the women toward the door.

"Go. Now." His hard tone allowed no argument.

Gertie pulled a reluctant Emma behind her, reaching the door an instant before a shot rang out.

"Go!" Quinn shouted as a stunned crowd turned their attention to the man now standing on top of a table, his gun waving back and forth. A quick glance around showed his two companions at opposite ends of the room, guns drawn.

"Ladies and gentlemen, we've joined your party for one reason." He narrowed his gaze, his features hardening. "We want your valuables, not your lives." He grinned at the loud gasp. "No one will get hurt as long as you do what I say. I want you to create two lines. One in front of each of my boys. Put your money and jewelry in the bags they're holding."

Quinn's gut clenched as he searched the room for his brother, Bram, thankful his sister, Heather, and younger siblings had stayed away. Catching the attention of Blaine and Caleb, he inched his way toward the back door. If he could get outside, he might be able to circle around to the entry and retrieve his gun, surprising the robbers as they left.

"You there." Quinn froze, his eyes locking with the man pointing a gun in his direction. "You aren't thinking of doing something foolish, are you?"

"Stay put, son. Our money isn't worth your life," Big Jim said, his face hard with anger. "We'll let Brodie deal with them."

The thought of his cousin riding after the robbers didn't sit well with Quinn, but Big Jim was right. If the outlaw decided to shoot, a stray bullet could go anywhere, hurting or killing women and children. Quinn took a decisive step forward.

"Smart choice." The man switched his focus to the crowd. "Line up, ladies and gentlemen. And don't be stingy."

Emma listened through the open window, her heart hammering in her chest. "Mother, I'm going to get Brodie. You stay here." Before Gertie could object, she lifted her skirt and took off toward the sheriff's office.

Paying little attention to her surroundings, she jumped onto the boardwalk, yelping when she collided with a hard body. Strong hands grabbed her arms, holding her upright.

"Miss Pearce. Are you all right?"

Relief washed through her as she looked up at the concerned gaze of Sam Covington, one of Brodie's deputies. Pulling from his grasp, she pointed toward the church behind her, sucking in a breath.

"Outlaws. They're holding everyone at gunpoint."

"How many?" Sam reached for his gun, checking the cylinder.

"Three that I could see, but there may be more."

"The sheriff is at the jail. Tell him what you told me, then stay put. Don't come back."

Sam hurried to the church, watchful for others who might be with the outlaws. As he got close, he slowed, glancing over his shoulder to make sure Emma entered the jail.

Sam first noticed the eerie quiet from a room full of people celebrating Christmas. As he looked into the entry, he spotted the gunbelts hanging on the walls, weapons still in the holsters. Moving past the entry, he stopped below an open window. Rising, he peeked into the room, seeing the three outlaws, as well as many friends. His anger rose when he saw them dropping money and jewelry into bags held by two of the outlaws. Sensing movement behind him, he swung around, gun at the ready.

Holding up his hands, Brodie came to a stop. "Whoa, Sam," he whispered. Dropping his hands, he pulled out his revolver as two other deputies, Nate Hollis and Jack Perkins, ran to join them. "What do you see?"

"Three men holding guns on everyone. They're collecting money and jewelry." Sam hesitated a moment. "Your family is inside, Brodie."

"Aye." Brodie swallowed before looking at his deputies. "Jack, go around back to the right. Nate, you go around to the left. They must have horses in the back. Let them loose, then wait for Sam and me to join you. Do not go inside. We'll wait for them to leave."

"Do you want us to wound them, or..." Nate let the thought trail off, knowing his meaning was clear.

"They're pointing guns at our friends and families. If they get away, we'll be sending them to do the same to other innocents." Brodie checked his gun once more, then glanced at his men, his face devoid of emotion. "Shoot to kill."

Waiting until the two left, Brodie leaned against the side of the building, sucking in air, letting it out in a slow breath. "We wait until they're ready to leave, make sure they don't come this way, then join Nate and Jack in the back. You ready?"

Sam nodded. "Let's get this done, Brodie."

"Thank you for your generous donations. As promised, my men and I will leave you now to continue your celebration." The outlaw jumped off the table, continuing to hold his gun. "I'd suggest no one tries to be a hero. We won't hesitate to shoot." Nodding to his men, they backed toward the back door.

Brodie didn't hesitate. "Head to the right, Sam. I'll go this way." Running to reach the back before the robbers left, he came to a halt at the sight of Gertie Pearce pacing by a side door. "You shouldn't be here, Mrs. Pearce. Please, join Emma at the jail."

She wrung her hands, shaking her head. "Big Jim is inside, Brodie. I can't leave him."

Taking hold of her arm, he turned her away from the building, his heart pounding, knowing the outlaws would come outside any moment.

"I can't let you stay. There is going to be gunfire. Please. I'm asking you to go."

Turning her toward the jail, he let go of her arm, watching her leave. Spinning and continuing to the back, he winced at the sound of gunfire, reaching the corner of the building to see his deputies with guns trained on the men coming out the back door.

"Hands up! There's no chance you'll escape." Sam's voice rang out. "Drop your guns. Now!"

Brodie added his voice to Sam's. "Set down your guns and turn around. No one needs to die here."

In an instant, the scene broke into chaos as one outlaw shot at Jack, who returned fire, hitting him in the chest. The other two dashed back inside, grabbing two people to use as shields, not seeing that Quinn, Blaine, Caleb, and Big Jim had already headed to the entry for their guns.

The crowd parted as the four men moved toward the unsuspecting outlaws, holding their guns at their sides. They stopped, hearing Brodie's warning.

"You don't want to add murder to robbery. Let those people go. Jail is better than a noose."

"The hell it is," the leader yelled back, tightening his grip on the older woman. Her body trembled in his grasp, her panicked gaze searching the crowd.

Quinn raised his gun. "Let them go, lads. You'll not be able to get away."

Without another word, the leader shot into the crowd, then screamed as a bullet from Jack's gun ripped through his neck. An instant later, the other outlaw hit the ground, his body riddled with bullets.

No one spoke as Brodie and his deputies moved forward, checking both bodies, then holstering their guns. Quinn turned to his cousins, letting out a shaky breath.

"Appears they're dead, lads." He glanced at Big Jim, whose drawn face grew pale as a hand came up to grip his chest. Quinn saw the blood seconds before Big Jim's eyes rolled back and he collapsed to the ground. A loud scream burst through the room.

"Papa!" Emma rushed forward, dropping next to her father. She lifted his head and placed it in her lap. "Papa, Mama and I are here." She looked up, her gaze locking on Quinn, her face streaked with tears. "Papa, please... Don't leave us."

Chapter One

MacLaren's Circle M Ranch
Two months later...

"I thought we'd never see you happy again, lad." Colin tipped the glass of punch toward Brodie, then took the flask Quinn offered, adding some much needed whiskey. They stood in the living room of the largest MacLaren ranch house, which had been built to hold every member of the family for large Sunday suppers and special occasions. Today, they came together to celebrate the marriage of Brodie and Maggie. "I know you thought you'd done what was honorable in letting her go, but it's obvious neither you nor Maggie would've ever been happy without the other."

"My decision to send her away seemed right at the time. It didn't take long to realize I'd made the biggest mistake of my life." Brodie watched his new bride as she talked to one set of relatives after another. The glow on her face made his chest constrict in love and pride. He'd never imagined this day when he arrested her for murder a few months earlier. Brodie leveled a serious look at Blaine and Quinn. "Now it's time you two eejits found good women and settled down."

Quinn grimaced. "Ach, marriage is fine for you and Colin. It isn't what I'm looking for—not for a good long while."

"Aye. I've no interest in any lass leading me around." Blaine's back straightened at the appearance of two women he didn't think would make it to the wedding.

"Sorry, lads. I agree with Brodie. It might do you two good to find a decent woman." Spotting Sarah, Colin set down his empty glass. "I'm off to spend time with my wife."

"I will say, if I thought she'd be interested, I'd stake a claim on Emma Pearce," Blaine said. "She is one bonny lass."

Quinn choked on his drink as his gaze moved around the room, landing on Emma and her mother.

"You all right, lad?" Brodie slapped him on the back, chuckling at the evil look from Quinn. "It's time I joined my bride." He took a step away, then turned back to Blaine, lifting a brow. "I hear the Pearce women have taken on quite a bit with Big Jim still laid up. They may welcome an offer to help...in case you want to claim her, lad." Brodie chuckled at the way Blaine's jaw dropped at the suggestion.

Blaine watched him walk away, considering his words. "Perhaps I should talk to Mrs. Pearce, find out—"

"If any of us helps, it will be me." Quinn didn't know where the words came from or why he said them out loud.

"You?" Blaine's eyes widened as he took a good look at his cousin, seeing something more than the disinterest he expected. "Are you interested in the lass, too?"

"Nae. As I said, I've no interest in settling down. My thoughts are on Big Jim and Gertie. They've been good to us since your da and mine were murdered. It's time to find out what we can do for them."

Blaine studied Quinn's face, noticing a spark in his eyes he'd never seen before. They'd never fought over a woman, and Blaine had no intention of Emma being the first. If his cousin had an interest in her, he'd step aside. No lass was worth causing trouble with family.

"If you do this, lad, be careful. Emma's a special lass. It wouldn't do to dally with her, then move on."

Quinn took a menacing step forward, his nostrils flaring. "I have no intention of *dallying* with her," he ground out.

Blaine held up his hands, palms out. "I want no trouble over this."

Quinn took a step away. Lifting a hand, he waved off Blaine's comments. "Ach, you're right. They're almost family. I have no interest in the lass." *She'd never have me anyway,* he thought as he watched Sam Covington walk up to Emma and her mother. She leaned toward him, commenting on something he'd said, causing Brodie's deputy to rear his head back with a roar of laughter. An unaccustomed flash of jealousy ripped through Quinn, then disappeared in an instant.

Blaine clasped him on the shoulder. "Why don't you talk to Mrs. Pearce? She might be more open than Emma to an offer of help."

Quinn nodded. "Aye. She can be one stubborn lassie."

Sam listened to Emma explaining the challenges of running the ranch with her father still bedridden. Finding her open, sincere, and quite engaging, he wondered at how no one seemed to be courting her. If he could get his thoughts off one particular MacLaren woman, he might be tempted. Unfortunately, his interest lay with someone he couldn't have and shouldn't even be thinking about.

"Brodie tells me your ranch is north of theirs."

"Yes, it is, Mr. Covington. The MacLarens recently bought a large section of land from Juan Estrada, which is north and to the east of us." Her gaze drifted past Sam to Quinn, who stood next to

Blaine, staring right at her. Lifting his arm, he touched a finger to his brow in a silent salute. She couldn't stop her lips from curving into a smile.

"Seems you're surrounded by MacLarens on three sides."

When she didn't respond, Gertie nudged her arm. "Emma, Mr. Covington was speaking to you."

"Oh, I'm sorry. I was just, um…thinking about something. What did you say?"

"Only that your property is surrounded by Circle M Ranch."

Sam turned at the sound of a distinctive laugh, knowing who he'd see. Bracing himself for the reaction he suspected, his body tensed when he saw Jinny MacLaren, her face animated as she spoke to Nate Hollis. He shouldn't care. Shouldn't wish it were him standing next to her instead of his fellow deputy. Forcing his attention back to Emma, he schooled his features, offering a polite smile.

"It is. In fact, I heard the family is trying to talk Brodie into coming back to take a more active role as the ranch expands. Would you then become sheriff, Mr. Covington?"

He froze. Brodie had never mentioned the possibility of returning to the ranch, and Sam had absolutely no desire to become the sheriff. The deal he'd made with Brodie was for six months, and the time was almost up. After he fulfilled his obligation, he'd be on the first steamboat to Sacramento, then on a train east. Nothing and no one could change his mind. Then he heard Jinny laugh again.

"I think you'd make a wonderful sheriff." Gertie nodded as she spoke.

"Thank you, Mrs. Pearce, but I haven't spoken to the sheriff about him leaving."

"Hello, Deputy Covington." Sam's breath hitched at the sound of Jinny's voice. Shifting, he made a slight bow.

"Miss MacLaren. I trust you are doing well."

"Yes, I am." Looking around him, she smiled at her good friend. "Hello, Emma, Mrs. Pearce. It's so good to see you. How's Big Jim doing?"

Sam stood next to Jinny long enough to enjoy the soft scent of lavender, listening to her enthusiastic tone as she talked with Emma. The longer he stood there, the more mesmerized he became.

"Hello, Sam."

Quinn's greeting shook him out of the trance, a state he often found himself in when around Jinny. Welcoming the chance to move away from her, he turned, extending his hand.

"Quite a wedding the MacLaren women put on for Brodie and Maggie."

"They do know how to plan a shindig." Quinn glanced over Sam's shoulder at Emma, who refused to meet his gaze.

Biting back a smile, he saw her eyes narrow, lips pursed as she worked to keep from moving her attention to him. Quinn had known for years she had feelings for him, although she'd never spoken of them. Instead, she pushed him away, kept a wall between them that hadn't existed when they were younger. He prayed she'd never seen the same desire in his eyes. Keeping his distance kept him from admitting how he felt, something he could never risk doing. What he *could* do was offer his help.

"Excuse me, Sam. I need to speak with Mrs. Pearce."

"It's time I head back into town and relieve Jack anyway. I appreciate being included in the party."

"You're always welcome, Sam."

Emma shifted on her feet, trying to calm the butterflies in her stomach as Quinn turned from Sam and stepped next to her mother. Without acknowledging her, he leaned down, whispering something in her mother's ear. Nodding, Gertie touched Emma's arm.

"I need to speak with Quinn for a spell."

"I'll come with you, Mama." She hoped her stringent tone worked.

"No need, Emma. Stay here and visit with Jinny. You've had so little time together since your father was shot."

Crossing her arms, Emma sent Quinn a venomous glare, the message clear. She knew he had purposely excluded her from the discussion. Sending her a bland stare, he feigned innocence, taking Gertie by the arm and escorting her outside.

"Now, Quinn MacLaren, tell me why I have upset my daughter by coming out here with you."

"I'm certain Big Jim would welcome the additional help, Quinn. We've been trying to find a foreman to replace the one who left a few months ago. I never thought it would take this long. Poor Emma has done her best to fill in, but she's young and doesn't yet have the respect of the men."

Even though he disagreed, he understood how the men felt. Few men were cut out to be a foreman, let alone a young woman of nineteen. No matter her experience, she would have a harder time being accepted as a boss.

"She'll disagree, but there's a lot Emma doesn't know. Maybe if Jimmy hadn't died..." Gertie's face took on a pained look as her voice trailed off. He knew she and Big Jim still felt the acute loss of their only son.

Quinn's throat tightened as he tried to swallow the loss he still felt at the death of his friend. Jimmy would've been twenty-three, the same as Quinn, if he hadn't died in a freak accident while searching for strays. His death had never made sense to anyone. Smart and cautious, Jimmy didn't take chances and could outride almost anyone. The only explanation providing any measure of peace was his horse had been spooked by a cougar or snake. Still...

"It won't be easy for Emma to accept you on the ranch." Gertie tapped a finger against her lips, her eyes narrowed in concentration. "Of course, I could tell her you've agreed to be our foreman until Big Jim recovers."

"I don't want your money. I just want to help for a short time." He didn't know how much time he could spend away from Circle M. With Brodie in town, his family couldn't take on all the work Quinn did.

"If you help, you'll get paid."

"But—"

"Not another word on it, Quinn, or we'll walk back inside and pretend we've never had this conversation."

Crossing his arms, he stared down at the woman who was older than his mother and stood close to a foot shorter than him. He'd never underestimate her, though. Gertie Pearce had more grit than most men he knew.

"I'll have to get my uncles' approval."

"You leave Ewan and Ian to me."

Quinn chuckled at the image of her cajoling his tall, broad-shouldered uncles into letting him leave Circle M to help out. "I'd like to hear that conversation." Quinn supposed he could give his wages to his uncles, allowing them to hire another ranch hand, something they'd been talking about.

Gertie didn't respond. Instead, she poked a finger at his chest. "It will be *your* job to figure out a way to work with Emma."

"It won't be easy."

Gertie's eyes flickered, a smile curving up the corners of her mouth. "Nothing worthwhile ever is."

"Are you all right, Emma?" Jinny watched her friend's face twist into a frown, wishing she knew the cause. "Did Quinn say something to upset you?"

Emma huffed out an exasperated breath. "Of course not. Your cousin couldn't possibly say anything to anger me. He never says *anything* to me at all."

Jinny sighed, understanding Emma's frustration. "Come on. Let's get some food. I want to hear all about Big Jim and how you're doing." Jinny took her elbow, parting groups of relatives and friends as they made their way across the room.

As they approached the table, she spotted Sam talking with Caleb and Blaine several feet away. A hint of irritation, along with a rush of excitement, passed through her when he lifted his gaze, nodding to her. Instead of responding, she turned away, hoping the heating of her face didn't show. Jinny knew she had to find a way to stop her heart from skipping a beat each time she saw the man.

Emma leaned toward her, lowering her voice. "I think Sam might have an interest in you."

Jinny scoffed. "He's being polite. Brodie is his boss and I'm Brodie's sister. Of course he's going to be courteous to me."

Passing Jinny a plate, Emma shook her head. "It's more than that. He watches you when he thinks you aren't looking."

Placing a spoonful of vegetables and slices of meat on her plate, Jinny turned her face away from Sam. "Emma, think about what you're saying. A man like him would never find me appealing as anything other than a casual friend." Leaving the table, they found seats along one wall of the living room, as far away from Sam as Jinny could get. "Besides, I overheard Brodie and Colin talking about him. Sam only plans to stay in Conviction a short time, returning home this spring. I don't know the details, but he's paying back a debt to Brodie by being a deputy. When the commitment is over, he'll leave.

"Now, enough about him. I want to hear about you...and Quinn."

"Quinn?" Emma laughed. "As I said, the man barely speaks to me. We see each other at church, special occasions, and once in a while in town when I ride in for supplies. Anyway, I have no interest in him."

Jinny studied her friend, seeing the lie on her face. "You aren't fooling me. I've known you too long." She scooped up some vegetables, chewing slowly, her gaze moving toward Sam, then shifting away when she saw him watching.

"He's your cousin. You know what people say about the way he spends his Saturday nights. Do you *really* want me to have an interest in him?"

Jinny bit her lip, the mischief gone from her face. "I suppose not. He does have a wild side."

"I doubt he'll ever consider settling down, and why should he? He, Colin, and Blaine practically run your ranch. Quinn has his pick of women, and no responsibilities beyond his work."

"You make my cousin sound like a worthless reprobate." Jinny knew she sounded surly, but he was family.

"You know that isn't what I mean," Emma breathed out. "It's just, well...he isn't someone who occupies my thoughts. I'm fortunate I don't have to see him every day the way you do." Taking a bite of still warm bread, she settled back into her chair. She wouldn't go as far as to express her thoughts on how arrogant and pigheaded Quinn could be. As Jinny knew all too well, those were traits owned by more than one of the MacLaren men.

"Look who's coming back inside." Jinny nodded toward the entry.

Quinn had Gertie's arm through his as they cut a path toward the two young women. His expression seemed wary, while Gertie wore a smile, something she hadn't done often since Big Jim had been shot.

"Your talk must have gone well, Mama." Emma didn't look at Quinn. Standing, she touched her mother's arm. "Why don't you sit down and I'll get you some food."

"Oh, I'm not hungry right now. I have the most wonderful news."

Emma saw her mother's hand slip from Quinn's arm. His expression signaled nothing as he took a step away. A warning she couldn't define shot through her.

"All right. Tell me what it is, Mama."

"We've found ourselves a new foreman."

No, no, no, Emma's mind screamed, suspecting where this was going, wanting nothing more than to run from the room. She shot a quick look at Quinn before turning her attention back to her mother.

"Who?"

She nodded behind her. "Quinn MacLaren."

Chapter Two

"Certain, are you, about working at the Pearce ranch?" Quinn's uncle, Ewan, Brodie's father, continued to saddle his horse, sparing his nephew a slight glance.

"Aye, I am. Big Jim spent a lot of time with us after Da and Uncle Angus were murdered. He even brought over a few of his men to help with branding. Mrs. Pearce spent days with Ma and Aunt Kyla, helping with cooking, laundry, watching the wee ones. We owe them."

"Aye, and that's the only reason your Uncle Ian and I are letting you go. Colin and Blaine also believe it's right of us to help them until Big Jim is fit to start working again." Ewan shook his head, chuckling as he led his horse out of the barn. "With you there, Gertie's hoping he might follow Doc Vickery's instructions and stay in bed longer."

Following Ewan outside, Quinn shot a look at Colin, Blaine, and Caleb, who stood by their horses, waiting to hear the decision. "Then I'll leave this afternoon."

"And the Pearce lass? Have you thought of how you'll work with her?"

Ewan's question didn't surprise him. Anyone who knew Emma understood her desire to take over the Pearce ranch one day.

"It won't be easy. She's a stubborn lass."

Ewan laughed. "That she is, lad." Sobering, he turned a serious gaze on his nephew. "You have a big job ahead of you. Stepping in for a short time won't be easy. You must earn the respect of the men, which I doubt will be a problem. Earning Emma's may take more time." Swinging up onto his horse, Ewan rested his hands on the saddle horn, taking one more look at Quinn. "I'll not hear of you disrespecting her. Do you understand me?"

He couldn't miss the double meaning—respect the work she did and keep his hands off. "Aye, Uncle Ewan. I understand you."

Nodding, Ewan reined his horse around, then turned back to Quinn. "You'll be here for Sunday supper." It wasn't a request.

"Aye, I will." Quinn's response died in the wind as Ewan kicked his horse into a gallop, taking the trail to town.

"What did they decide?" Colin stepped beside him, Blaine and Caleb lagging a few paces behind.

"He and Uncle Ian gave their blessing. They could do nothing else after the talk Gertie had with them at Brodie's wedding."

"They'll do whatever they can for the Pearce clan." With so much work to do as winter turned to spring, Blaine hated to lose Quinn, yet he understood. "And the lads will step up to do what's needed," he said, referring to Camden, Bram, Fletcher, and Sean.

The four were about the same age their older cousins and brothers were when they rode to Oregon to bring Sarah to Circle M. Colin, Quinn, and Brodie spent months away while Blaine reluctantly stayed behind. There had never been a choice. As Colin's younger brother, Blaine had been expected to take up a good portion of the work during their absence. The best part of the trip, other than bringing Sarah back, was seeing Caleb again, inviting him to join them at Circle M.

"Between you and me, the lads won't have a choice."

"Aye, Colin." Blaine accepted the extra work when Colin left to find Sarah. He'd taken on more when Brodie became sheriff. He didn't mind and never complained. There were times, though, when he wondered if he'd ever be able to fulfill his own dreams. "Caleb and I will let the lads know."

Watching Blaine and Caleb leave, Quinn turned to Colin. "I'll finish the job we started yesterday, then leave after dinner. I want to talk with Gertie and Emma before meeting the men."

Hearing resignation in his voice, Colin studied Quinn's face. "Are you certain you want to do this?"

Quinn shoved his hands in his pockets and lowered his head, as if studying his boots. "Aye. I'm sure."

"If not, Blaine could go in your place. I'm sure Gertie would be happy either way."

Quinn glanced up, remembering Blaine's comment about courting Emma. He might not want to spend day after day near her, but he'd never let Blaine get that close to her.

"Nae. Gertie asked me and I accepted. It will give me a chance to see Big Jim each day, reassure him of how the ranch is doing. If he knows the work is being taken care of, it might help him recover faster."

Colin opened his mouth to say something, then thought better of it. What he wanted to say wouldn't help, and might even hurt if Quinn knew what he was thinking.

Quinn watched the struggle on Colin's face. For a long time, he'd thought his cousin suspected how Quinn felt about Emma, but he'd never uttered a word. Crossing his arms, he cocked his head.

"Say it." He waited for Colin to respond, knowing it might take a while. Colin had always been one to consider his words before speaking them aloud, a skill Quinn wished he possessed.

"It's not my business."

"Ach. I know something's got you bothered. I want to hear it before I ride off."

Colin rested fisted hands on his hips. "All right. It's Emma."

Quinn let out an uneasy laugh. "You've got your woman, Colin. You don't need two."

"Don't be daft. My concern is for Emma."

"And what do you think will happen to her?"

Colin shifted to face him, his voice lowering. "She's a sweet lass...an innocent, Quinn. Don't be breaking her heart."

Lowering his head, Quinn swore, more out of frustration with his own feelings than Colin's warning. Looking up, his expression haunted, he locked gazes with his cousin.

"I'd never do anything to hurt Emma."

"Not intentionally. You've known for a while how the lass feels about you. You don't have to admit it, but I'm thinking you feel the same."

Quinn didn't respond as he worked to control his conflicting feelings.

"All I'm saying is to keep your hands off her. Do what you must to do the job, then come home." Colin rested a hand on Quinn's shoulder. "You're an honorable lad."

"Are you sure? Some believe me to be a loon."

Colin's hearty laugh broke the gloomy mood. "Aye. You may indeed be a rascal, but you're a good-hearted one, and your word means something to you. All I'm suggesting is to be careful around the lass."

Nodding, Quinn felt his body relax. He knew Colin would never breathe a word of this to anyone—not even Brodie or Blaine. The thought gave him a sense of comfort and another reason to stay with his plan of keeping distance between him and Emma. Nothing good could come from their mutual attraction.

"I still don't understand why we need Quinn MacLaren at the ranch." Emma crossed her arms as she paced around the spacious kitchen, her cup of coffee forgotten on the table. Today, she'd put on some old pants her mother had altered and an overlarge shirt—her choice when working around the ranch. "Aren't we doing all right without him?"

Gertie continued to slice the vegetables she'd later add to the stew for dinner. Other than to sleep, Emma hadn't stopped ranting about Quinn since the decision to hire him. Gertie didn't blame her daughter. If Big Jim hadn't been so insistent they needed a man to run the ranch, Gertie would have never mentioned it. It had been a blessing when Quinn volunteered. They'd never accept free labor, but they wouldn't turn away a young man Big Jim respected.

"Mama, did you hear me?"

Gertie smiled to herself. "I'm sorry, dear. What did you say?"

Emma stopped pacing, dropped into a chair, and picked up her now cold coffee. "I asked you if we were doing all right without Quinn."

Setting the knife down, Gertie wiped her hands on a towel and turned around. Crossing her arms, she leaned against the counter. "You've had no problem with us looking for a new foreman. Why is it you have so much difficulty with Quinn taking the job until we find someone?"

"Because he has his own work at Circle M." Emma didn't meet her mother's gaze, choosing to stare into the almost full cup.

"And?"

"Isn't that enough?"

"No, it's not. He offered to come by as often as needed to make certain the men were doing their work. Neither Ewan nor Ian had problems with him helping. Don't forget. We're paying Quinn for the work."

Emma didn't respond. She couldn't share her real reason for not wanting Quinn at the ranch.

"Your father is concerned you and I are taking on too much." Gertie wouldn't tell her he also didn't believe the men accepted her as their boss while Big Jim was laid up. "If he's worried about the ranch, he'll push himself to return before he should. Doc Vickery made it clear your father needs more time, at least another month, and I'm going to see that he gets it." Her voice broke on the last. "We almost lost him, Emma. That should be enough reason for us to accept Quinn's help."

Setting her coffee aside, Emma stood, feeling horrible for upsetting her mother. She'd only been thinking of herself and what she felt for Quinn—had always felt for him. It was a secret she'd never share with anyone.

"I'm sorry, Mama." Reaching out, she pulled her mother into her arms, squeezing tight before stepping back. "You're right. We need help and Quinn is the perfect person. Besides, Papa trusts him."

"So do I, Emma. You must learn to do the same."

Emma mucked her horse's stall, muttering to herself, not caring if anyone heard. She'd agreed to stop complaining about Quinn. It didn't mean she had to like it, though. Continuing her internal rant, she sifted through the last section of hay, throwing manure into the nearby wheelbarrow. Tossing the pitchfork aside, she muttered a curse.

"Such a nasty word coming from such a pretty mouth."

Spinning around, her jaw dropped at the sight of Quinn leaning against the stall, amusement flickering across his face.

Emma fisted her hands, placing them on her hips. "What are you doing here?"

"If I'm not mistaken, I work here." His grin widened.

"Then why aren't you?"

Chuckling, he bent to pick up the pitchfork, then walked to the stall's back wall, scooping up a pile Emma had missed. Tossing it in the wheelbarrow, he set the pitchfork aside, then pushed his hat off his forehead.

"I was enjoying watching you, lass." The minute the words left his mouth, Quinn knew it had been a mistake.

Straightening, Emma crossed her arms, her eyes sparking. "We don't need another lazy dunderhead around the ranch."

"Dunderhead? And where did you hear such a term?"

Walking toward him, she stopped less than a foot away, poking a finger into his chest. "From you." Turning, she grabbed the wheelbarrow and rolled it past him, then glanced over her shoulder. "Are you going to stand around the rest of the day, or are you going to get to work?"

Emma didn't slow her pace as she pushed the wheelbarrow out the barn's back door, unaware

Quinn watched as she continued on a well-worn path. Dumping the contents, she returned to the barn, letting out a shaky breath when she found no sign of him. His absence didn't last long.

Leading her horse outside, Emma groomed and saddled Moonshine before swinging into the saddle. Reining toward the house, she jerked to a stop. Quinn and her mother stood on the porch.

"Emma, come on over here." Gertie signaled for her to join them.

Groaning, Emma continued to the house, not dismounting. "I'm riding to the north pasture."

Gertie moved to the edge of the porch. "Quinn is going with you. He needs to meet the men."

Emma should've known she wouldn't be able to ride out without him tagging along. She needed to accept he'd be part of her life until her father recovered. It didn't mean she had to make it easy for him.

"Hurry up then. I don't have time to wait around for you."

Reining Moonshine around, she kicked her into an easy jog, not looking to see if Quinn followed. A minute later, she heard the sound of a horse coming up behind her.

"Are you trying to lose me?"

Emma glanced at Quinn sitting atop his beautiful stallion, Warrior. They were a magnificent combination. Both strong and haughty—a feast for the eyes. Warrior was known to be one of the fastest horses around, besting his competitors in every race she knew about.

Accepting she and Moonshine could never outrun them, Emma shook her head. "Not at all."

They rode in silence, neither glancing at the other. Leading him on a trail he'd never ridden, they traveled over rolling hills and crossed two streams, stopping at the top of a rise. The herd grazed below. Several hundred head of cattle moved about the open pasture, their mawwwing sounds drifting up the hill to where they sat.

"Where are your men?" Scanning the area, Quinn couldn't see a single ranch hand.

"Good question. Let's find out." Taking a direct path to the herd, she pulled up as they got closer. "This doesn't make sense. I sent them out here right after breakfast."

"How many men?"

"There are six working for us. We only have one herd, so all the men should be here." An instant later, Emma heard the sound of raucous laughter. "Did you hear that?"

Quinn's gaze shifted toward a copse of trees a hundred yards away. "Aye. It came from over there." He held up his hand to stop her when she started to ride out. "Wait. Let's go in slow, see what the lads are up to."

A few minutes later, they stopped, finding the men sitting in a circle, passing around a bottle of whiskey while playing cards.

"I'll go in first."

"No. It's my ranch."

Quinn knew how she must feel, but it didn't change the facts. "It's Big Jim's ranch. He and your mother hired me as foreman, which means you do as I say." He ignored the red tinge of anger creeping up her face. "You can follow, but I'll do the talking. When I signal, you can ride forward. You won't have six men working here when I'm through."

As much as it pained Emma to admit it, Quinn was right. No doubt her parents would agree with him. Being foreman trumped her position as their daughter—at least concerning ranch business. Biting her bottom lip, she nodded.

Riding forward, he got within twenty feet, surprised no one had noticed him.

"Appears you lads have a lively game going."

Cards dropped and the whiskey bottle disappeared as the men jumped to their feet.

"You want to tell me what you're doing?" Quinn looked at each face, surprised to find not one appeared to be over eighteen.

"And who the hell are you?" A tall, lanky man stepped forward, his thick Irish accent indicating his heritage.

"I'm Quinn MacLaren, the new foreman. The man who decides whether you'll have work after today."

A series of quick explanations and half-hearted apologies followed. Quinn wasn't impressed.

"Whose whiskey?"

"Mine." The lanky ranch hand held out the bottle.

"And the cards?"

"Also mine."

"I'm guessing it was your idea to pull all the lads off their jobs to hide back in here to gamble. Am I right?"

For the first time, remorse showed on the young man's face. "It was." His voice was rough, resigned, as if he suspected what Quinn would say before the words were out. He was wrong.

"What's your name?"

"Finn O'Sullivan."

"Where are you from?"

"County Cork, Ireland."

Quinn nodded, glancing at the others. "The rest of you, tell me your names, ages, and where you're from."

Including Finn, four came from Cork. All made the long journey across the Atlantic together, traveling across the country until they'd found work at the Pearce ranch. One came from

Louisiana to escape the war, and the last hailed from Texas. They ranged in age from sixteen to nineteen. Right now, all six looked as if they wanted to be anywhere except standing before him. Quinn motioned behind him.

"Put the whiskey and cards in the saddlebag, O'Sullivan."

When Finn stepped away from Warrior, Quinn took one more look at the young men.

"This is the way it will be, lads. If you want to stay on the Pearce ranch, you'll give Big Jim a full day's work for the wage he pays you. Cards are for after supper. No whiskey, except what you get in town on Saturday nights. If you can abide by these terms, you're welcome to stay. If not, ride out now." When no one moved, Quinn glanced behind him, seeing Emma a few feet away, irritated she'd ignored his order to stay back until his signal. "All right. I assume you all need work. Until you pull another eejit stunt like this or don't play by the rules, you can stay."

A collective sigh rippled through the group, Finn seeming to be the most relieved.

"Who of you has more than a year experience working on a cattle ranch?"

Holler Gibson, the boy from Texas, stepped forward. "I grew up on a ranch. My folks raised cattle."

Quinn nodded, wanting to learn more about his experience. At least he had one solid ranch hand he could count on. "Appears most of you have a lot to learn. I'll explain what you'll be doing each morning. Mrs. Pearce will provide breakfast, food to pack if you're out with the herd all day, and supper in the bunkhouse at night. Can you all handle a gun?"

All six nodded. Quinn somehow doubted how accurate they might be, but it was a start. He looked at Emma.

"Miss Pearce and I have been good friends a long time. She'll be treated with respect. If I hear otherwise, you'll not like the consequences. Do you understand what I'm telling you?"

Six heads bobbed up and down. He didn't need to look at Emma to know she'd be seething at his comment. Too bad. She'd have to accept his way of dealing with the men while protecting her.

"Get your horses. Your work starts now."

Chapter Three

Reining her mare to a stop, Emma slid to the ground. Her normally upbeat demeanor faded the longer she stayed, watching the men follow Quinn's orders without hesitation. She'd left, giving the excuse she needed to get back to help with supper. Getting away from Quinn had been the real reason.

It irritated her how easy it had been for him to step into the role of foreman and for the men to show their respect. She'd worked alongside them for months, taking the foreman role after her father was shot, and not once had she seen the quick response the men gave Quinn. They liked her, of that she had no doubt. Seeing her as an extension of her father, though? Not at all.

Picking up the hoof Moonshine favored, she dislodged a small stone, then dropped the leg, stroking the mare's neck. Emma took several deep breaths, working hard to push aside her frustration and the all-too-real temptation of being around Quinn. The crush she had as a girl had grown into something more, although she refused to call it love.

Running a hand down Moonshine's withers and back, she couldn't remember a time when the mare hadn't been in her life. Big Jim had given her to Emma on her seventh birthday, saying it was her job to care for the three-year-old filly. Twelve years later, they were still partners.

At fifteen, Moonshine showed signs of slowing down. Emma knew it wouldn't be long before she'd have to choose another horse to handle the hard riding required, letting the mare live out the last years of her life at a quieter pace.

She had her eye on a year-old colt sired by Warrior, Quinn's stallion. It had been her pleasure to be at Circle M the night the foal was born, holding her breath as Quinn worked with his cousins, Sean and Fletcher, to ease the mare's stress. She'd never seen three men work so well together, as if they were of one mind.

Even now, standing alongside Moonshine, she felt shivers of excitement as she remembered that night. The Pearce ranch survived by raising and selling cattle. Emma's passion was horses. She'd never been able to convince her father to do more than keep enough horses for the remuda, but she hadn't given up. Getting Warrior's colt would be a start.

The night of the Christmas church party, the same night Big Jim was shot, her father had spoken to Ewan about buying the animal. She wondered if Quinn's uncle had ever mentioned the conversation to him.

Feeling a renewed sense of peace, Emma swung back into the saddle. Maybe something good could come from Quinn working at the ranch. At supper tonight, she'd ask about the colt, beginning her crusade to work out a deal with the cocky cowboy. She didn't know what his terms would be, but she knew it wouldn't be too hefty a price if it meant fulfilling her dream of owning the colt.

Quinn sat atop Warrior, scanning the evening sky before riding down the last hill to the Pearce ranch. Three men had been left to guard the herd, the other three riding well ahead of him. He'd worked them hard, never giving an inch. In return, he got what he believed might be the first full day of labor from the young men. Their exhaustion clearly showed in the slump of their shoulders and slow pace of their horses.

He felt good about his first day as foreman. Except for the tension with Emma, Quinn believed he'd made the right decision to offer his help. Approaching the house, he spotted Gertie waving for him. His plan to eat and bunk with the men had been pushed aside by her easy grace. Gertie had informed him a room had already been prepared in the house and he'd take his meals with the family. She'd accept no excuses.

"Good evening, Mrs. Pearce." Dismounting, he glanced up at the porch. Even though it made no sense, he felt a wave of disappointment that Gertie stood alone. "Did Emma make it back?"

"A long time ago. She's finishing getting supper ready. Stable your horse, then come inside. I want to hear all about your first day."

Quinn didn't know what Emma may have told her mother, but it didn't matter. Gertie would form her own opinions about his work and the way the men responded. Removing the tack, he brushed Warrior, then took his time getting him fresh hay and water.

Peeling off his shirt, Quinn doused his head with water, feeling the taut muscles revive as it streamed down his chest and back. Shaking off the moisture, he pulled a clean shirt out of his saddlebags, then stopped at the sound of footsteps followed by a gasp.

"Oh. I, um..."

Slipping into the shirt, he turned, leaving the front open. Emma had her back to him. "Is there something you needed, Emma?"

"No. I mean, yes." She took a deep breath, turning, hoping he didn't notice the flush she felt on her face. "Mama says it's time to come in for supper."

Buttoning his shirt, Quinn would've chuckled if she wasn't trying so hard to hide her red cheeks. "Don't tell me you've never seen the ranch hands with their shirts off."

Crossing her arms, Emma glared at him. "Of course I've seen men without shirts."

"Just not me, right, lass?"

Biting her lower lip, she remembered the colt's birth. By the time it was over, he'd shucked his shirt, his back and chest gleaming with dampness. He'd been so busy, she'd been able to hide her reaction.

"I've seen you without a shirt, Quinn," she shot back, seeing the surprise on his face. "The night your colt was born. Now, if you want to eat, I'd suggest you get inside." Lifting her chin, she spun around, leaving him to watch her retreat.

He tucked his shirt in, then grabbed his hat. It had been a while since he'd seen Emma turn such a pretty shade of red. Each time it happened, his body responded just as it did tonight.

If it had been any other woman, one he wasn't honor bound not to touch, he would've stepped closer, taking her in his arms. He'd given his word—not just to Colin, but to Uncle Ewan. They knew him better than he knew himself.

Quinn lived for whatever adventure would surface each day. There wasn't a task he couldn't complete or a woman who could resist his charms.

The bigger the challenge, the better he liked it. And he never backed down. The one exception was Emma.

He was impulsive and brash, eager to take action. Some would even say foolhardy and wild at times. Emma didn't have a reckless bone in her body. All her actions were expected—no surprises, nothing spontaneous. As much as he wanted her, they'd never mesh. Emma needed someone more like her—reliable, unassuming, and supportive— not a man who looked for excitement and spurned anything too comfortable.

"Are you coming, MacLaren?"

Quinn couldn't stop the chuckle at the use of his last name. She had always called him Quinn, and he loved the way it rolled off her tongue. Maybe it was Emma's way of creating a wall, a barrier neither could breach. Taking the porch steps two at a time, he smiled. He might not be able to act on his feelings, but there was no reason he couldn't enjoy himself during his time at the ranch.

"Thank you, Mrs. Pearce. I can't recall ever having a better berry pie." Quinn leaned back in his chair, touching the edge of his coffee cup.

"Go on. I happen to know your mother and all the MacLaren women make wonderful pies. In fact, my crust recipe came from your Aunt Kyla."

"And I'll be telling them you're ready to go up against the MacLaren clan at the next church bake off."

Gertie crossed her arms, feigning anger. "Don't you go telling them that, young man. Besides, I always enter my special cake."

"And it always wins," Quinn commented with a smile.

Emma tapped her fingers on the table, listening to the two banter back and forth, her mother laughing. It felt good to hear it after months of worry over Big Jim. They'd thought he might join them for supper tonight, but he couldn't navigate the stairs.

"I've been thinking, Mama. Why don't we make up the downstairs for Papa? Now that Quinn is here, he could help us get him moved. Papa might be able to join us for meals or sit outside if he doesn't have to worry about the stairs."

Quinn nodded. "I can help whenever you're ready. Getting him outside is a great idea, Emma." He looked at his empty plate and pushed his chair from the table. "I'll help with the dishes, then I'm going to get some sleep. The men will be ready to head back out at dawn."

"You go on, Quinn. Emma and I will get the dishes."

"Mama? Do you mind if I have a word with Quinn first?" Emma stood, ready to follow him outside.

Quinn's eyes widened at her request.

"Go ahead, dear. I'll be in the kitchen."

"Do you have a minute, Quinn?" He nodded, following her into Big Jim's study. "I can pour you a whiskey if you'd like."

"Nae. What I want right now is sleep. But we can talk for a bit if that's what you want." Under no circumstances would he talk in private with Emma with a glass of whiskey in his hand.

"Well, um..." She bit her lip, unsure of how to say what she wanted.

"Lass...just say it." He turned to face her.

"It's about your new colt."

"Champion?"

Emma clasped her hands in front of her and nodded. "Yes."

"And?"

"I want to buy him."

Of everything she could have said, this was the last thing Quinn expected. He thought she'd rail at him for ignoring her most of the day or for warning the men away from her. But Champion?

"And what would you be needing a colt for? You have Moonshine and a respectable remuda.

Champion is for breeding and hard work, not for pleasure."

She almost choked on the slight. "Pleasure? Is that what you think I do all day, MacLaren? Ride around picking flowers or shopping in town?"

He held out his hands, palms toward her. "Ach, settle down, lass. You know that's not what I meant. But you buying Champion makes no sense unless you're wanting to start breeding horses."

She blinked a few times, her lips forming a thin line.

Quinn's eyes widened before his gaze sharpened. "Does Big Jim know?"

Her eyes crinkled in confusion. "Know what?" She gripped her hands together in front of her, forcing herself not to fidget under his scrutiny.

Cocking his head, his mouth curved up at the corners. "That you want to breed horses?"

"I didn't say—"

"Emma, you are the worst liar I've ever met. Fact is, you can't even tell a small fib without your eyes giving you away." He took a step closer, lifting her chin with his finger. "Tell me. Does Big Jim know?"

Emma jutted her chin out, shaking her head as she took a step away. "No, and you aren't going to tell him. I've got some money saved, although I'm certain it's not enough. I was hoping we could make some kind of deal. You tell me your terms and I'll do all I can to meet them."

Without thinking, he inched forward, his face growing somber, his eyes darkening with desire as be bent toward her. "Trust me, sweetheart. You do not want to hear my terms."

Emma gasped, sucking a breath. "I…"

Groaning, he stepped away, his voice hard and tight. "Enough of this talk. I'm in need of sleep, not a conversation with a lass about a horse." He grabbed his hat from a hook, then turned. "I'll see you tomorrow."

She held out her hand, trying to get his attention. "Wait, Quinn."

"Nae, Emma. Champion *will* be the foundation of a solid breeding program. But it will be at Circle M, not here." He slammed his hat on his head, stomping outside and into the dark.

"Have you seen Nate this morning?" Brodie slipped into his coat as one of his deputies, Jack Perkins, poured a cup of coffee.

"Nope. Saw Sam, though. He's having breakfast over at the Gold Dust Hotel." Jack scratched his jaw, his brows furrowing. "Now that I think on it, Nate usually has breakfast with him."

"As far as you know, both still take rooms at the Gold Dust, right?"

"Yep. Both are on opposite ends of the second floor." Jack walked to the back, glancing at the empty cells. "Been quiet around here since those outlaws tried to rob the folks in December. Mrs. Pearce came into town a couple days ago. Stopped by to say Big Jim is doing better. Every time I think of him being shot, I want to kill those three varmints again."

"You're not the only one who feels that way, lad. We're lucky no one else was shot and Big Jim didn't die. You did real well that night, Jack."

Looking up from his cup of coffee, the young deputy blushed. "Just doing my job, Sheriff."

Slipping on his gunbelt, Brodie thought of Quinn. He'd come home for supper and to get more clothes the previous Sunday. After a week at the Pearce ranch, he'd seen a marked improvement in the men's work and Big Jim's health. Quinn hadn't mentioned Emma once.

"I'm riding to the docks and Chinatown. Stay here while I'm gone." Brodie opened the door, then stopped. "When Nate comes in, tell him to wait for me. I need to speak with him."

"Sure thing, Sheriff. Anything else you want me to do?" Jack jumped up from his seat, setting down his cup, splashing tepid coffee over the sides.

Brodie chuckled. "Nae. When I get back, I'll have you do rounds in the north end of town."

"You can count on me."

Brodie shook his head as he stepped outside. No matter the day, hour, or situation, Jack never lost his enthusiasm. He'd never met anyone like him. Brodie knew how fortunate he was to have him, as well as Sam and Nate.

Unfortunately, Sam wouldn't be staying much longer. In a matter of weeks, he would fulfill his obligation to Brodie and head out, moving on to a life away from Conviction. He didn't look forward to replacing Sam. His intelligence, wit, and even temperament, as well as his experience working for Allen Pinkerton, were invaluable. Finding someone to take over when he left wouldn't be easy.

For now, he had to learn what bothered Nate. Brodie didn't know what to make of the changes in the deputy. Although subtle, he'd witnessed mood swings, bouts of nausea, and occasional confusion. Nate brushed Brodie's concerns aside, attributing them to lack of sleep and possible food poisoning.

With the town growing, each deputy focused on a certain area of Conviction, making it a point to know the people and the businesses. Nate now kept track of what went on at the docks and in Chinatown. In preparation for his departure, Sam transitioned the docks to Nate over the last week. More than once, Sam had noticed the same changes in Nate that Brodie witnessed. Today, Brodie hoped to convince the man to visit Doc Vickery.

"Sheriff? May I have a word with you?"

Brodie had grabbed Hunter's reins, preparing to mount, when August Fielder reined to a stop alongside him. An attorney, he also owned blocks of the town, a cattle ranch, and gold mines. In addition, he held a large piece of land in partnership with the MacLaren family, which Brodie assumed would be the topic of their conversation.

"Good morning, Mr. Fielder. Would you like to talk in the jail?"

"Actually, there is a new restaurant near the docks I'd like to try if you have the time."

"I was just headed in that direction."

Mounting, Brodie rode next to August, his gaze shifting, hoping to spot Nate. He'd seen no sign of his deputy by the time they stopped.

Six tables took up most of the front area of the restaurant, the aroma of Chinese food wafting from the kitchen causing Brodie's stomach to growl.

"Sounds as if you're in need of food as much as I am." August motioned to the one empty table.

"Ah, Mr. Fielder. Welcome. Welcome." A thin, short man walked from behind a counter, a broad smile on his face.

"Hong Wo, this is Brodie MacLaren, our sheriff."

Brodie held out his hand, not recognizing the man he guessed to be in his forties. "Mr. Wo."

"Hong Wo, please. Yes, yes. I've met your deputy."

"Nate Hollis?"

"The man with one arm." Hong Wo smiled, although Brodie detected something in his eyes before it quickly disappeared. "I bring you two specials." He bowed and scurried off without waiting for August to reply.

Taking seats, Brodie's gaze followed the man as he rushed into the back, his mind working. After meeting with August, he planned to stay and talk with Hong Wo a bit longer.

"From what I know, he makes one dish each day. His special." Leaning forward, August settled his gaze on Brodie, his jovial attitude turning serious. "I won't waste time. I've come to speak with you about the land grant your family and I bought from Juan Estrada."

"Aye. I thought that might be the reason."

"Good. It makes it easier since you already know what I'm going to ask." August sat back when Hong Wo approached with two plates overflowing with food.

"You like these." Hong Wo smiled, then retreated to the kitchen, returning a moment later with two cups and a pot of tea. "Eat. Eat. I bring you more if you want." Bowing, he left them to their meal.

"He's optimistic. I like that in a man." August picked up a fork and took a large bite. Chewing, he nodded at Brodie. "Hong Wo is right. I think you'll like it."

Brodie dug in, finishing his in record time, then pushed the plate away.

"Well, that was superb." August finished the last of the tea. "Brodie, you've done an excellent job as sheriff. You haven't been doing it a year and we already see considerable improvement."

"Aye, Mr. Fielder. You told me the same last week." He crossed his arms, waiting for August to get to the point of their meeting.

"True. And, I assure you, nothing has changed. Well, almost nothing. It has come to my attention that Sam Covington may be leaving soon. He's a good man. The town doesn't want to lose him."

"By *town* you mean the town council."

"Correct. At the same time, with the purchase of land from Juan Estrada, the partnership is in dire need of someone with your ranch experience." August paused a moment. He never would've approached Brodie if he hadn't been a partner with the MacLarens in the additional sixty thousand acres. "You're a man of many talents, Brodie. Sam, well...he's suited for one role—enforcing the law."

The more August spoke, the more Brodie's jaw tightened. Yes, he had done a good job as sheriff, bringing in excellent men as deputies. The four of them worked well as a team. He hated to see Sam leave, but what August implied didn't sit well either.

"You're asking me to quit so you can offer the job to Sam."

August held up his hands. "I would never ask you to resign. No one knows better than I how much you wanted this job, how much you've always wanted to be a lawman." He took a breath and leaned forward, resting his arms on the table. "I'm asking you to consider taking on a larger, quite important role in the Fielder/MacLaren partnership. If you do, you'd need to give up the role as sheriff."

"And, in your mind, Sam is the logical replacement."

"Yes, he is."

His father, Ewan, and his uncle, Ian, had already talked to him more than once about moving back. Colin, Blaine, and Quinn, along with the younger MacLarens, were doing well. According to the elders, though, they still needed his skills.

"You know Sam wants to leave. He has no intention of staying in Conviction longer than necessary to fulfill an obligation he agreed to with me. He's always planned to return home, maybe even pick up with Pinkerton again."

"I've heard rumors, yes. It doesn't change the fact he could change his mind if given the right incentive. And you need to keep in mind the long-term benefits of returning to the ranch. You would be a wealthy man, MacLaren. Beyond what you could ever make as a lawman."

Brodie shook his head. "Money isn't why I do this, or why I'd take any job."

"All I'm asking is for you to think about it. Even if you decide to return to the ranch after Sam leaves, we can track him down." August reached into his pocket, dropping money on the table. "You think about it. Talk to your wife and family."

"And Sam?"

"No one will say a word to him until you've made your decision." August started to leave, then turned back. "If you decide to stay on as sheriff, there'll be no repercussions. We'll continue on as we have and you'll still receive my full support."

Brodie stayed at the table, watching as the man who'd promoted him for the sheriff position walked out. He'd wondered who would be next to put additional pressure on him to return to the ranch. So far, it had only been his father and uncle. Colin, Blaine, and Quinn had stayed out of it, for which Brodie was grateful. August Fielder setting him down and talking so freely had been a surprise.

Scrubbing a hand down his face, Brodie decided to speak with Wo later and walked outside. He loved his job, but Fielder's comments had him wondering if taking the badge in the first place had been as selfish as it now felt. Swinging up on Hunter, he reined the horse around, heading toward his house, hoping Maggie hadn't left for her daily errands. He needed to see his wife, talk to her, share all Fielder had said. It wouldn't take long. Certainly the town could get by without him for an hour.

His mind focused on Fielder's words, he rode down the street, his gaze straight ahead, thoughts of Nate temporarily forgotten.

Chapter Four

Pearce Ranch

"The last I saw Emma...I mean, Miss Pearce, she rode north with Finn." At sixteen, Jory Walsh was the youngest of the Pearce ranch hands. His experience with cattle compared to those of the other three from County Cork, which meant he had not nearly as much as Quinn wanted. "She needed help locating a group of strays she saw scatter yesterday."

Quinn cursed under his breath. Emma knew better than to ride out without telling him. The lass had been a pain in his side ever since he'd refused to discuss selling the colt. She did her work and took care of whatever he asked of her, all the while with a saucy grin on her face. The same grin that made him want to throttle her and kiss her at the same time. If he weren't careful, the woman would make an eejit out of him before he returned to Circle M.

"How long ago?"

"About three hours, Mr. MacLaren."

"I told you to call me Quinn, Jory."

Jory's face, covered in freckles, colored a bright red, almost the same shade as his hair, which reminded Quinn of ripe carrots.

"Should I fetch them for you?"

"Nae. If they don't return by the time we leave for supper, I'll take Holler and go look for them. You go on and join the rest of the lads."

Jory kicked his horse into a run, not waiting for Quinn to change his mind.

Waiting until Jory disappeared over a hill, Quinn pulled a canteen from his saddlebag, taking a swallow. He'd accomplished a lot in a short time, including jeopardizing his fragile friendship with Emma. They were civil with each other, not letting on about the friction resulting from their discussion about Champion. If Gertie noticed, she said nothing.

He'd known Emma wanted the colt. Big Jim had said as much to Uncle Ewan, who'd told Quinn. With Warrior as the sire, Ewan made it clear the decision would be up to Quinn and no one else. If he sold Champion to anyone, it would be the Pearces. He'd sought opinions from Colin, Blaine, Fletcher, and Bram. Although they understood Emma's dream of breeding horses, all encouraged Quinn to keep the young horse, letting Bram train him at Circle M.

Reining Warrior around, he cut north in the direction Emma and Finn had ridden. He had at least two hours of daylight left and he meant to spend it trying to find them. Quinn had lied to Jory. He had no intention of waiting to see if they showed up with the missing cattle before the men left for supper. Emma being out with Finn after dark wasn't going to happen. Not tonight—not ever.

Emma glanced up at the sky, noting the sun making its descent over the western hills. To her complete frustration, they'd yet to find any strays. Worse, Finn had turned his considerable Irish charm on her. She figured most women would be flattered by his attention. As entertaining as it was, his efforts were a waste of time on her.

"I was certain we'd find the missing cattle by now." Emma looked around at the vast expanse of pasture, the missing cattle nowhere in sight.

"We can keep searching as long as you want." As it had much of the day, Finn's attention focused on Emma. "We've at least a couple hours of daylight left."

"No, Finn. It would be best to head back and start again tomorrow." Emma looked to the west, shielding her eyes from the retreating sun. "We don't want to be this far out when the sun sets. Follow me. I know a shortcut."

Navigating Moonshine into a forest of cedar and pine trees, Emma took a trail her father had shown her years before. She always enjoyed riding through this section of their land. It provided a diversion from her usual chores around the ranch, giving her needed solitude. Today was different. She felt on edge, her senses on alert, as if something weren't quite right. Following the familiar trail, her body tensed at the unmistakable guttural growl of a mountain lion.

"We've a cat nearby." Finn rode up beside her.

When the sound came again, Moonshine danced around, Emma working to control the horse. "We need to get out of here." Emma knew the danger of being stalked by a cougar, had seen what one had done to a ranch hand years before.

"He won't come after us, will he?" Finn reached behind him, pulling a rifle from its scabbard.

Hearing another growl, Emma spotted the mountain lion crouched on a rock above them, ready to spring. A shout from behind had her turning, seeing Finn level his rifle at the cat. Before he could pull the trigger, a shot rang out, striking the animal in mid-air.

A scream tore from her throat as the dead cat landed close to Moonshine. Panicking, the mare bucked, sending Emma to the ground. Lifting her head, she felt a wave of nausea before a sharp pain flashed in her head, propelling her into darkness.

"Emma, can you hear me?"

She recognized the slight Scottish brogue, vaguely aware of a hand moving in front of her eyes. Emma tried to raise her head, wincing at the stab of pain.

"Nae, lass. Don't move your head. You've a knot on it that needs tending."

Her eyes opened to slits. "Quinn?" she groaned.

"Aye. You've had a nasty fall."

Emma felt the dampness of the hard ground seeping through her clothes, her head swimming as she tried to think. She remembered riding with someone. Squeezing her eyes tight, an image of Finn appeared, along with the mountain lion.

"Where's Finn?"

"I've sent him after Moonshine. She bucked you off, then ran."

"The cat..." She whispered the words, as if she weren't sure of her memory.

"Dead."

"I need to get up." Reaching her hand out, she waited until Quinn took it in a strong grip.

"Slow, lass." He slipped a hand behind her back, helping her sit up.

Staring ahead, the forest swam before her. Feeling herself sway, Emma tightened her hold on Quinn's hand.

"Do you want to lie back down?"

She shook her head, gasping at the bolt of pain. "Did I hit a rock?"

"I don't know. You were already unconscious by the time I got here."

"Where did you come from? Weren't you with the herd?" It hurt to talk, to think, to move. "Did you shoot the mountain lion?"

"Aye. I had the best shot and took it. As soon as Finn returns, you and I will ride back to the ranch."

"And Finn?"

"I'll send him to find the other lads and let them know what happened. I think you should see Doc Vickery."

"No, Quinn. I'll be fine. I've handled worse."

He chuckled, shaking his head. Reaching out, he swept back a strand of hair from her cheek, securing it behind her ear. "So strong and brave."

Brushing his hand away, she scoffed at the description. "I'm neither. I do what anyone else would to keep a ranch running. I'm nothing special. Just another ranch hand."

Quinn's chest tightened, his eyes softening. "Ah, lass. You are so much more than another ranch hand."

He searched her face, his gaze drawn to her full lips. Glancing up, their gazes locked as his head dipped lower.

"Found her about a mile away." Finn's voice shattered the moment.

Standing, Quinn turned to see him slide to the ground, the reins to his horse and Moonshine in one hand.

"I need you to ride back to the herd, tell the men what happened, then leave for the ranch. Take Moonshine with you."

Finn nodded at Emma. "Is she all right?"

Quinn pinned him with a hard glare, his expression showing his extreme displeasure. "Aye, Emma will be fine. I'm taking her back to the ranch." His voice grew cold, unyielding. "In the future, you wait for an order from me before you take off. It makes no difference if Emma is the one doing the asking. I'm the foreman and I give the orders. When you ride out with her, you're responsible for her safety, but I'm responsible for both of you."

Finn opened his mouth, then shut it. Nodding, he took one more look at Emma, then swung up on his horse and left.

"He didn't do anything wrong." Emma touched the knot on her head.

Quinn's anger at what almost happened to her, and between them, shifted to Emma. "He took you away from the herd, stayed out until almost dark, and didn't protect you. The lad is a walking calamity. And you aren't much better."

If her head didn't hurt so much, she would have railed at him, screamed at his high-handed manner. He had no right to blame Finn. Going after the strays had been her idea, not his.

"You're a brute, MacLaren."

"Aye. A brute who saved your life." Slipping his arms under Emma's knees and behind her back, he lifted her. "Now, let's get you back to the ranch."

Emma complained the entire ride back, saying she could've handled Moonshine and didn't need to be cradled in his arms as they rode back on Warrior. Quinn listened, his only response being to hold her tighter against his chest.

He liked the feel of her in his arms...more than he should. As much as he enjoyed the time away from Circle M and the ability to manage a ranch with little meddling from others, he knew his time at the Pearce ranch would soon end.

Big Jim improved each day, taking breakfast and supper with the family. Most evenings, he and Gertie sat on the front porch, talking of their plans for the future. At least that's what Gertie said. Somehow, Quinn thought there might be more to it. After the death of their son, Jimmy, Quinn had taken for granted the couple would finish their lives on the ranch, leaving it to Emma and whomever she decided to marry.

The thought of her with someone else disturbed Quinn a great deal. He wanted her more than any woman he'd ever known, yet knew they were too different to ever make a life together.

Settling down with one woman had never been important to him. His entire family expected him to marry and have children. Quinn didn't know if he'd ever be able to commit to one woman. If he couldn't promise to commit, he'd never agree to marry.

"What on earth?" Gertie raced down the steps, running up to Warrior. "What happened?"

Quinn handed Emma down, letting her mother wrap an arm around her waist to steady her.

"A cougar took an interest in Emma. Moonshine spooked, bucking her off, leaving a knot on her head. You may want to send for Doc Vickery."

"It's not that bad, Mama. I'm fine...truly."

Gertie ignored her, looking over her shoulder. "Quinn, would you mind sending one of the men for the doctor?"

"I can go."

"No. I'd prefer you stay here. One of the men is fine."

Quinn watched them walk through the front door, the need to put as much distance between himself and Emma fighting against the need to stay close. Being near her won out. A few minutes later, the men rode in, Finn volunteering to ride into town.

Climbing the steps, Quinn knocked, then entered. Gertie had told him more than once to come inside and not worry about waiting for her to answer the door. He hadn't quite been able to barge in as if it were his own home. The knock was a compromise.

"Did someone go for the doctor?"

"Aye. Finn volunteered. If Doc is available, they should be here within an hour. Where's Emma?"

"She's none too happy, but I insisted she rest a spell. I'm making her tea and broth, which she'll hate." Gertie grinned. "That girl never did take to either one." She ladled broth into a bowl, holding it toward Quinn. "Would you mind taking this up to her?"

"I, uh…don't know that I should." He knew being alone with Emma, in her bedroom, wasn't proper. Besides, he had no desire to spend more time with her until he got himself under control. Without even trying, she caused him to act overprotective and possessive.

Gertie grinned, handing him the broth. "Oh, go on. I'll be up in a few minutes with the tea. It would be best if she isn't up there alone too long."

Taking the broth from her hands, he trudged up the stairs, not looking forward to the reception he'd get. Knocking, he waited.

"Come on in, Mama." When the door swung open to reveal Quinn, she gasped, eyes widening. "What are you doing here?" She pulled the blankets up under her chin, her grim features showing her displeasure.

Looking behind him, not seeing Gertie, he sighed. "Your ma asked me to bring this up to you." He held it out, not moving toward her.

"Well, I can't eat it from over there. Just set it on the table." She nodded to the bedstand.

Quinn focused on the bowl, his hands trembling as he tried not to make a fool of himself by spilling it. Making the mistake of taking his eyes off it for an instant to look in her direction, his boot caught on the rug. He lurched forward, spilling most of it over the sides of the bowl and onto the rug. Cursing under his breath, he glanced at Emma, her hand over her mouth, eyes crinkling. Before he could take another step, she burst out laughing.

"Now, what do we have here?" Gertie stepped into the room. Moving around Quinn, she set the tray down, then bit her lip when she saw the reason for Emma's laughter. "Oh dear. I'll get her some more. You just go ahead and have a seat until I get back. And, Emma, don't you be teasing him. It could've happened to anyone."

"I'll be glad to get the soup." Quinn started for the door.

"If you want to help, clean up the mess." She grabbed the towel tucked into her apron, handing it to him.

Kneeling, he mopped up the moisture, glad she'd prepared broth and not her famous stew. Standing, he checked the rug, thankful the colors and weave hid what he'd been unable to clean. His gaze wandered to Emma, seeing her still grinning.

"It's not that funny, lass."

"Maybe not to you, but it made me feel better." She touched her temple, wincing. "Although laughing isn't much fun with my aching head."

Crossing his arms, his face sobered. He didn't want to think about what would've happened if he'd been a minute slower finding them. The cat's impact could've broken her neck before Finn got off a shot.

Shifting, she grabbed the pillow to pull it behind her back, groaning when it slipped out of her grasp and landed on the floor.

"Let me do it." Quinn picked up the pillow, making adjustments until Emma leaned back against it. "Better?"

"Yes. Thank you. Um, you don't need to stay. I'm sure Mama has supper ready, and I know you must be famished."

"Nae. I'll stay as Gertie asked." Grabbing a chair, he pulled it around, straddling it, resting his arms on the back. They sat in silence a couple minutes before he asked what had been bothering him.

"What possessed you to ride off with Finn?"

Glaring at him, she crossed her arms. "I didn't know I needed *your* permission to ride after strays or *your* permission on who went with me."

"Is that so? Then I don't believe you understand my job around here. Should I explain it to you again?"

Gritting her teeth, she leaned toward him. "I don't need you to explain anything."

"Because one word from me, lass, and you'll find yourself cooking, cleaning, and mending, instead of out on the range."

"How dare you threaten me." She spat the words out, showing no trace of her normal good nature. Turning her back to him, she scooted to the other side of the small bed.

Quinn smirked, although he felt no pleasure in pushing her. Lowering his voice, he tried to get her to listen. "Nae, lass. You misunderstand. It's no idle threat. Big Jim was quite clear. You either follow my orders or you'll spend your days in the house."

Emma sucked in a breath, turning back toward him. She saw compassion, not the look of triumph she expected. Her head throbbed, but her heart hurt more. "You're lying." Her voice held disbelief. "Papa would never stop me from riding. He knows how much I love the ranch."

"Aye. He would not stop your riding, but your days as a ranch hand will end—at least until I'm gone."

Forgetting her state of dress, she pulled the covers back, swinging her legs to the side. "Then leave. We don't need you here. We've never needed you here."

Quinn's gaze moved from the fierce features of her face to the thin nightgown, then to the bare legs dangling over the edge of her bed. His mouth went dry at the sight of pale, creamy skin. Swallowing a ball of desire, he groaned, pulling his gaze up to meet hers.

"Uh, lass...I think..." He gripped the back of the chair.

Emma glanced down when he hesitated, realizing what had caught his attention. Without uttering a sound, she yanked her legs up, pulling the blankets over them. "I think you should leave."

Standing, almost toppling the chair to the ground, he stepped away. "Aye, lass. It's best I leave."

She nodded, her composure returning. "Good."

"For tonight anyway." He walked into the hall, then turned. "I'll not be leaving the ranch until I've fulfilled the pledge I made to Big Jim."

"What pledge?" Her gaze narrowed, brows scrunching together.

"I promised to stay until he's fully recovered. I'll not be going back on my word—no matter how much you wish I would."

Chapter Five

Circle M

"Quinn. I was beginning to think my oldest son would not be joining us." Audrey turned her cheek for his kiss before wrapping her arms around him. Stepping away, she studied his face. "You're exhausted, lad. Take a seat and I'll bring you some tea."

"Nae, Ma. Tea isn't what I'm needing."

Cocking a brow, she nodded toward the study. "You know where your da used to keep his whiskey." She turned to walk back into the kitchen. "One only," she called over her shoulder.

Watching her leave, he removed his gunbelt, hanging it and his hat on hooks near the entry. Opening the study door, he glanced around, noting how almost nothing had changed since his father had been murdered while he, Brodie, and Colin had traveled to Oregon to retrieve Sarah. While still young, she and Colin had promised themselves to each other. Neither had ever forgotten their vow. When they returned to Circle M, it was to find out Colin's father, Angus, and Quinn's father, Gillis, had been murdered. After more than a year, Quinn still felt the same surge of pain followed by anger when he saw the empty chair behind his father's desk.

Taking a shaky breath, he walked to the cabinet where the whiskey had always been kept. Pulling down a glass and opening the bottle, he poured until the liquid touched just below the rim, then held it up to the morning light streaming through the window.

"To you, Da." He tilted the glass toward the sunlight, then took a sip. Ignoring the painful lump in his throat and the ache in his chest, he took another, leaning against the desk. He thought of the last time he saw his father, waving goodbye to them as they rode north. The three cousins had seen it as an adventure, although the trip was also the most important mission of Colin's life. Taking one more glance over his shoulder, Quinn had seen his da raise a hand, the grin on his face belying the fear he felt for his son. Everyone had concerns about the three young men traveling hundreds of miles. At the time, no one knew how misplaced the fear was—until Angus and Gillis had been gunned down.

"Ah, there you are, Quinn. Fletcher and I thought we saw you ride in." Bram joined him in the study, oblivious to the mental journey his brother had been on. "Where's Warrior?" He slapped Quinn on the back, then slumped into a chair.

Quinn pushed away from the desk and poured a second glass of whiskey, ignoring his mother's request. "Already stabled. I didn't see anyone. Where were you two?"

"On the eastern hill. We rode up there with Cam and Sean after church. Fletcher swore he saw a group of strays head up that way last night."

"And?"

"Nothing. Sean told him the cattle wouldn't use their energy climbing a hill when they could get away on flat ground." Bram laughed, remembering the good-natured ribbing Fletcher had endured. "So, are you done yet?"

Quinn tilted his head. "Done with what?"

"Your commitment to Big Jim. It's been a month and we're in need of you here."

Pinching the bridge of his nose, Quinn finished the whiskey, then set the glass down. "Doc says another two weeks, maybe longer." Letting out a frustrated breath, he took a seat in the chair next to Bram, cradling his head in his hands.

"The lass must be a handful."

Quinn dropped his hands, glancing at Bram, wanting to knock the smirk off his face. "I've no issue with Emma."

"Not if you've already bedded her."

In an instant, Quinn had Bram on his feet, gripping his collar, their faces inches apart. "You'll not be talking about her like that. Not now, not ever." He shoved Bram back into the chair, then turned away.

"So it's true." Bram straightened his shirt, then stood.

Whipping around to face his brother, Quinn took a step forward, ready for a fight. "What's true?"

Bram didn't back down. Instead, he moved closer to Quinn, his voice more conciliatory than taunting. "You *do* want the lass."

The words vibrated through Quinn. He wanted to deny them, pretend what he felt for Emma was only friendship. After a month in her presence, he knew it would be a lie. Nodding once, his pained gaze locked on Bram.

"Aye." Quinn turned back to the window, watching the activity around the barn.

"And you've chosen to say nothing."

"Aye. Emma doesn't know."

Walking up beside him, Bram clasped his shoulder. "And why not? The lass has always been daft for you. Big Jim and Gertie treat you as if you're already part of their family. What more do you want?" Dropping his hand, he moved to stand in front of him. At nineteen, Bram was four years younger, just as broad shouldered, and a scant inch shorter. It took no effort to see the pain flash across Quinn's face.

"I've no desire to settle with one woman. Emma, well…she's so bonny, so sweet…"

"Not much different from the lasses here at home, Quinn."

"Nae, but different from the women *I* spend my time with."

"They're a diversion for you, nothing more. Emma could be your life, the same as Colin and Sarah, or Brodie and Maggie. Don't you want what they have?"

Quinn scoffed. "And what do you know of love or commitment?"

Bram folded his arms, his feet spread shoulder width apart. "I'm a year older than Colin was when he made his vow to Sarah. I'm older than Da when he and Ma married. We're surrounded by love every day on the ranch."

"And look at Ma's life now. Da is dead. She'll grow old alone, without him by her side. Same with Aunt Kyla. Losing Angus almost killed her." Backing up, Quinn paced a few feet away. "I've no desire to fall in love, then have it all ripped from me."

"You forget. Ma has her children, as does Aunt Kyla. Within a short time, Colin and Sarah will give her a wee bairn. You're the oldest. You'll be giving Ma the same someday, maybe with Emma."

"Nae, Bram." The resignation in Quinn's voice stunned his brother. "You, Heather, and the others will be the ones providing Ma with wee bairns. Me? I'll be content with my work on the ranch, growing Circle M into the largest spread in California. I'll leave growing the family to you."

"And you'll stand aside to see Emma choose another? What if it's Blaine?"

Quinn's face reddened, his jaw hardening. "Emma would never choose him."

"Nae? If you turn your back on her, are you so certain she wouldn't choose a fine lad like him, or even another MacLaren? And if she does, would you be able to stay here, watching as she built a life with one of our cousins?"

He wanted to believe Emma wouldn't choose another MacLaren because he was the one she cared about, maybe even loved. Still, Bram's questions rippled through him, forcing Quinn to consider answers he didn't want to accept.

Getting control of his inner turbulence, he stalked to the door. "The lass will do whatever is right for her. If it's another MacLaren, I'll live with it." His chest constricted on the lie, making it hard to breathe as he left the study and walked outside.

Bram placed a hand on the window, watching Quinn storm to the barn. Moments later, he rode out, pushing Warrior into a gallop, as if the devil were on his tail.

"Perhaps the devil at your heels is just what you need, lad," Bram whispered.

Quinn rode for over an hour, traveling north into the hill country separating Circle M from the Pearce ranch. If he continued, he'd be back on MacLaren land, the portion of the Mexican land grant they'd bought from Juan Estrada. The same land Uncle Ewan and Uncle Ian wanted him and Brodie to oversee.

Quinn blew out a breath, feeling the familiar pang of guilt. With Brodie in town and him helping the Pearces, the added burden fell to Colin and Blaine. As experienced as Bram, Fletcher, Sean, and Cam were with cattle and horses, none had held a foreman position, which was what the additional land required.

His family had thought he'd be done with the commitment to Big Jim and Gertie by now. He'd thought the same. Quinn also believed he could handle being close to Emma. He'd been wrong. Bram's insight into how he felt about her had shaken him, made him wonder who else knew the truth. But it was only the truth from his perspective. Emma had never spoken of her feelings, and with their rocky friendship, whatever stirrings of desire she might have felt for him had no doubt been shattered.

Pushing his hat farther down on his forehead, he began to rein Warrior west until the unmistakable blast of gunfire and a deep rumbling through the ground had him whipping his gaze to the north. The sound had been so faint, he'd almost missed it, but he still felt the ground vibrating. Grabbing field glasses from his saddlebag, he scanned the land before him.

Moving his gaze left to right, then back again, he'd been about ready to believe he'd imagined the sound when he heard more shots. This time, Quinn's gaze focused on movement to the northwest. Locking on the object, he blinked a couple times to confirm what he saw, then cursed. A herd of about fifty cattle were being moved, and MacLaren men weren't the ones driving them.

Jamming the field glasses back into the saddlebag, he pulled his rifle out of its scabbard. Tightening his grip around it, he kicked Warrior into a gallop, holding the reins in his other hand as he rode low over the horse's neck. They were less than a mile away. If luck were with him, he'd get close enough to get off a few shots before they realized what was happening.

Coming up behind them, Quinn sat up in the saddle, raised the rifle, and fired. The man at the back of the herd toppled to the ground as Quinn sighted on a second rider and squeezed off a shot, missing. The next one hit its mark. The rider stayed in the saddle, clutching the horn. Another rustler came up next to him, then turned, seeing Quinn approaching.

Shouting a warning to the others, he drew his gun and aimed. Quinn reined Warrior hard to the left as bullets whizzed past. Coming to a stop, he raised the rifle, aimed, and fired, clipping a shoulder, failing to knock him from his horse. He'd stopped one and hit two others, but the rest were still in control of the herd, pushing them farther and farther away.

Roaring a frustrated curse, Quinn kicked Warrior into a gallop, refusing to give up. To his right, he became vaguely aware of a cloud of dust. Taking his eyes off the rustlers ahead of him, he looked over his shoulder, stunned to see Fletcher, Bram, Sean, and Cam racing toward him. A calm certainty claimed him. They might not get the rustlers. The herd, however, wasn't lost.

"*Creag an Tuirc*!" The MacLaren war cry split the air behind him as all four pushed their horses.

Guiding Warrior with this knees and thighs, Quinn lifted the rifle once more. Aiming, he squeezed off his last bullet, missing his target, but seeing the man rein away. The other outlaws followed, leaving the herd to their frantic stampede.

"Quinn!"

He turned to see Bram gesturing for him to follow their cousins. He nodded, knowing they had to mill the cattle. Getting them to circle into themselves would be the only way to stop the spooked charge. Fletcher and Cam took the lead, Sean and Bram close behind, riding alongside the herd, turning the cattle into themselves. The action allowed the horses to slow their frantic pace. The men continued their efforts, Quinn joining them, as the animals bunched together, slowing until the circle tightened.

"Holy Mother of God," Bram breathed, coming alongside Quinn, who wiped a sleeve across his forehead.

"Where did you come from?" Quinn asked his brother.

"Ach. Did you think I'd let you ride off after what was said? The other lads rode in as I started to follow you. They wouldn't be denied coming along, so..." Bram shrugged.

"Does Ma know I left?" A stab of guilt sped through Quinn. He knew how much Sunday suppers meant to their ma. Months ago, his sister, Heather, had taken a job at a nearby ranch and returned for Sunday meals every few weeks. The pain on their ma's face when Heather didn't arrive was plain to all. Quinn leaving had been selfish, and foolish.

"I'm not a complete eejit. I told her you had to check on something and would be back in time to eat. And you aren't making a liar of me, big brother." Bram flashed a smile, bringing a slight grin to Quinn's face.

"Aye, you're a wise lad all right." Quinn glanced around, seeing Fletcher ride up to them.

"It's going to take time getting the herd. Why don't you two go on along. No sense Aunt Audrey getting worked up about you being late for supper."

Bram dragged his hat off his head, running a hand through his hair. "That leaves just three of you to bring the herd back. No. We'll not leave you with such a burden."

"There's less than fifty head. We can handle them."

"I'm certain you can, Fletch. But you've not just the cattle to worry about." Quinn scanned the horizon. "The rustlers may return. We'll not leave you to worry about the herd and them."

Fletcher nodded. "Then we best get moving or there'll be no food left by the time we get home."

Exhausted, Quinn flirted with the idea of staying home, sleeping in his own bed, instead of riding back to the Pearce ranch. He could rise before dawn and still make it back before the men rose for breakfast. Instead, he saddled Warrior after supper and left.

It had been good to see Heather ride up, offering a bright smile to all except Caleb. The two had been at each other from the day they met. It seemed they had been born to fight. His cousin, Jinny, believed it was their way of pushing each other away, too afraid to admit their feelings. Quinn scoffed at the idea of either Heather or Caleb being scared of anything. Then he thought of his feelings for Emma. It gave him something to occupy his mind on the ride back to the Pearce ranch.

Riding into the barn, he dismounted, grabbed a lantern and lit it, placing it on a hook before unsaddling his horse. His movements were slow and mechanical from years of experience taking care of Warrior.

The entire ride back, his mind jumped between the rustlers, and where they'd strike next, and Emma. He worried about her taking off again, putting herself in danger. The thought of her getting hurt, or taken by men like the ones they chased today, gnawed at him.

"I wondered if you'd decided to quit."

Quinn spun around. Emma stood not six feet away, wrapped in a thin coat, her arms crossed. He took a couple steps toward her, surprised she'd gotten so close without him knowing.

"I didn't hear you come in."

She walked closer, closing the distance until they were a foot apart. She hadn't seen the complete exhaustion on his face or the slump of his shoulders until now. He'd been working from dawn until late each night, doing what her pa hadn't been able to do since Jimmy's death. The ranch was in better shape than ever, the ranch hands having a competence they lacked before Quinn arrived. Even though she still felt some justification for her actions, all she'd done was make his life harder.

Reaching up, she swiped an errant strand of hair from his forehead. The rush of feelings when her fingers touched his skin, caused her face to heat. She licked her lips as a pulsing sensation rushed through her. Dropping her gaze to his eyes, her heart tripped at the intensity of his stare. His gray-blue eyes turned stormy, the color of the night sky when lightning ignited the heavens.

Her stomach fluttered and heart raced when he said nothing, continuing to study her. Before she could step away, Quinn's hand came up, his fingers wrapping around her wrist, pulling her close.

She didn't flinch. Didn't try to pull away or break her gaze. Instead, she leaned forward, almost touching his chest.

"Emma…" He breathed her name out, almost as a prayer.

She could see the vein in his neck pulse, hear the almost desperate agony in his voice. Still, she didn't move away.

"What is it, Quinn?"

Searching her face, he sucked in a shaky breath, seeing trust and so much more. Lowering his head, he stopped an inch from her mouth, wanting her to pull back, needing her to meet him.

Lifting her chin, she placed her other hand on his chest, splaying her fingers wide. Her lips parted an instant before Quinn's touched them.

His actions were gentle, a mere caress before becoming more urgent. Letting go of her wrist, he wrapped his arms around her, aligning her body with his. Melting into him, she lifted her arms around his neck, drawing him down on a deep sigh.

Quinn had never tasted anything so sweet, so perfect. The waves of passion consuming him should have been a warning to step away. Instead, he traced the outline of her lips with his tongue, coaxing her to open, groaning when she allowed him access.

He had wondered if she'd ever been kissed. Now he knew. A sense of satisfaction gripped him as he deepened the kiss, knowing she'd never given this to another man. He could feel her fingers threading through the hair at the nape of his neck, sending a shiver of need straight through him. All this time, he'd denied his feelings for Emma, pushed her away, warning himself he wasn't right for her. Tonight, with her in his arms, her kisses overwhelming his senses, he realized the truth. He wanted more...so much more of her.

Breaking the kiss, he drew back, sucking in a ragged breath. Lifting her chin with a finger, he chuckled.

"Open your eyes, Emma."

When she did, the air ripped right out of him. Bram, Colin, and his Uncle Ewan had been right. Even without words, he knew she loved him.

"Emma, lass, you are so bonny." Quinn leaned forward, placing another kiss on her cheek. Gripping her shoulders, he stepped away, shaking his head. "We cannot do this." Pain sliced through him at the desolate look on her face. He wanted to explain, make her understand. Instead, he dropped his hands and took another step back, needing distance.

Her eyes, still glassy, closed tight, then opened. Swallowing the lump of disappointment at his words, she nodded. "I understand. I'm not the type of woman you want."

His eyes widened, a frown turning down the corners of his mouth. "I don't know what you mean."

Wrapping her arms around her waist, she turned to walk away. Within three steps, a hand grabbed her from behind, stopping her.

"I want to know what you mean, Emma."

She couldn't meet his gaze, humiliation at his rejection controlling her actions. Shaking her head, Emma pulled from his grip. "It doesn't matter." She tried to smile, knowing she failed when she saw what looked to be pity on his face. Lifting her chin, she jutted it toward him and shrugged. "It meant nothing. I've never been kissed before, and you seemed the perfect person to be my first." She wanted to choke on the lie. Whirling around, she marched out of the barn and to the house, the door slamming behind her.

His arms hanging limp at his sides, he watched her retreat. He'd been thoughtless and cruel when he didn't mean to be. Emma was the most beautiful woman he'd ever known. Not just outside, where she shone like the sun pushing away the dark clouds, bathing his world in light.

She was equally as gorgeous on the inside, with a huge heart and endless energy. And her smile...

Quinn sighed, thinking of the smile he'd come to expect. A smile that had all but disappeared since he'd come to work for her parents. And now he'd tasted her, knew how perfect and incredibly sweet she was. Revealing how he felt, how he ached to be with her, would bring nothing but heartache to both of them.

He'd told Bram the truth. Watching how his ma had mourned his father, how Aunt Kyla had mourned the death of his Uncle Angus, he'd vowed to never be drawn into a trap where his heart could be ripped from his chest. Quinn didn't understand how any man believed finding love could remove the emptiness from his life. He only knew what he saw when love disappeared, snatched away as a thief takes what belongs to someone else.

Firming his resolve to keep a safe distance until Big Jim healed, Quinn grabbed the lantern, extinguishing the flame. No matter what Gertie might say, he'd bunk with the men tonight and every night until his work here ended. Kissing Emma, holding her, had been a huge mistake. Now, each time he saw her, he'd think of the way she felt in his arms...and what he'd given up.

Chapter Six

Emma turned, punched her pillow, then shifted to her side in an effort to get comfortable. After leaving the barn, she ran straight upstairs, ignoring her mother calling from the living room. Three hours later, Quinn still hadn't come inside, and she hadn't gotten a minute of sleep.

When he hadn't returned from the Circle M before dark, Emma grabbed a book, sat by her bedroom window, and waited, dozing off at some point. Hours later, a noise from outside woke her. Seeing Quinn ride up, she'd grabbed a coat, slipped into boots, and dashed outside, coming to a stop when she saw him with his back to her. Emma hadn't meant to surprise him, only to let him know her mother had saved food if he were hungry. Wanting to lessen the tension between them, she tried to make a joke about him quitting. The look on his face hadn't been what she expected.

He'd stunned her when he pulled her to him. Anticipation replaced shock as she relaxed into him, sending up a quiet prayer. For years, Emma had fantasized about what it would be like if he ever held her, kissed her. She hadn't been disappointed. The kiss had been everything she'd ever dreamed of from the man she'd always wanted. Then he turned her away.

A silent tear rolled down her face. Emma knew she wasn't a ravishing beauty. No one would ever call her stunning, or even striking. Pretty and lovely were terms people used to describe her, along with vivacious, energetic, and kind. Until tonight, she'd always been happy with those descriptions. For Quinn to want her, she knew she had to be much more than pretty.

Emma had heard the stories about him, the women he'd been seen with, and his trips to Buckie's Castle. According to the town gossips, the women he escorted were older, widowed, experienced, and beautiful.

She'd seen him at the Gold Dust Hotel once. Her parents had treated her to supper there when she'd turned eighteen a year before. It had been a wonderful evening until partway through dessert. Her heart had plummeted when Quinn walked in alongside the most stunning woman Emma had ever seen. The pie she'd been enjoying no longer tasted so delectable. Setting down her fork, she'd excused herself, citing the need for some fresh air. Unfortunately, Quinn had spotted her leaving, walking out behind her.

He'd been cordial, asking about her parents and the ranch, standing outside with her a few minutes before excusing himself to return to his table. Watching him walk back inside, her chest tightened when he took the hand of the newest woman to capture his attention. Emma hadn't eaten at the Gold Dust since.

A year later, she still hadn't learned her lesson—until tonight. Throwing off the covers, she walked to the window, looking up at a cloudless sky glittering with brilliant stars. She'd held on for years, hoping and praying Quinn might one day see her as more than the younger sister of his deceased friend. After waiting so long, Emma had gotten her wish tonight, a moment before all her dreams were shattered.

Drawing in a deep breath, she made the toughest decision of her life. Emma would let him go, try to be the friend he wanted, and bury the love she felt deep inside. Others had asked to court her. She'd turned them all away. No longer. Starting tomorrow, she'd do her best to begin anew, even if it meant leaving Quinn MacLaren behind.

Four days later, Quinn stomped about the barn, saddling Warrior, getting ready to ride out with the men and Emma. After what happened, he'd expected her to be angry. Instead, she'd been pleasant, agreeing to anything he asked without complaint. If possible, her smile had become sweeter, her eyes brighter when they spoke, even if their discussions only included a few words.

At meals, she laughed at his jokes, spoke of the work around the ranch, and praised his abilities. He saw the Emma everyone in Conviction knew and loved. But it wasn't the passionate woman he'd held in his arms a few nights before. Her friendliness no longer signaled they were friends. Their bond had been severed, leaving a hole in his heart the size of a full moon. And it was all his fault.

Grabbing Warrior's reins, he stormed outside, then slowed his pace. Finn stood next to Emma, probably telling her one of his Irish lies, making her laugh. As he got closer, Finn let out a whoop.

"I'll see if Ma and Pa will let us use the wagon."

"Using their wagon would be grand. If you'd like, I'll go speak to them."

"There's no need, Finn. I'll tell them you've asked me to supper. I'm certain they'll be glad to get me off the ranch for an evening."

Quinn's jaw tightened, his nostrils flaring. Finn intended to court *his* woman. Worse, he wanted to throttle Emma for agreeing to have supper with him.

Knowing his anger was misplaced, Quinn fumed as he walked closer, narrowing the distance between the three of them.

"Ah, MacLaren. I didn't hear you come up." Finn flashed him a victorious smile. Quinn squelched the urge to wipe it off with a quick punch to the jaw.

"Aye. I see you've time to spare, Finn. I'd like you to take Jory and check the far eastern boundary. It's close to where the rustlers tried to take part of the MacLaren herd last Sunday. I want you to look for anything suspicious. Emma will be working with me today."

Emma's jaw dropped, but she stayed silent.

"But, boss, yesterday you said for me to take Emma and Jory and ride west."

"And now I'm telling you different. Is there a problem, O'Sullivan?"

Finn cast a disappointed look at Emma, then shrugged. "No problem, boss. I'll get Jory." Mounting, he took off, casting one last look over his shoulder at Emma.

Emma bit her lip, willing herself to keep her tongue in check. "And what, may I ask, is it you want me to do today?"

Shifting his gaze from Finn's back, he looked at Emma, his body reacting instantly. He'd fought his immediate response to her each day since their time in the barn. Right now, all he felt was growing anger. "Get Moonshine saddled. We'll ride out as soon as you're ready." Tossing Warrior's reins over a post, he took the steps into the house, leaving her to gape after him.

Glad Big Jim and Gertie were working on ranch business in the study, he stalked to the kitchen. Filling a glass from a pitcher on the table, he gulped down the water in a few quick swallows. Setting the empty glass aside, he scrubbed a hand down his face, muttering a curse, chastising himself. Now that he'd made his intentions clear, he had no business interfering in her life.

Quinn didn't see a way he could ever give Emma the happiness she deserved. Pushing her away had been the best solution. But upon hearing Emma accept Finn's invitation, he couldn't stand aside to allow the young rogue to be alone with her at night without an escort. In truth, it was Big Jim and Gertie's decision as to whether she went with Finn unaccompanied. Had he lived, Quinn knew what Jimmy's opinion would have been at seeing his impressionable sister fall under Finn's spell. He would've fought like hell to keep them apart.

Quinn had to find a way to thwart the lad's plans without garnering more of Emma's wrath.

His mind began to work. Quinn couldn't talk to Big Jim or Gertie about it. Instead, he'd need to come up with another way to thwart O'Sullivan's plans to get Emma alone.

"Are you going to tell me what our plans are for today?" Emma couldn't hide her sarcasm as they took the trail to the northwestern border of the ranch. Quinn may have had good reason for sending Finn off with Jory. Not catching the rustlers pretty much assured they'd regroup and try again, maybe going after her family's cattle.

Quinn glanced at her, then turned his gaze ahead. "We're heading to the northwestern border."

Groaning, she fixed a smile on her face. "Yes, I can see which way we're riding. My question is why? We already moved the herd south, closer to the ranch."

"The count was off. I'm hoping to find the missing cattle."

"Finn and I already tried. We found nothing—not a trace." Her brows furrowed. "How many are missing?"

"Your father estimates about twenty."

"Twenty? I saw no more than five or six run off."

Quinn looked at her, his mouth twisting into a smirk. "That's why we're riding north. To try and figure it out. Any more questions?"

Emma opened her mouth to deliver a sharp retort, then thought better of it. No sense getting into another argument with Quinn. What did she care if they rode north, east, or west? If his answers didn't make sense, what did it matter? All she needed to do was get through the next few days, not antagonize him, and wait. He'd be gone soon. She could get on with her life as if the last months hadn't happened—as if Sunday night in the barn hadn't happened.

She shook her head. "No more questions."

The trail meandered north, west, then turned north again, leading to the area Quinn wanted to search. Big Jim told him of a particular gully at the extreme northwestern corner of the ranch where cattle seemed to cluster. He'd also mentioned a ravine not far away. Another favorite of cattle that wandered off.

As they got closer to the edge of the property, Quinn reined Warrior to a halt, looking around. The gully should be straight ahead, the ravine to the right of it. His senses perked up at sounds coming from the direction of the gully. He glanced at Emma. She nodded, indicating she'd heard it, too.

"Ride behind me, and try to keep Moonshine quiet."

Quinn picked a path toward the gully, then dismounted, indicating for Emma to do the same. He pulled the field glasses from his saddlebag, then checked each of his guns. Unlike his brother or cousins, Quinn preferred a gunbelt with two holsters. He'd won the set in a card game a few years before, practiced until he became proficient with both hands, and wore it most days.

Leaving the horses, they continued forward. Steep walls, created by a combination of heavy rains and erosion, framed both sides of the gully. From where they stood, it appeared to be about a hundred yards deep and fifty feet wide, forming a rough circle that narrowed to about ten feet wide at the entrance. In the center, a small herd of cattle grazed on a sparse strip of grass. Crouching, Quinn and Emma looked around.

"I don't see anyone," she whispered from behind him.

"Neither do I." He didn't like it. If rustlers took them, at least one man would've been left behind to guard them. Counting, he came up with eighteen head, close to the number Big Jim anticipated. "Go back to the horses and wait for me, Emma. I'm going to climb to the top of the gully and look around."

"Shouldn't I go with you?"

"Nae. I want you able to ride out if anything happens." He saw her shake her head. "Emma, it's important you do this. I need to know you're safe, lass."

"If there's gunfire, I won't leave you alone. Please don't ask me to." She crossed her arms, her gaze fixed on him.

Quinn blew out a breath. "Lass—"

"No. I won't leave. You might as well accept it, or let me go with you."

"You are not going with me, and that will be the end of such talk."

"Then it's settled. I'll wait with the horses, but I won't leave." Her mouth formed a smug smile.

"Ach. Someday you'll push me too far." He glanced at the gully, then back at Emma. "Go on with you now."

Her eyes glittered in triumph before she turned her back on him and headed toward the horses. When she glanced over her shoulder, Quinn had already disappeared.

The walls of the gully were about fifteen feet high. An easy climb, but it would leave him exposed. Before Emma left, he'd spotted a trail. Taking it would put him at the top without being spotted.

Removing the gun from his right side, he started up. It didn't take more than a couple minutes to reach the top. Lying on the ground, he looked around, surprised to see flat ground, a few scattered bushes and trees, and nothing else. No men or horses.

Holstering his gun, Quinn hurried back down. Coming to a stop, a slow grin spread across his face. Emma held Warrior's reins, stroking his nose while whispering to the horse. Most women avoided the large, powerful stallion, too scared to get close. Not Emma. She treated him the same as any other horse—with respect and affection.

"He seems to like you."

She whipped around to face Quinn, her eyes wide as if she'd been caught doing something she shouldn't. "I was just, well..." She bit her lower lip, then turned back to Warrior. "He's such a beautiful horse. I hope you don't mind."

Walking up to her, he watched his horse nudge Emma's shoulder, a sure sign Warrior welcomed her touch. *The same way I do*, Quinn thought. Letting out a low groan, he took the reins.

"The fickle beast likes you. The only woman who's ever been around him is Heather. Men are normally all he'll let get close."

Emma shrugged. "Well, your sister is a superb rider."

"Aye. So are you. Perhaps he senses it in you."

She smiled at the compliment, then sobered. "You've always been a charmer. Your horse is no different."

His stomach clenched, seeing the light in her eyes dim. "Emma..." Reaching his hand out, he let it drop when she stepped away.

"Did you see anyone?"

"Uh...nae. Nothing. It seems the cattle strayed here on their own. Big Jim told me about this place. He said a few find their way here every so often."

Her eyes widened, then clouded over. "Papa told you of the gully? I wonder why he never showed it to me."

Quinn hated seeing the flash of pain on her face. "I think he just remembered it this morning when he told me about the missing cattle. No doubt he's not been here for years."

"With Jimmy, no doubt. They went everywhere together." She sucked in a breath, then grabbed Moonshine's reins, forcing a smile. "I suppose we'd better get these ornery animals back to the herd before dark."

Quinn watched her mount before swinging up on Warrior. "Aye. We should go."

"Finally. I was beginning to think you two had decided to spend the night with the herd." Gertie stood on the porch, arms crossed. "The other men got back a good hour ago."

"We found the strays, Mama. They were in the gully at the north edge of the property."

"Oh my. I haven't heard of that place for a long time." Her face took on a wistful look. "Jimmy and your father used to ride up there, stay a few days, then come home. I think it was their time to get away from everything."

"Including you and me." Emma climbed the steps, coming up next to her mother.

Gertie smiled. "It was just their time, honey. Men need to get away sometimes, talk the way they want without a woman interfering. It's the way of it. Right, Quinn?"

He looked down at his boots, uncomfortable with what seemed to be a personal conversation. "I suppose so, Gertie."

"Let's get you two inside. Big Jim and I have already eaten, but I saved you plenty. He'll want to hear about the missing cattle."

"Did Doc Vickery come out today?" Quinn inhaled the aroma of cooked meat as they entered the kitchen.

"He couldn't make it. A family who arrived on the morning steamship had a sick child. He sent a message saying he hopes to come out tomorrow."

"Papa's still doing better, isn't he, Mama? I mean, Quinn won't have to stay much longer, right?" Emma took a seat at the kitchen table, Quinn pulling out a chair across from her.

"Anxious to get rid of me, lass?"

Emma felt her face heat. She looked at him, then quickly away. "I'm certain your family is ready to have you back, especially with rustlers in the area."

"If we're causing a hardship with your family, Quinn, please don't feel you must stay. I'm certain we'll be all right." Gertie placed plates of food in front of each of them, then wrung her hands in the apron that was as much a part of her as the men's hats and kerchiefs were to them.

Quinn held a forkful of meat mid-air, looking up at her. "I'm not leaving until Big Jim is fully recovered."

Gertie's face relaxed and her hands stilled. Patting him on the shoulder, she turned back to the stove. "We appreciate what you've done more than you know. I'm afraid we'll never find a way to repay you."

Swallowing his food, Quinn took a sip of milk, then set down the glass. "You'd insult me if you tried. I'm doing this because I want to, and you need the help." His gaze locked on Emma. He knew she'd been watching him, thinking he wasn't aware of her scrutiny. If he were a different man...

"Quinn. I thought I heard you in here." Big Jim clasped his shoulder, then placed a kiss on Emma's cheek. "Did you find them?"

"We did, Papa. They were right were you told Quinn they'd be."

"The gully." Big Jim shook his head as he sat at the table. "I don't know how those animals find it. Jimmy and I used to run across them when we'd ride the lines." He crossed his arms and leaned back in his chair. "Thank you, Quinn."

Quinn saw Emma's face fall. Pushing his plate away, he met Big Jim's gaze. "Emma's the one you should thank. It took both of us to find and bring them home. She's the one who'll be taking over when I leave." He didn't miss the look Gertie shared with her husband. "What is it, Big Jim?"

The older man sat forward, resting his arms on the table, and clasping his hands. He sighed, casting an apologetic glance at Emma. "I suppose there isn't a better time to say this, sweetheart. Your mother and I have made the decision to hire a foreman. Someone with years of experience. A man we can count on—" He stopped when Emma jumped up from her chair, her face red with anger.

"You've hired an outsider to run the ranch? What about our plans for you to be in charge and me to act as foreman?" She slammed her hands on the table, startling everyone. "You said if I worked hard, did all you said, I could take over the job." Her voice rose with each sentence, her body shaking. "You *promised* me, Papa."

Holding his hands up, Big Jim looked as if he'd been slapped. "You're still young, Emma. There's plenty of time—"

"No. There's no more time. I love you, but I'm through believing what you tell me will happen. You'll never have faith in me, will you?"

He didn't answer, his lips thinning.

"Answer me, Papa."

Her mother stepped forward, glancing at her husband, then Emma. "That's enough. Your father's made a decision, and you'll have to learn to live with it."

Emma shook her head. "Yes, I'll learn to live with it. But it won't be here." Shifting her gaze from her mother to her father, she ran out of the room.

"Emma, wait." Big Jim started to rise, stopping when Gertie placed a hand on his shoulder.

"Let her be. She'll think about it. Tomorrow, she'll be back to the Emma we all know."

"I don't know, Gertie. This may have been too much for her."

She offered a regretful smile, not budging from what she believed. "Trust me. Tomorrow, Emma will be riding Moonshine with the men, tonight's argument forgotten."

Quinn sat frozen in his seat. When he offered to help, Big Jim had told him Emma would be taking over when he left. She'd counted on her father's words, believed what he promised would happen. A ball of anger formed in Quinn's stomach. He ached for Emma, understood the sense of betrayal.

"What do you think, Quinn?" Gertie sat next to him, a hopeful look on her face.

"It isn't my business how you run your ranch. I'll be gone as soon as Doc Vickery gives Big Jim approval to get back to work."

"Surely you have an opinion," Gertie persisted.

His jaw worked. They should've expected Emma's reaction. Announcing it in front of someone other than family added to her humiliation.

"I believe we'll all know more in the morning." Standing, he picked up his plate, taking it to the sink. "I'm bushed. Thank you for supper." Quinn couldn't muster a smile.

Walking outside, his stomach churned. He wanted to dash upstairs, talk to Emma, help her through what he knew would be a painful night. She had done her best to hide the hurt he'd caused her, but Quinn knew. A day didn't go by when he didn't regret what happened in the barn, the words he'd said. No matter how much he believed them, any kind of rejection stung. Now this.

Checking the barn one last time before bunking down, he walked back outside, glancing up at Emma's window. The curtains were open enough for him to see her moving back and forth in her room, dropping what appeared to be clothes on the bed. Crossing his arms, he planted his feet shoulder width apart, his face set. What he saw didn't bode well. The good girl, the one everyone could count on to do what was right and expected, might shock them all.

Chapter Seven

Quinn woke with a start. He'd slept near Moonshine's stall in the barn, not trusting what Emma might do. Gertie's declaration all would turn out fine didn't assure him in the least. He'd never seen Emma so hurt or broken.

Blinking, he pushed himself up and looked around. Moonshine was still in her stall, paying him no attention. As his gaze moved around the barn, he began to relax, finding nothing amiss. Then his eyes landed on the rail where he kept his saddle. It and his bridle were gone.

Racing to the pasture behind the barn, he scanned the area, then let out a string of curses. She'd taken Warrior.

"Eejit," he growled as he ran back inside the barn. Grabbing Big Jim's saddle and tack, it took him no more than a few minutes to saddle a spirited gelding. Swinging into the saddle, he debated a moment about telling her parents, deciding it would be better to find Emma and bring her back. Kicking the horse into a gallop, he headed toward Conviction, hoping his instincts of where she'd go were right.

He'd been wrong. Emma didn't go to see Brodie's wife, Maggie. They'd become good friends since the wedding. His cousin promised he'd keep watch, sending word if he found her, asking if he wanted to press charges for stealing his horse.

"I *should* press charges to teach her a lesson." He ran fingers through his hair, then muttered a curse. "What's she thinking, Brodie?"

The sun touched the eastern hills, the two watching as they sipped coffee on the top step of Brodie's porch. The one bedroom house he and Maggie lived in was provided by the town. It met their needs for now.

"She isn't."

Quinn smacked his cousin's skull. "Aye, I understand that much."

Brodie touched the back of his head, grimacing. "Ach, no need for violence."

"Where else would Emma go? I doubt she has much money, and she has no other relatives in town."

"Friends?" Brodie asked, resting his arms on his knees, cradling the cup in his hands.

"Nae. Lillie Gleason moved to San Francisco with her family." Pinching the bridge of his nose, Quinn thought a moment, then abruptly stood. "Jinny."

"My sister?"

Quinn nodded. "Aye. You know your da and ma would let her stay the night."

Brodie chuckled, then stood. "And Jinny will do her best to make sure Emma stays as long as she wants."

"Uncle Ewan and Aunt Lorna will get word to the Pearces." Quinn let out a breath, then finished his coffee, handing the empty cup to Brodie. "I'd best get home and make certain we're right."

"You may be the last person Emma wants to see right now. I'll ride out, then come by the Pearce ranch on my way back to town. Maggie wants to spend some time with Sarah anyway, see how she's doing."

"That's right. The wee bairn is due soon."

"Aye, and from what Blaine says, you don't want to be around Colin right now. The lad isn't handling it too well."

Quinn grinned. "Ach, you know our mothers won't let anything happen. With all the wee bairns born into the family, only two were lost." His face sobered, recalling the pain everyone felt at the loss. "They'll not let it happen again." Walking down the steps, he picked up the gelding's reins. "When you ride to the Pearce's, bring Warrior."

"It's a wonder the lass could handle the beast."

Quinn's mouth formed into a thin line. "Emma is an excellent rider and good with horses.

Mention it to your da. Maybe he'll let her work with Bram and Fletcher a bit...until things cool off with Big Jim and Gertie."

"I'll speak with Da, and bring Warrior back to you." Brodie crossed his arms, his face taking on a grim expression.

Quinn cocked his head. The two were as close as brothers, could sense each other's moods. "What is it?"

"We need to talk. Not now, but soon."

Quinn nodded, smiling. "Saturday night. You buy drinks, and Maggie makes supper."

Reining the horse around, he took the trail back to the Pearce ranch, wondering what he'd say to Big Jim and Gertie, more than a little concerned about their reaction.

Big Jim rose on shaky legs. "I'll ride over there now and get her."

"Nae. Wait until Brodie lets us know what he finds. Emma may not even be there."

"Is that what you believe, Quinn?" Gertie walked over to her husband and slipped an arm around his waist.

"Nae. I think Emma is at Circle M." He looked at both of them, knowing they wouldn't like what he said next. "If she is, it may be best to let her stay for a bit."

"That's ridiculous. Emma belongs here, not with your family."

"Gertie, you asked Quinn's opinion and he gave it to you." Big Jim leaned against the edge of a chair to keep his balance. "You and Emma have always been friends, Quinn. Why should we allow her to stay at your ranch?"

Quinn walked to the window, knowing the men had already taken off to start their day. He felt a stabbing pain, knowing Emma should've been out there with them, a bright smile on her face. Turning, he forced himself to show no emotion.

"You won't like my answers."

"Probably not, but I want to hear them just the same." Big Jim's grim features indicated the grief he felt at the decision he and Gertie had made.

"Emma is nineteen, a woman, able to decide what she wants. More than that, she's an excellent rancher with good instincts and better skills. I know you both believe she's still a girl, but let me assure you, she isn't, and hasn't been since Jimmy died."

Gertie sucked in a breath, gripping her husband's hand.

"Go on," Big Jim said.

"She's a hard worker, loves the land, and is willing to do whatever it takes to make this ranch a success. That doesn't mean she's ready to lead the men. Right now, I do believe the ranch needs a more experienced foreman. I haven't met the person you hired, so I have no opinion of him, but I do know Emma. She wants to breed horses, the same as we do at Circle M." Quinn stepped closer, his voice softening. "If she's at the ranch, I'll see she gets to work with Bram and Fletcher. She'll be surrounded by experienced ranch hands who'll respect her and treat her as one of their own. Emma may need this time away. When she's ready, she'll come home."

Silence blanketed the room. Big Jim eased himself into a chair, his tan face turning pale.

"It's my fault she's gone," Gertie whispered.

"No, Gertie. If anyone's to blame, it's me." Big Jim scrubbed a hand down his face, taking a moment to compose himself. "I promised her the job, then didn't explain to her why I changed my mind."

Quinn lowered himself into a chair across from him, leaning forward. "Why did you decide to hire an outsider?"

Big Jim's red-rimmed eyes met Quinn's gaze. "The longer it took me to heal, the more I realized how much more Emma had to learn. Part of it was watching you with the men. You know what you're doing, Quinn. Any ranch would be lucky to have you. Emma...her heart is in the right place, but I've done the girl a disservice by protecting her from the tough realities of ranch life. I've also done nothing to make the men see her as anything other than my daughter. They like her well enough, but respect? She's got to earn it. I'm afraid she doesn't quite know how."

Quinn rested his arms on his legs, clasping his hands. "If she's at Circle M, I'll help her learn."

He didn't know why he'd said it. Any of the MacLaren men would be a better teacher than him. Being around Emma messed up his mind, fogged his thinking. He'd talk to Colin. Together, they'd decide who'd be best to guide her.

A knock on the door had Gertie walking to the front. "Brodie. Come in. We've been expecting you."

He removed his hat, following her into the living room, nodding to Big Jim and Quinn.

"Well?" Quinn asked.

"Emma's at the ranch with my parents. She wants to stay."

Gertie's hand flew to her mouth as her eyes moistened.

"What does Ewan say about it?" Big Jim reached over, clasping his wife's other hand.

"Da and Ma are fine with her being there as long as she wants. She'll be staying in Jinny's room." Brodie looked at Quinn. "Emma wants to work while she's there. Da wants to talk to you about what's best for the lass."

Quinn nodded. He'd expected his uncle to say as much.

Brodie looked at Big Jim, then Gertie. "Tell me now if there is a problem with Emma staying at Circle M. Da and Uncle Ian made it clear they want no issues between the families."

"If we don't agree?" Gertie asked.

"I'll make sure she returns. But it doesn't mean she'll stay." Brodie fingered the brim of his hat, glancing at Quinn.

"I think our girl should come home, Jim."

He squeezed her hand. "I want Emma back here as much as you, Gertie. If it were up to us, we'd bring her home. As hard as it is to accept, she's a woman who needs to make her own decisions." Looking at Brodie, he nodded. "She'll stay at Circle M."

Letting go of her husband's hand, Gertie walked up to Brodie, her eyes full of sorrow. "You tell her to come home when she's ready."

"Aye, Mrs. Pearce. I'll let her know. If you don't mind, I need to speak with Quinn before I leave."

Quinn followed Brodie outside, walking down the steps to stand next to Hunter.

"Warrior's in the barn, still saddled. Thought you'd want to take care of him yourself."

"Thanks, Brodie. I'll try to get over to the ranch before supper tonight to speak with your da."

"And Uncle Ian." Brodie swung up on Hunter.

Quinn sighed. "Aye. Doc Vickery is coming out today to check on Big Jim."

"Drinks at Buckie's Saturday night. Maggie will have supper for us afterward, so you might as well plan to stay the night. We can ride to the ranch together after church Sunday."

Slapping Hunter on the rump, Quinn stepped away. "I'll be there."

Hooking thumbs in his pockets, he watched Brodie ride off. It had been a long night, a tough morning, and the day wasn't half over. He needed to take care of Warrior, then meet the men who were out with the herd. He'd sent Holler and another hand to check the north border again, not wanting to assume the rustlers had moved on.

Brodie had heard, through August Fielder, the Union troops were making progress against the South. Their partner in the land acquired from Estrada speculated the war would be over within months, perhaps even weeks, warning Brodie to expect a significant increase in people migrating west. Quinn knew many would be looking for work and a fresh start. If they didn't find it, he knew they'd do whatever necessary to survive, including stealing cattle and robbing banks. The outlaws who died trying to rob the people at Christmas might just be the start.

"Whiskey?" Ewan MacLaren set four glasses on the table, then filled each.

Quinn and Colin sat on their uncle's sofa, Uncle Ian across from them. Supper with Quinn's ma and siblings had been what he needed to relax, forgetting the turmoil at the Pearce ranch, if only for a few hours. He'd hoped to see Emma when he rode over to Ewan's house after supper. So far, there'd been no sign of her.

Nodding to Ian to close the study door, Ewan handed each man a drink.

"Thank you for riding over tonight, Quinn. I know you've been doing a lot for Big Jim and Gertie."

"No more than I'd be doing here, Uncle Ewan." Quinn sipped the liquor, readying himself for wherever the discussion led.

"I'll get right to it, lad. With Brodie in town, we need you back here. Any word on Jim's health?"

"Doc Vickery came out today, along with Hugh Tilden, the new doctor who moved here. He and Vickery worked together in Union Army field hospitals."

"I haven't met him yet," Ian said, leaning forward in his chair. "What did they say?"

Quinn rolled the glass between his fingers and thumb, studying the liquid as it coated the sides. "Big Jim's as healed as he'll ever be."

"What does that mean?" Colin set his glass down and stood, stretched his arms above his head, then paced around the room. Bram had mentioned their cousin doing this more often as the time for his baby's birth got closer.

"He'll need to use a cane to get around. Riding won't be an issue, but he's done doing anything more physical than dealing with the men. They told him to take it easy."

Ewan chuckled. "You know he won't."

"Nae. He's too anxious to get out of the house and back on a horse. It's good he has a foreman starting the day I leave."

Ewan leaned against his desk. "Have you met him?"

"Nae, and Big Jim didn't give me his name. I don't like it, but it's not my ranch. Something just seems...off."

"Ian and I will ride over as soon as we can. It might be easier for us to find out how Big Jim is doing, learning more about the new foreman. It's important to know who's working the land next to you."

Quinn emptied his glass, set it down, then stood. "If you've nothing else..."

Ewan leveled a gaze at him. "Sit back down, lad. We need to talk about Emma."

Rubbing his eyes with the palms of his hands, he groaned, lowering himself into the chair. "What about the lass?"

Ewan cast a look at Ian, then back at Quinn. "Bram and Fletcher said they'd let her work around them and the horses."

"Good. She was born to work with horses."

"That isn't all, Quinn. We need extra help with the herd. She's experienced and is happy to help."

"I'm certain she will do whatever you ask."

Ewan crossed his arms, his face devoid of expression. "She'll be working with Blaine."

Quinn jumped up from his seat, his jaw tight. "The hell you say."

Colin moved up next to him, placing a hand on his cousin's shoulder. "Calm down. You know we can't just let her loose. Someone needs to ride with her."

"Not Blaine," Quinn countered, his voice rough.

"You aren't here and neither is Brodie." Colin dropped his hand, stepping in front of Quinn. "I have to keep watch on the expanded herd on the old Estrada land or I'd take her with me."

"I'll be back in a few days."

"She starts with Blaine tomorrow." Ewan took a step forward, halting when Colin held up his hand.

"I'll take over when I get back." Quinn crossed his arms, his face turning to stone.

Colin lowered his voice. "Quinn, the lass doesn't want to work with you. You'll be working with me when you get back."

Quinn glared at Colin, then shifted his attention to Ewan and Ian. They knew, the same as he did, that Blaine had an interest in Emma, talked about courting her. Quinn had turned her away and had no claim on her. It didn't mean he wanted to watch his cousin with her.

"I have to get back." Quinn stormed toward the door.

"Wait, Quinn."

"I heard what you said, Uncle Ewan. I don't need to hear any more." Slamming the door behind him, he didn't even notice Emma and Jinny sitting in the living room.

"Quinn?" Emma stood, taking a hesitant step in his direction. He glanced over his shoulder, his eyes blazing.

"I've no time for you now, lass. Ask Blaine your questions. I'm certain the lad will be more than willing to answer them." Grabbing his hat and gunbelt, he turned his back on her as he opened the door and walked into the night.

Emma's jaw dropped as she looked at Jinny. "What did I say?"

"I'm afraid it isn't what you said to Quinn. It's what you told Colin."

Emma's stomach lurched. She'd been angry with her parents, still hurting from Quinn's rejection when Colin asked her who she'd like to ride with. *Anyone but Quinn.*

"You've got to learn to be careful about what you say around here, Emma. The men will take you at your word." Standing, she came up next to her, placing an arm around her friend's shoulders. "Don't worry about Quinn. His reaction tonight says much more than what he said to you at the ranch."

Emma's face colored, her voice dropping to a whisper. "Shhh, Jinny. No one else knows about that night."

"And no one will hear anything from me. But I knew Da and Uncle Ian were going to tell him you'd be riding with Blaine. I didn't expect him to be happy with the news." Jinny smiled, dropping her arm. "Storming away from you says a lot."

"You're right. It says he hates me."

Jinny laughed. "I don't think so, Emma. Just wait until he returns to the ranch." She clasped her hands in front of her. "This is going to be real exciting to watch."

Chapter Eight

Conviction

"You've not touched your whiskey. Something wrong?" News traveled fast. Brodie had already heard about Quinn's reaction to Blaine being the one to ride with Emma.

"I've a lot on my mind," Quinn murmured, cradling the glass.

Brodie rested his arms on the table. "Sorry, lad. Anything you want to talk about?"

Quinn shook his head. "Nae." He lifted the glass, taking a slow sip. His gaze clouded before his eyes cleared and he looked at Brodie.

"Did you meet the new foreman?"

"Aye. He rode in today before I left. Boyd Doggett. Ever heard of him?"

Brodie thought a moment. "Nae, but I can check wanted posters if it will make you feel better."

"I'm more curious than worried. Big Jim said he got Doggett from a ranch in Colorado. People he'd known for years. They didn't fire him. He wanted to see California, so they sent Big Jim a telegram, asking if he knew of anyone looking for a foreman."

"Seems it all worked out."

Quinn shrugged, knowing time would tell if Boyd stayed around. "What did you want to talk about?"

"Circle M."

Quinn sat up straighter, leaning forward. "What about it?"

"Fielder thinks it's time I quit my job and return to the ranch."

Nothing Brodie said could've surprised Quinn more. "Why? You're the best sheriff this town has ever had."

"Fielder told me the same. He isn't forcing me out. It's a suggestion."

Quinn snorted. "The man who hired you is making a *suggestion*? What's his reason?"

Brodie glanced around the room, noting the tables filled with ranch hands enjoying their one night away, gamblers stuffing their pockets with hard-earned money, and working women draping themselves over the men. It may seem odd to most, especially his family, but he loved being a lawman. Each morning, he woke up looking forward to whatever happened, good or bad. It hadn't been long enough to burn a hole in his heart or turn him into a cynic.

"It's simple. I'm needed on the ranch. The herd more than doubled with the purchase of Estrada's cattle."

Quinn's eyes narrowed. "I hadn't heard about buying the herd."

"Estrada spoke with Da, Uncle Ian, and Fielder not long after you left to help the Pearces. They came to an agreement before Fielder spoke with me. Most of Estrada's vaqueros found work elsewhere. A few asked to stay and have been offered jobs. Colin and Blaine can't keep up, and Fletch, Bram, Sean, and Cam aren't ready to lead ranch hands." He sipped his whiskey, his gaze focusing on the liquid left in his glass.

"Caleb is ready."

"Aye, but he's not a MacLaren. Da and Uncle Ian aren't ready to pass along the responsibility to anyone who isn't family. I have to consider what Fielder said."

"Surely you'll not quit being sheriff. It's what you've dreamed of doing since you were a young lad." Quinn scrubbed a hand down his face. "Ach. Of course you'll quit. You'll do whatever is needed for the family."

"As would you."

"Aye. The difference is I love working on the ranch. It is my dream, as being a lawman is yours." He sat back on a deep sigh. Reaching for the bottle in the center of the table, he filled their glasses. "Don't make your decision yet. My work for Big Jim is over, so I'll be back at Circle M tomorrow. I'll work with Colin, which will allow Blaine to work the original herd." Swallowing the whiskey, his chest squeezing, he thought of Blaine riding alongside Emma. "Give it a month, lad. Make sure of your decision. We can all still fulfill our dreams."

Brodie tipped his glass toward Quinn and smiled. "I'll give it a month if you'll do something for me during the same time."

Quinn cocked his head, his gaze narrowing. "You know I'll do anything."

Brodie tossed back the whiskey, then leaned forward. "If you want to run a ranch, build your own dream, you'll need a woman who will share it with you."

Quinn rubbed the back of his head. "If this is about Emma, I've already told the lass I've nothing to offer."

Brodie nodded, still not able to understand Quinn's thinking. Pushing back his chair, he stood, squaring his shoulders, sending a hard look at his cousin. "Blaine has every intention of courting her. All I'm asking is for you to be sure, lad. There *will* come a time when you can't turn back."

"Glad you're back." Blaine clasped Quinn's shoulder. They sat next to each other at Sunday supper, directly across from Jinny and Emma, Blaine unaware of the glances passing between Quinn and Emma.

"No more than I am to be here." Taking the bowl of potatoes, he took a large helping, handing it to Blaine. "I'll be working with Colin."

Blaine turned his gaze to Quinn. No one had to tell him something wasn't right between him and Emma. He could tell by the way the two avoided each other.

"I can stay with Colin if you'd rather work with Emma."

"Nae. The uncles have made their decision." Quinn raised his voice enough for Emma to hear, keeping his gaze on Blaine. "Besides, it seems Emma prefers working with you." A small amount of pleasure passed through him when he heard her suck in a breath.

"The lass has good taste." Blaine flashed a smile toward Emma, whose face colored before she turned to talk with Jinny. A chair scraping across the floor claimed everyone's attention.

"Welcome home, Quinn." Ewan stood at the head of the table, Ian beside him. "It's good to have you back."

Quinn nodded, glancing around the oversized table in the house they'd built for Colin's ma and da. The room was big enough to accommodate well over twenty people. The table had been a work of love, everyone having a hand in finishing it. The chairs were occupied by family, the people he cared most about.

Quinn hadn't realized how hard it would be for him to be so close to Emma, still wanting her, with Blaine ready to stake a claim.

Ewan nodded at him once more before sitting down. "Brodie told us you met Big Jim's new foreman."

Emma's head snapped up, her gaze locking on Quinn's. He hadn't been back long enough to tell her about the man, but had planned to do it in private.

"Aye. Boyd Doggett. He came from a ranch in Colorado." Quinn didn't say the ranch hands seemed to take to him right away.

Clearing her throat, Emma licked her lips, then looked at Quinn. "What did you think of him?"

Quinn's voice softened, as did his features. "Doggett's older, late thirties, maybe forty. Gertie told me he grew up on a ranch in Texas. He's been a foreman for a while."

A sadness washed across her face before she looked down at her plate. "Good. I'm glad they found someone they trust."

The table fell silent. No one wanted to interfere in another family's business.

Jinny settled a hand on Emma's arm. "It's good you came here. You'll get to help Bram and Fletcher with the horses, which is what you've always wanted."

"And when you're ready, you can take the skills you learn back to your ranch," Ewan added, understanding the disappointment Emma felt, although he believed Big Jim and Gertie made the right decision.

Emma looked around the table, her chin jutting out. "There's so much to learn. I don't plan on going back...at least not right away."

"Then you'll stay as long as you like. Hardworking ranch hands are always welcome." Colin smiled at her as he reached for Sarah's hand, grasping it in his much larger one.

"Aye. Colin is right. Perhaps this is where you're supposed to be." Blaine cast a quick look at her, then went back to finishing his meal. Quinn stilled, not missing the implication of Blaine's comment or the stark look on Emma's face.

A strange sensation wrapped its way around his heart as he continued to watch Emma. Quinn didn't want to draw attention to either of them. He did know he needed to get her alone, try to fix the tension between them. And it needed to be done tonight.

Fletcher and Jinny walked back to their house with Kenzie, their eleven-year-old sister, and nine-year-old twin brothers, Clint and Banner. Emma walked behind them, thinking about Boyd Doggett and Quinn's description of him. She recalled the argument with her parents where she'd stormed out, packed her belongings, and left. A week later, Emma could admit her actions were rash. Her parents had made the right decision to hire someone with more experience, although the feeling of betrayal still stung.

"Emma, wait."

Glancing over her shoulder at the sound of the familiar voice, she turned. As always happened, her heart raced at the sight of Quinn. Her brain pulled her in one direction, telling her to accept his decision to let her go. Plaguing every waking moment was her hopeful heart, urging Emma not to give up.

"What is it, Quinn?" Hands clasped together, she stood still, waiting.

Quinn stopped a foot away, close enough for her to see the gleam in his eyes and hesitant set of his mouth. He seemed nervous, which surprised her. Always confident, he never let anything bother him, least of all a woman he had no interest in.

Exhaling, he finally met her gaze. "Would you have time to walk with me?"

She glanced behind her to see Fletcher and Jinny had stopped, staring at them.

"They'll go on. I'll walk you back to Uncle Ewan's when you're ready." Quinn raised a hand, signaling them to head home.

"What if I'm ready now?"

He saw the mischief in her eyes, something he hadn't seen in weeks, and smiled. "You're not."

Quinn didn't wait for her response, placing a hand on the small of her back, guiding her toward a fenced pasture. Dropping his arm, he opened the gate. They stood just inside, watching several MacLaren horses ranging in age from the colt born a few months before to a three-year-old filly. All were part of the small herd Bram and Fletcher had started to build.

"They're so beautiful," Emma breathed out as she took a few cautious steps forward, Quinn right beside her. "I still can't believe how lucky I am to be working with Bram and Fletcher." The smile she flashed at him sucked the air from his lungs, causing his steps to falter. "I know you talked to your uncles about letting me learn from them.

After all that's happened, I'm surprised you wanted to help me."

His throat constricted. What he wanted to say and what he should say were completely different. Bram and Brodie were right. He couldn't stay at the ranch and watch Blaine court her, standing aside as she fell in love with his cousin. Yet he couldn't leave the ranch he loved, the life he'd always wanted. Quinn had never felt so conflicted.

Staring at her, he studied a face clouded with confusion. "We're friends, Emma. At least I *hope* we still are."

He watched her expression still for a brief moment, her voice becoming soft, wistful.

"Yes. We're still friends." Her gaze returned to the horses, Quinn noticing the slight slump of her shoulders. Causing her pain had never been his intention.

Crossing his arms, he followed her gaze, the corners of his mouth curving upward when the two youngest of the herd danced around each other, then quieted.

"It's obvious you were born to work with horses. Big Jim is one of the best men around with cattle. Horses? They're a necessary part of his work, nothing more."

She drew in a deep breath, her gaze never leaving the horses. "My father and I have had the same conversation more than once. He's content to spend his time on cattle and doesn't see the potential of offering better horse stock. Jimmy believed as I do." Emma shifted toward Quinn. "When he died, Father lost all interest in breeding horses, other than to supply the remuda."

"When you return, it will be your job to convince him otherwise."

"What makes you think I'll ever go back?"

"They're your family, lass. All families have disagreements. It's not cause to shut them from your life." Placing a finger under her chin, he coaxed her to look at him. "About what happened in the barn…"

Emma stepped away, not interested in hearing whatever excuse he might want to make. "Nothing significant happened, Quinn. It was just a kiss between friends."

His eyes flashed, jaw hardening. "Is that what it was to you?"

Locking her gaze with his, she crossed her arms. "Of course. We've known each other a long time, always as friends and nothing more. Besides, I know about the women you see in town. I'd never delude myself into thinking I could ever offer you what they do."

Quinn's jaw dropped. He never expected her to compare their friendship to the fleeting acquaintances of a few women he escorted. Their company filled a short-term need, paling in comparison to what he felt for Emma. He had to find a way to correct her impression.

Glancing over his shoulder, irritation flared when he spotted Blaine approaching.

"We'll finish this discussion another time, and don't believe we won't. It's time to get you back to Uncle Ewan's."

Placing a hand on her back, Quinn turned Emma toward the gate, closing it behind them as Blaine stopped a few feet away. Shoving hands in his pockets, Blaine looked out at the horses, then at Emma.

"We'll need to get an early start tomorrow. Uncle Ewan wants us to ride the eastern property line and check for strays."

Quinn narrowed his eyes. "Only the two of you?"

"Nae, Quinn. Caleb will be riding with us." Blaine hesitated a moment. "You're welcome to come along."

"Nae. I'm riding with Colin tomorrow." He glanced at Emma, then took a few steps away, telling himself what he was about to do was for the best. "I've got to finish up in the barn. Can you walk Emma back to Ewan's?" The broad smile on Blaine's face almost had him changing his mind.

"Aye. It would be a pleasure."

Emma's eyes flickered as Blaine cupped her elbow, guiding her toward Ewan's. Her heart twisted as she shot Quinn a quick look over her shoulder. He stood motionless, arms hanging loose at his sides, a bleak expression on his face.

She'd been so hopeful when he asked her to walk with him. Now she felt like a fool. Pulling away from Blaine's relaxed grasp, she clasped her hands behind her back.

"He's hard to understand."

Emma turned her gaze to Blaine. "Who?"

He chuckled. "Quinn. He's always said he doesn't plan to settle down and marry."

Her eyes widened. "Do you believe him?"

Blaine glanced at her, then shook his head. "Nae. He's more tied to the land than any of us, which tells me he's already settled down. The lad just hasn't accepted it."

They walked a few more steps in silence.

"And marriage?"

"Ach, who knows? Like I said, his reasons are sometimes difficult to understand. It may have something to do with Uncle Gillis dying."

"I'm certain losing his da was hard, but I wouldn't think it would change the way he thinks about marriage. Your father was murdered with Gillis. Colin married Sarah anyway, and you..."

A sly grin crossed his face. "Aye, lass. I plan to marry someday. Finding the right lass? That's another story."

Nudging him with her shoulder, Emma smiled. "When you're ready, I'm certain you'll have no problem attracting the right woman. Besides, I know of at least—" She clamped a hand over her mouth. Emma couldn't believe she'd been ready to blurt out the names of at least two young women who'd be thrilled to have Blaine court them.

"You know of at least *what*?" Blaine prodded.

Dropping her hand, she refused to meet his gaze, feeling her face flush. "Nothing."

"Sounded like more than nothing, lass."

"All I'll say is when you're ready, I don't think you'll have any problem finding a suitable woman."

Blaine didn't respond, keeping his gaze focused on the house ahead, for which Emma was grateful. She didn't need anyone to tell her Blaine had an interest in her. He hadn't even tried to hide it. As was true of all the MacLarens, he was handsome, smart, and worked hard. Any woman would be honored to have Blaine court her. Any woman except her. She hoped he didn't ask because she had no desire to hurt him.

Emma had already given her heart to one MacLaren. Even after what Quinn had said, she couldn't seem to break her thin thread of hope and leave her dreams of loving him behind.

Chapter Nine

"I'm sorry, Mr. Pearce. There isn't much more I can do."

Big Jim didn't reply as he held the bank notice telling him of the eminent foreclose if he didn't pay off the loan due three months earlier. Gertie knew nothing of the credit he'd taken out not long after Jimmy died. There'd been no reason to tell her. He'd made the payments on time every month until several hundred dollars remained. It might as well have been a few thousand.

The money he'd set aside for the loan had gone to pay Quinn's wages, which he gave directly to Ewan—an agreement Big Jim had insisted on with the elder MacLaren. Now the money went to pay Boyd Doggett, the new foreman. The bullets Big Jim had taken at the Christmas social impacted ranch profits more than he ever imagined.

Deegan James sat forward, his arms on the desk, hands clasped. "I'd have to get the board's approval, but I might be able to go another thirty days."

The slender, fair-skinned banker had moved to Conviction from St. Louis. After meeting with a group of investors, the decision had been made to open a branch of the San Francisco Merchant Bank—in competition with the Bank of

Conviction, the other financial institution. August Fielder was the major shareholder.

At first, Big Jim had felt guilty about bypassing the bank where he held a position on the board. Now he felt grateful, not wanting his friends, men he respected and admired, to know the extent of his debt. Nodding, he stood.

"I'll take the thirty days. I'd appreciate it if no one else knew about this."

"Of course. I'll let you know the decision within a few days." Deegan walked around his desk, extending his hand. "I don't want your ranch, Mr. Pearce. My understanding is cattle prices are stable right now." Meaning if the cattle could get to market soon, they might fetch enough for Big Jim to pay off the loan and put some money into savings.

Big Jim looked at the banker, who stood several inches shorter than him. "Boyd and I plan to start moving the herd next week. I'm fortunate to have a buyer in Sacramento."

"I wish you a safe, profitable trip." Deegan held the side door open for Big Jim, the exit leading to the walkway between the bank and mercantile next door. It was the same door used by several of his customers who preferred to keep their dealings with the bank discreet.

Picking up the notes he'd made, Deegan walked into the main lobby, pausing at his secretary's desk. "Please add these to Mr. Pearce's file. As always, Mrs. Ulster, this information is confidential."

The young widow nodded. "Of course, Mr. James." She read his notes, taking a moment to add the information to a journal before slipping the paper into Big Jim's file. With little thought, she opened her bottom drawer, set the journal inside, then turned the key. Placing it in her top drawer, she returned to her other work, her mind already occupied on the stew she planned for supper.

Boyd moved his gaze around the circle of young ranch hands. All were greenhorns except Holler, who'd grown up on a ranch and been on several cattle drives. Finn and Jory were hard workers, intelligent, and quick to learn. The other two young Irishmen did their best, but he didn't believe they'd stay on after the cattle drive. Boyd already had to fire the boy from Louisiana when he caught him drunk while on the job. He hoped the other five would stay until they reached Sacramento.

"Holler, I want you and another man to check the brands on each of the animals we'll be moving to Sacramento. Any issues, you bring them to me."

"Yes, sir. I'll work with Finn."

Boyd looked at the other three ranch hands. "The rest of you will be working with me. We're going to cull the herd, separating those we'll be taking from those that aren't ready to sell. The ones going on the drive will be moved into the large corral for Holler and Finn to check." He watched heads nod, knowing none of them had ever done the job before. "Follow my lead and we'll get through this today. Mr. Pearce intends to move the herd to Sacramento in a few days."

"Do we all go on the drive, boss?"

"Yep, Jory. I need all of you. You'll be paid when we get the herd to Sacramento."

"Will you be needing us all to come back?" Finn glanced at the others, their expressions blank.

"There's work if you return. If not, let me know after we deliver the herd. You can take your pay and head out." Boyd didn't expect all of them to return. It was a rare drive when he didn't lose some of the men once they'd received their pay. "Let's get to work."

He watched Finn and Jory, talking in hushed tones, walk to their horses. The other two Irishmen walked behind them, immersed in their own conversation.

"We should move on, Finn. Find work in San Francisco or another cattle ranch closer to the ocean."

"I've no mind to leave yet, Jory. The work here is good, and Big Jim pays us fair." He glanced over his shoulder at Boyd. "Doggett knows his business and can teach us much. There's no reason to go."

Jory glared at him, his voice low and fierce. "You're thinking of the Pearce gal instead of what we planned."

Finn stopped, waited until the other men walked past, then shoved Jory into the shadows. "We'll not be speaking of Miss Emma. She's gone."

"For now," Jory hissed.

"It doesn't matter how long she stays away. The girl is not for me." He took a step closer, his face hardening. "We need the work. When we've saved enough, we'll leave."

Finn would never admit how much Emma had come to mean to him before she left to work at Circle M. His reputation in Cork had been that of a rake, never spending more than a short period with any gal, taking what she offered before moving on. The warmth he felt radiating from Emma made him want to own a piece of it, wrap his arms around it, and never let go. As a poor immigrant boy with nothing in his pockets, only a dream to keep him going, he accepted a girl such as Emma was out of his reach. Someday, though...

"What of the others?" Jory nodded toward the two who were now yards ahead of them. His words pulled Finn's attention back to the present.

"We brought them with us from Cork, as we agreed. They'll be making their own plans once we reach Sacramento."

Jory placed fisted hands on his hips, glaring at Finn before letting his gaze fall to the ground, accepting his cousin was right. The other two were friends who wanted to travel with them to America. He and Finn had agreed to bring them along. They fulfilled their promise and owed them nothing more. He let out a frustrated breath before glancing up.

"I'll return with you after Doggett sells the cattle, staying through the summer. After that, I make no promises."

Finn watched Jory storm away, wondering what had gotten him so all-fired mad. After their first week working for Big Jim, they'd agreed to stay at least two years, learn the business, save money, then decide about moving on. In his mind, nothing had changed. Clearly, Jory didn't see it the same. Talking sense with his cousin never worked when anger took over. Finn would wait. There'd be time enough to figure out what ate at Jory between now and the time they returned from Sacramento. And if what Finn suspected came true, they and Holler would be the only ones coming back.

"Do you have the list?" Giles Delacroix leaned his heavy frame against the doorjamb, smoke from a cheroot streaming from his mouth to disappear into the night air. He wore all black, but they weren't the clothes of a gunslinger. His were made of fine cloth, the vest brocade with silver threads, the boots of fine, polished leather. The only color came from his deep red beard, which matched his hair, and the handkerchief in his coat pocket.

"I have it right here." Chester Bailey patted his coat pocket, taking a seat next to an old wood stove. A worn pallet topped with a thin, dirty mattress made up the rest of the furniture in the small cabin miles from Conviction. "Do you have the money?"

Giles tossed the cheroot on the floor, grinding it out with the heel of his boot, then pulled a pouch from inside his vest. Taking a couple steps, he tossed it on top of the stove.

"It's all there...as we agreed. Now, I'd like the list."

Chester stood, grabbed the pouch, feeling the weight, then smiled. Taking the list from his pocket, he reached out to hand it to Giles, grimacing when the man encircled his wrist in an iron grip.

"The information better be accurate. You won't like the consequences if I find you've manipulated anything." Giles dropped Chester's wrist, but not before seeing the beads of sweat forming on the man's forehead.

"I'd never do anything so foolish, Mr. Delacroix." His voice shook as he took a few steps backward. "I value my life too much."

"Glad to hear that." Giles opened the paper, scanning the four names and balances owed.

"All of them have been extended a few weeks—"

"I can see that," Giles interrupted.

Chester cleared his throat. "I doubt any will be able to come up with the money to pay the balances. There is always a chance, though. Mr. Pearce is taking his herd to Sacramento this week. If he gets a good price..." He shrugged, his words trailing off.

"And the others?"

Chester pulled a handkerchief from his pocket, mopping his brow. "Widow Jones barely keeps food on the table and hasn't paid her only ranch hand in two months. I couldn't find out anything on the other two."

Giles nodded, slipping the list into a pocket. "You've been most helpful." His gaze narrowed as he leveled a stern look at Chester. "I expect to hear from you if anything changes."

"Yes, sir. I'll get word to you the usual way." Chester pulled the door open and stepped outside, glad to have accomplished what Giles asked. His work for the man was finished. In a few days, Chester would take the steamboat south, with no intention of ever returning to Conviction.

Circle M

Exhausted and ready for a hot meal, Emma slid off Moonshine. Grabbing the reins, she followed Blaine and Caleb toward the barn, stopping and looking behind her when she heard shouting.

"What's your Uncle Ewan waving in his hand?" Emma asked.

"I've no idea." Blaine handed his horse's reins to Caleb, then dashed toward his uncle. "What is it?" he shouted.

Ewan smiled, holding up a piece of paper as he closed the distance between them. "August Fielder made sure we heard the news."

"What news?"

"Lee surrendered to Grant. The war is all but over." Ewan glanced over Blaine's shoulder, seeing Caleb and Emma running up.

"What happened?" Emma held a hand to her stomach, praying whatever news Ewan had wasn't about Quinn. Seeing his relaxed features, the tilt of his lips, she realized it couldn't be anything bad.

Ewan handed the message to her. "The South admitted defeat. Lee and Grant signed papers somewhere in Virginia. August Fielder believes it's only a matter of time before President Lincoln declares a Union victory. The nation may finally have peace."

Caleb snickered. "Until the next time men want to take something away from others."

Ewan raised a brow. "You don't believe we can have peace?"

"I'd like to, but we all came here from Scotland. When did *we* ever see a time of peace?" Caleb's family had come to America a few years before the MacLarens. Although his brogue was slight, there was no mistaking his Scottish roots.

"Aye. You may be right, lad. But America is different. People here want the same things— honest work, a safe place to raise their family, a chance to end up better than the life they had before."

"Perhaps. Seems to me they go about it in different ways." Caleb shoved hands in his pockets, looking at the distant horizon. "We'll see the kind of people who move here once peace is declared. I've a feeling we'll get as many bad as good coming this way."

"Don't be so negative, Caleb." Emma tapped him on the arm. "I'm sure many more good people than bad will seek a new life in the west. Don't you think, Mr. MacLaren?"

Ewan crossed his arms, thinking over Caleb's words. "What the lad says has merit. We could get the same border ruffians we saw in the old country. Those who lost homes and families. They didn't care how they ate, even if they had to steal or kill to do it." He took the paper from Emma's hand, noting the way the mood had shifted. "Ach. We'll worry about that another time. Today is a day to be happy. I should let Kyla and Audrey know. We'll celebrate at Sunday supper."

"It's good to see him in better spirits. Uncle Ewan's been in a sour temper since Brodie took the job as sheriff." Blaine walked next to Emma on the way back to the barn, his arm brushing hers until she casually stepped away, creating some distance.

"Will Colin and Quinn spend the night on the range?" Emma hoped her comment sounded casual, as if the answer didn't matter.

Blaine glanced at the darkening sky. "Nae. If I know the lads, they'll be back before supper. With the wee bairn on the way, Colin won't sleep apart from Sarah."

Emma made quick work of removing Moonshine's saddle before brushing her down and letting her out into the pasture behind the barn. "I'm going inside to see if I can help with supper."

"Quinn said he's having supper at Ewan's house tonight, so make sure there's plenty." Caleb chuckled. "I've never seen a man eat so much in such a short time."

Emma glanced over her shoulder and smiled. "I'll let Lorna know."

Caleb waited until Emma couldn't hear him before turning to Blaine. "Your ma invited me to supper tonight. Let her know I appreciate it, but I've other plans."

"Riding over to the Evanston ranch to see Heather, are you?"

Caleb cocked a brow as he swung onto his horse. "I didn't say anything about Heather."

"Aye, you didn't. You know, the lass won't like you checking on her." Blaine brushed the dirt from his pants as he walked out of the barn.

Caleb flashed a bright smile. "Widow Evanston invited me over tonight to meet her niece visiting from back east. Fletcher and Bram already met her. They say she's a real pretty thing."

Blaine threw his head back and laughed. "You *are* determined to die young, aren't you, lad?"

Caleb touched two fingers to the brim of his hat. "Can't think of a better way to leave this earth than looking at a pretty lass." He reined his horse around, still hearing Blaine's laughter as he took the trail south.

Chapter Ten

"Do you mind passing me the potatoes, Emma?"

Quinn's smooth, deep voice washed over her, the same as it had each time he came over for supper with Brodie's family. Jinny sat to the left of her, the younger siblings, Kenzie, Clint, and Banner, taking their regular places to her right. Ewan's wife, Lorna, sat across the table, Fletcher next to her, Quinn on his left. By all appearances, it seemed a normal evening meal. To Emma, it was anything but.

With a nod, Emma picked up the bowl, passing it around the table to Quinn. He'd arrived moments before Lorna announced supper was ready, apologizing for being late before washing up. Other than the request for vegetables, all his conversations had been with Fletcher, Jinny, or Ewan.

"Did you and Blaine enjoy yourselves today?"

Emma's fork stilled in her hand. She'd never heard such an edge to Quinn's voice. She slowly brought her gaze up to meet his, setting her fork down.

"Blaine, *Caleb*, and I found a few strays. I can't say I enjoyed it, but it's work that must be done." Clasping her hands in her lap, she leaned forward. "I must say, Blaine never left my side, which I found quite comforting." She found a small amount of satisfaction at the way Quinn's cocky grin faded, his lips drawing into a thin line. "He's a good rancher. I'm certain I'll learn a lot from him."

"That so?" Quinn stabbed a piece of meat with his fork harder than intended, stuffing it in his mouth, chewing slowly.

"Why yes. He seems to be quite an accomplished rancher. One of the best I've seen."

Quinn swallowed, his jaw still working as if he wanted to say more. Instead, he held back his words, taking another bite of meat, not noticing how everyone's eyes shifted between him and Emma. After a few awkward moments, Fletcher cleared his throat.

"Seems you'll be working with Bram and me tomorrow."

Emma's eyes lit up as she pulled her gaze from Quinn and turned her attention to Fletcher. "I'm looking forward to it. I know there's a lot to learn."

Jinny almost laughed when she saw Fletcher's mischievous grin. "You know, lass, it could take a long time to learn everything Bram and I know." He cast a quick look at Quinn, seeing his cousin's face darken. "Best to plan sunrise to sunset with one of us for several weeks, maybe months."

"Emma will have left long before then," Quinn grumbled, unable to swallow another bite.

"I have no idea when I'll be leaving. As long as I'm welcome here, there's no reason to rush off. Right, Jinny?"

Her friend patted her arm. "Of course, Emma. You know you're welcome here as long as you want. And Fletch is right. You should plan to get up early each day so you can work closely with him and Bram. I'm certain Blaine plans to spend a great deal of time working alongside you, as well."

Quinn had heard enough. Tossing down his napkin, he pushed from the table and stood. "I've got an early day. Thanks for supper, Aunt Lorna." He nodded at Ewan, then walked to the front door, not sparing a glance at Emma.

"You're welcome any time, Quinn," Lorna called out as Jinny leaned toward Emma, talking in a whisper.

"You should go after him."

"No, I don't think—"

"Emma, trust me. Go now, before he gets too close to his house."

Emma flashed a look at Lorna, then around the table. Taking a breath, she stood. "Would you excuse me a minute?"

"Take your time. Jinny, Kenzie, and I can get the dishes." Lorna's gaze caught Ewan's. She could tell they were both thinking the same.

Emma grabbed a coat before dashing out the front door and hurrying down the steps. "Quinn, wait."

He didn't slow his stride, making no indication he'd heard her.

"Please, Quinn. Wait."

He ignored the sound of her running toward him, his mind churning with conflicting thoughts. His chest tightened at the thought of Emma spending each day with his brother or cousins, believing he should be the one teaching her what she needed to know. He should be the MacLaren she went to for advice. Pushing her away had been painful, but it had seemed right a few weeks ago. After seeing the pain his mother went through dealing with his father's death, Quinn made the decision he wanted no part of the pain that came with loving someone the way he would a wife. There would already be enough pain if he lost any of his family. Losing Emma, though...he didn't think he could handle it.

Quinn lengthened his stride, wanting her to give up and turn back toward the house. Disappearing into the barn, he walked to Warrior's stall without stopping to light the lantern. He knew Ewan's barn like he knew his own. All he wanted was to get his horse and ride home, shut the door to his bedroom, and give his mind some rest.

He didn't hear any more from Emma as he put the saddle and bridle on Warrior. Grabbing the reins, he turned to leave, halting when he saw her standing at the entrance to the barn, silhouetted by the moon's light.

"Didn't you hear me calling?" She was breathless, her hair falling from the bun at the back of her head, soft tendrils framing her face.

Quinn's breath caught at the sheer beauty before him. Emotions warred within him, the same as they'd done for weeks...no, years. He'd struggled with his feelings for her ever since his father died, always able to brush them aside, believing his decision was the best for both of them. Looking at her tentative smile, the sheen in her eyes, he wasn't so certain now.

Dropping the reins, he stepped toward her, not knowing what he meant to do.

She watched his slow, determined movements, uncertain whether to stand her ground or walk to him. Taking a step forward, the moonlight illuminating him, she could clearly see the struggle on his face, the silent conflict he fought.

"Quinn, I..."

Stopping in front of her, he placed a finger to her lips as his other arm snaked around her waist, pulling her flush against him. Their lips were a breath apart as he lowered his mouth to hers.

There was no hesitancy as she wrapped her arms around his neck, drawing him down, taking all he gave her.

Tightening his arms around her, he splayed his hands on her back, deepening the kiss. He'd never felt anything so right, her body fitting his perfectly. Her kisses set him on fire, causing his heart to pound in a wild rhythm.

Moving a hand up, he held the back of her head steady, allowing him to devour her the way he wanted. He'd lain awake more nights than he could count, thinking of Emma, imagining the two of them together and how he wanted to love her. Stroking her back, his hand moving to settle on her hip, he could feel her tremble, sensing she needed him as much as he needed her, yet his mind continued to chastise him. Tonight, he ignored it.

Breaking the kiss, he moved his lips across her cheek to the sensitive spot behind her ear. Her soft mews told him how much she enjoyed his touch, the fevered movements of her hands on his back encouraging him to continue.

Reclaiming her mouth, he reached down, grabbing the edge of her dress, drawing it up until his hand felt the warmth of her thigh. The touch of her heated skin, the way she squirmed against him in an attempt to get closer, caused his hand to still.

If they continued, he'd end up taking her here, in the barn.

Dropping her skirt, he broke the kiss, resting his forehead against hers, both of them panting for breath.

"We cannot do this here, lass. I'll not take you on the ground." He saw the confusion on her face.

"But I want this, Quinn. I want you to make—"

Again, he placed a finger to her lips. "Don't say it, lass." Resting both hands on her shoulders, he took a step away. Studying her face, watching her struggle with what she perceived as another rejection, he bent down, kissing her once more before turning to pick up Warrior's reins. Without another word, he walked past her to the entrance of the barn, then mounted.

"Quinn?"

He sucked in a breath, knowing he couldn't ignore the plea in her voice. "What is it, Emma?"

She licked her lips, taking a few steps toward him. "Do you love me?"

Exhaling on a sigh, he tightened his grip on the reins, narrowing his gaze at her. "Aye, lass. I have for years."

Emma wrapped her arms around her waist, her body frozen in place as she watched Quinn rein Warrior around and ride off. He didn't look back, leaving her to wonder if she'd heard him right. If she did, what did it mean?

Willing her legs to move, she walked back to the house, silently stepping inside and taking the stairs with leaden legs. Entering the bedroom she shared with Jinny, Emma stepped inside, closing the door on a silent click.

Setting down the book she'd been reading, Jinny slipped off the bed. "Did you catch him? What did he say?"

Emma would've laughed if she didn't understand the sincerity of Jinny's questions. Pulling her arms out of her coat, she tossed it aside, then walked to the dresser. She poured water into a large bowl and picked up a towel, intending to soak it in the cool water. Then she thought of Quinn's kiss. Setting the towel on a hook, she placed a hand to her mouth, still able to feel the vibrations from his touch. A shiver ran through her at the feelings coursing through her body as he held her, stroked her back, kissed her with such intensity, she thought she'd burst. Sucking in a shaky breath, she turned around.

"He said he loved me."

"What?" Jinny's voice was louder than intended.

Emma moved toward her, placing a finger to her lips. "Shhh. They'll hear you."

Jinny clamped a hand over her mouth. She hadn't intended to say it so loud. The fact is, she hadn't expected to be so surprised. Dropping her hand, she wrapped her arms around Emma, then pulled back.

"I knew it. I knew Quinn loved you. He has since we were in school." Grabbing Emma's hand, she led her to the bed. "Sit down and tell me what happened."

A few minutes later, Emma finished by telling Jinny what Quinn said before he rode away. *Aye, lass. I have for years.*

Jinny studied her face, then cocked her head. "You don't seem as excited as I thought you'd be."

"I don't know why I feel so confused. Quinn said the words, but he didn't seem happy about admitting it, as if it were painful to say out loud." She glanced at Jinny. "Do you think he loves one of those women in town, but thinks he loves me, too?"

"No. Never. Quinn isn't like that. If he said he loves you, he does. And I've no doubt he knows you love him." Jinny stood, pacing around the room a few times before coming to a halt. "You know him as well as anyone. He can be driven and hard, act like a scoundrel, then turn around and charm you. Down deep, though, he may be one of the most sensitive of the family."

"I don't understand." Emma drew her knees up, circling them with her arms. "Explain what you mean."

"Well, on the outside, Quinn's tough. Maybe the toughest of all the MacLarens. I do believe he'd kill a man without a second thought if he believed his family or those he loved were in danger."

Emma's brows drew together. "Any of the MacLarens would do the same."

"True, but they might hesitate. Not Quinn. He makes up his mind and that's the end of it. And he never changes his mind once he's made a decision. I don't know if it has to do with some sense of honor or standing by his word, but it's easier to blow up a bridge than get that man to reverse a decision."

"I know he's stubborn..."

"Stubborn doesn't begin to describe him, Emma. It can be downright irritating. But, under it all, he has a vulnerable heart. One he wants to protect. The more I think on it, the more I believe it has to do with his da being murdered and having to watch Aunt Audrey struggle so much. He and his ma have always been close, even before Uncle Gillis died. After his death, Aunt Audrey had a difficult time, withdrawing into herself. It took her a long time to accept his death. I think a part of Quinn closed up, too, as if he'd built a wall around himself, not letting anyone outside the family get close."

Emma shook her head, not grasping all Jinny said. "He's always joking around with his brothers and cousins. There are days he doesn't seem to have any worries at all."

"Ach, that's his way of hiding what he feels." Jinny leaned against her dresser, crossing her arms. A moment later, she pushed away. "There's one person who might say something...if he knows. He may not tell you, but he might talk to me."

"Who?"

"Bram."

They talked into the night, plotting how to get Bram to talk. He and Jinny were close. If he knew anything about Quinn, he might confide in her. At least Jinny hoped he would.

Emma didn't believe it. The MacLaren men were loyal to the extreme. From years of watching them, she knew Quinn's confidantes were Colin and Brodie...and, once he got older, maybe Bram. He was also close to Blaine, but Emma knew he didn't confide in him like the others. That was another reason she'd never allow Blaine or any MacLaren, except for Quinn, to court her. It would split the family, create problems she wanted no part of.

After a while, Jinny's breathing became deep and regular. For Emma, sleep didn't come. Her thoughts continued to return to Quinn holding her in his arms, his hands moving over her body. She'd felt odd sensations, an ache she couldn't describe, a need causing her to squirm against him. The more he caressed her, the deeper the ache became until she'd felt desperate for something, although she didn't know what.

Emma and Jinny had never talked about what it would be like to be with a man. Neither had any experience. She wondered if Jinny had the same fears mixed with anticipation she did. Her heated embrace with Quinn was as far as she'd ever gone, igniting a craving she didn't understand. Uncaring if her desires were considered wrong, she wanted to explore them with Quinn.

Finally, her body and mind gave in to sleep, a hand resting on her chest, her body fevered from the images her vivid imagination produced.

Quinn tossed and turned hours after midnight, still deriding himself for admitting his true feelings. It had been an impulse, one he now regretted.

When she'd called his name, her gaze locking on his as she asked the one question he didn't want to answer, Quinn could not refuse her. He'd spoken the truth. Now he didn't know what to do.

Tossing off the blankets, he poured a glass of water, emptying it in a few gulps. He couldn't purge the way Emma felt and tasted from his mind. Their brief encounter in the Pearce barn hadn't been as passionate. More of a tentative step toward what he knew they both wanted. If they'd gone much further tonight, he knew they would've ended up on the ground, coming together in a hurried coupling. He refused to take Emma that way the first time.

Scrubbing his face with both hands, he moved to the window, scanning the sky. When he, Colin, and Brodie were younger, they'd lay outside at night, pretending they were explorers, using stars to guide them to their destination. They journeyed everywhere on those nights, fighting imaginary enemies, taking no prisoners.

When Blaine got older, he joined them. It was then the stories became brilliant in their detail. The heroes were bigger, braver, more handsome, and unstoppable—the villains vile, cruel, and not deserving to live.

Blaine called them the Three Musketeers after a book Uncle Ian read them. Blaine took the part of d'Artagnan, a reckless, brave, and clever young man seeking fame and fortune in Paris. Colin became Athos, the oldest, a battle-wizened musketeer who never recovered from his marriage, finding comfort in copious amounts of wine. Brodie was Aramis, a handsome young man who fought what he believed to be his true calling—religion, and women who sought his attention. Quinn became Porthos, a young musketeer fond of fashionable clothes and driven to make a fortune. Although the least intellectual of the four, Porthos compensated by using his considerable charm, strength, and cavalier attitude.

Quinn smiled, remembering how much fun they had. Blaine sometimes read out loud, often weaving stories more adventurous than those in print. Years later, he found he missed the freedom they had and the stories with wonderful adventures. He'd once asked Blaine if he ever thought of doing something other than ranching. Colin's brother had shrugged, shook his head, and walked away.

Feeling better, Quinn turned back to the bed, the sight reminding him of Emma. His actions and words tonight were reckless, yet true. Worse, he knew Emma would hold them close to her heart, expecting more from him than he might be able to give. He needed time to think, sort out the mess he'd created, and make decisions he intended to keep. To achieve this, he needed to distance himself from her.

Colin had asked if he'd be willing to stay at the old Estrada ranch with Caleb, work with the men who'd stayed. If Sarah weren't about ready to deliver, Colin would go. He needed people he trusted to take over until the baby arrived. First light tomorrow, Quinn would ride Warrior to the new ranch.

Chapter Eleven

Emma winced at the bright sunlight. Pulling the covers over her head, she closed her eyes, intending to return to sleep until hard pounding on the door had her jumping out of bed.

"Emma, are you all right?"

She stumbled around, grabbing clothes, pulling them on as fast as possible. "I'm fine, Mrs. Maclaren."

"Bram and Fletcher are waiting for you in the barn. They asked me to let you know."

She pulled the curtain open, grimacing at the sight of the bright sun sitting midway up in the sky. Hurrying to the door, she pulled it open. "I'm so sorry. I must have overslept."

"Jinny told them you had a rough night." Lorna turned to go downstairs, Emma following.

"Why didn't she wake me?"

"You were so sound asleep, you didn't even stir when she got up. We thought it best to let you sleep a bit longer."

Grabbing a hat, Emma started for the front door.

"Oh no, lass. You don't leave until you eat."

"But..." She followed Lorna into the kitchen, the aroma making her stomach growl.

"Don't be arguing with me, lass. You'll eat first or you won't be working with the horses."

Emma sighed and slumped into a chair, then smiled, appreciating the eggs, bacon, and toast Lorna set down in front of her.

"You eat every bite. I know how hard those lads are going to work you today. You'll need all of it to keep up. And, lass, you don't have to be ladylike about it."

Emma laughed, scooping up a forkful of eggs and stuffing them into her mouth. She kept at it until she'd eaten every bite. Lorna picked up the plate before Emma could stand.

"Now, off with you."

Paying no attention to her appearance, she dashed outside and down the steps, looking up to see Bram and Fletcher standing by the horse pasture, leaning against the fence, arms folded.

"Glad you could join us, Emma."

She glanced at Bram, feeling her face redden. "I'm so sorry. What can I do?"

"Is that all you're going to say?" Fletcher asked.

"Well, I..."

"You're not going to give us some long explanation?"

"No, Fletch. It would just waste more time. Let's get working." She walked past them on her way to the barn.

"Uh, lass?"

Emma turned at Fletch's voice. He pointed toward the pasture. "We're working in there this morning."

"Of course." She felt like such a fool, and on her first day with Bram and Fletcher. With any luck, they wouldn't say a word to Quinn about her sleeping so late.

"We'll start by going over each of the horses, their age, sire, and dam." Bram took the lead when they entered the pasture, walking toward a mare and colt. "That is Shamrock, Heather's mare, and Champion. He's about six months old."

Emma nodded, her voice softening. "I know."

Bram looked at her, his brows knitting together before he grinned. "Ach, I forgot. You were here when he was born."

"It was the most amazing sight I've ever seen." She glanced at Bram, then Fletcher. "We've had fillies born on the ranch, but we've never gotten a colt. I know how much you wanted one."

"Aye. Warrior, Chieftain, and Galath are used to sire. Shamrock and mares from the remuda are the dams. Champion will be the future of the breeding program." Fletcher walked up to Shamrock, running a hand down his cousin's mare. "Heather is riding a mare from Widow Evanston's ranch. I know she's anxious to get her own horse back."

Emma looked up at a couple riders coming from the north. "Is that Colin and Quinn?" She'd done her best not to ask about him, but seeing the riders had her heart beating faster.

Bram pushed the brim of his hat up. "Nae. It's Cam and Sean. Colin is working around here today. Quinn and Caleb left early for the old Estrada ranch. They'll be staying there."

"Staying there?"

"Aye. We need to have men with experience over there to work with the Estrada vaqueros who decided to stay when we bought the land and herd. Quinn and Colin are the best we have, but Caleb is close. With Sarah being so near delivery, Colin doesn't want to be too far away. Fletch, stay here with Emma while I talk with Sean and Cam."

Emma watched Bram walk away, then turned to Fletcher. "How long do you think Caleb and Quinn will be gone?" Emma walked alongside him toward another mare and her filly.

"Quinn said he'd be there a month, maybe more. They're staying at a smaller hacienda Estrada built years ago for him and his wife. Colin says it's in good shape. They'll need to bring in additional supplies, but it will be better being close to the ranch hands."

"I'm sure they'll be back for Sunday suppers." Emma tried to calm the tightness in her chest.

Fletcher stopped, looking down at her, his face laced with sympathy. "No, lass. Quinn told Aunt Audrey he wouldn't be here for several weeks. Caleb may be riding back, but I'm certain he isn't the reason you're asking."

The air whooshed from her lungs, disappointment clear on her face for a brief moment before she masked it with a slight smile. Looking up, she met his gaze. "I was curious, that's all. It doesn't matter one way or another, except who's available to work the ranch."

Fletcher studied her face, then nodded. Irritation burned through him at the way Quinn treated such a wonderful lass. His cousin could be an eejit sometimes. Riding off without a word of explanation after what Quinn had admitted to Emma the night before wasn't right. Then again, Fletcher wasn't supposed to know about it. He'd forgotten something in the barn, stopping when he saw Quinn and Emma together. Fletcher moved into the shadows, thinking it was about time Quinn made his move. Then he swung up on Warrior, telling Emma he loved her before riding away. All seemed to be going good for the two. Then came the news this morning about Quinn's decision to stay away. Colin swore he hadn't been ordered to do it by Ewan or Ian. It had been his choice.

"They have a remuda up there. Bram and I talked about riding north sometime, checking what they have and what they'll need. You may want to ride along."

Emma didn't know why she struggled with the answer. She wanted to see Quinn, be near him. After last night, she thought he'd welcome her presence. The true answer seemed clear in the decision he'd made this morning.

"Thank you, Fletcher. I believe I'll ride with Blaine when you and Bram check the remuda. There's a lot I can help with at Circle M." She increased her pace, moving past him, glancing over her shoulder and forcing a smile. "I've held you and Bram up long enough. I'm ready to learn all you can teach me."

Conviction

Giles Delacroix studied the face of the man across the table. It had been serendipitous how he'd been introduced to him through an acquaintance he'd first met playing cards on the steamboat headed for Conviction. When Giles asked if he knew of anyone who could be trusted to carry out some unusual business, the man studied him, asking more questions before mentioning Doggett, a man who had been in the area a short time. A meeting between Doggett and Delacroix had been arranged within a day of docking.

"What do you have for me?" Giles glanced around the crowded restaurant in Conviction's Chinatown, glad to see everyone lost in their own conversations, paying no attention to the two of them.

Several cities had a sizeable number of Chinese. Rumors were Conviction's Chinatown was the third largest in the state, consisting of restaurants, laundries, poultry and fish shops, and apothecaries selling healing concoctions, as well as discreet personal services.

"Widow Jones won't be a problem. She has children to feed and one man working for her, who she hasn't paid in quite a while. He didn't hesitate when I offered him your deal, saying it wouldn't be a problem talking the widow into taking it."

"When?" Giles picked up the teapot on the table and topped off his cup.

"I meet with him again in two days. He's optimistic about her selling."

"What about the two smaller ranchers?"

Doggett leaned forward, a smile stretching across his face. "Both have agreed to sell on your terms. You provide whatever they need to sign and the money. I'll do the rest."

"No. I'll meet with them myself. They won't know who I am, other than a man who has the ability to solve their money problems." Giles sat back, crossing his arms. "You'll go with me."

"When?"

"I'll have what's needed tomorrow. Now, tell me about the Pearce ranch."

A smirk crossed Doggett's face at the mention of Big Jim's property. "He's certain selling the cattle in Sacramento will bring enough to make the loan current. The drive starts in a few days."

"The cattle can't reach Sacramento."

"It's taken care of."

Giles leaned forward, resting his arms on the table. "I want to know what you have planned."

Doggett glanced around, making sure no one listened. "More than one Pearce ranch hand is unhappy. I made a proposition. Trust me, Delacroix. You'll have the Pearce ranch within a couple weeks."

Giles nodded, reaching into his pocket to pull out a pouch, handing it to Doggett. "For your efforts. I must say, I'm impressed with what you've been able to accomplish in such a short time."

Doggett slipped the pouch into his pocket. "It wasn't hard. People will do anything when they're desperate."

Nate Hollis sat at a corner table in the restaurant, his red-rimmed eyes trying to focus on the people in the room. He felt light-headed, his motions sluggish. Brodie's deputy had come here for one purpose—well, two actually. Hong Wo had already delivered part of it, which still sat untouched on the table, his stomach churning at the sight of it. No matter. Nate knew he had to eat, even if his body ended up rejecting it.

Taking a few small bites, he rested his back against the chair, absently rubbing the stub of his left arm with his right hand. There were times he could still feel his left hand, surprise gripping him when he'd look down to see his arm severed just below the elbow. People told him how lucky he'd been to lose only his arm in the battle that claimed hundreds of lives.

Most days, he would agree. Today wasn't one of them. It had been years, yet the pain pulsed through him as if it had happened yesterday, burning until he didn't think he could bear it much longer.

In an attempt to relieve the dull ache that had plagued him for days, Nate kneaded the stump of his left arm, feeling an immediate sense of relief. Blinking a few times, he picked up his fork, catching movement at the table a few feet away. A rotund man, dressed in finery not associated with

Conviction, passed a pouch to his companion, who wasted no time stuffing it into a pocket. He briefly wondered at the exchange before Hong Wo appeared and nodded at him.

Without a word, Nate slid his chair back and stood, following Hong Wo toward the back of the restaurant. On instinct, he took one more look behind him at the two men, committing their faces to memory.

"Come, Mr. Hollis," Hong Wo encouraged as he held the curtain open for him.

Nate nodded, ready to complete the second purpose of his trip to Chinatown.

"This will work well." Caleb stepped through the door of the hacienda where he and Quinn would be staying. He stood in the center of the front room, taking in the older home. "Looks like the kitchen is at the back. Bedrooms must be down the hall to the right. Seems clean. Someone must have been taking care of it."

Quinn listened, not caring about the layout or cleanliness. All he wanted was to fall onto any bed available and sleep, even though he already knew it wouldn't come. Thoughts of Emma had plagued him last night and all day as he and Caleb worked with the men. He still believed he'd made the right decision, putting distance between them so he could figure a way to ease out of the confession made in a moment of weakness.

Quinn had spoken the truth. He couldn't imagine ever loving another woman the way he did Emma. Nor could he imagine giving his heart away only to have it shattered when tragedy tore Emma away from him, as he believed it surely would. The dangers of ranch work were vast. Being thrown from a horse, bitten by a rattlesnake, lost in an unexpected storm, or trampled by stampeding cattle were daily concerns, happening more often than most city dwellers wanted to believe. Those dangers didn't include rustlers or outlaws who thought nothing of taking a human life.

Some might consider his fear of loss a weakness. To Quinn, it was a necessary part of what kept him functioning each day.

"I've thrown my gear in the first bedroom. You have a choice of three others." Caleb walked up beside him. "Are you all right? You've not seemed yourself today."

"Fine."

He walked down the hall, taking a room a couple doors down from Caleb and tossing his gear inside. Removing his hat, he ran a hand through his hair, sucking in a ragged breath. He already missed her.

Caleb stood in the doorway. "We need to order supplies soon. The place is empty of food and anything else we'll need. I can take one of the men and ride to town tomorrow."

"I'll go. I need to speak with Brodie, and I'd like to ride by the Pearce ranch, see how Big Jim is doing." Quinn opened his saddlebags, pulling out a flask. Removing the cap, he took a long swallow, then held it out for Caleb, who hesitated.

"You sure you don't want it all? Seems you may need it more than me."

Quinn took one more quick sip, then shook his head. "Nae. I'm done."

Caleb took a healthy drink, handing it back before being tempted to drink more. "Do you want to talk about what has you so bothered?"

Quinn shot him a disgusted look. "Nae. There's nothing to talk about. Just tired and hungry."

Caleb knew it was a lie, but decided to ignore it. "I've the food your ma prepared in my saddlebags." Walking to the bedroom where he'd left his belongings, he returned a few minutes later. He set each item aside as he unwrapped it. "Meat, bread, dried fruit, boiled eggs..." He took out the last item, unwrapped it, and smiled. "Your ma's sugar cookies. We will eat like kings."

"Aye, until you start cooking. Then we may starve."

"Have either of you seen Nate?" Brodie sorted through the wanted posters, pulling out those he'd learned had been arrested or killed, but his mind wasn't on the outlaws. It was on the man he'd become increasingly concerned about. He hadn't seen much of Nate for several days, and what he did see worried him. His one hand shook slightly, his eyes rimmed in red, as if he hadn't slept in days.

"Not since early afternoon. He planned to eat at Hong Wo's, then ride through the dock area." Sam sat at the desk, trying to focus on cleaning the guns in front of him.

"Nope. Not since this morning when he came in for coffee." Jack pulled off one of his boots, shook out a stone, then slipped his foot back inside.

"He say anything?"

"Like what, Sheriff?" Jack stood, stomping his boot on the ground.

Brodie crossed his arms, lifting a brow, his voice hard. "Anything, Jack. I haven't seen my deputy in almost three days."

Jack took a step away at the unexpected harsh tone. "Well, uh...let me think." His gaze moved about the room as he tried to remember what Nate had said. "Like Sam already said, he was going to Chinatown, same as he's done each day. There and the docks, just like you told him to do, Sheriff."

Brodie shook his head, dropping his arms to his sides. "Did you see him afterward? I rode around the docks and Chinatown yesterday and saw no sign of him."

"No, sir. He didn't come back while I was here. But you had me taking care of business out near Stein Tharaldson's end of town. You remember? The vandalism Stein reported."

Brodie let out a breath, leaned against his desk, and pinched the bridge of his nose. "Yes, Jack. I remember."

Jack nodded, tightening his gunbelt around his waist before picking up his hat. "I'd better start my rounds. You never know what might happen." He didn't wait for Brodie to respond before hurrying out the door, as if he couldn't get away fast enough.

Sam had stayed quiet, listening to the exchange, seeing Brodie's irritation rise. He understood what his boss wanted and the reason for his questions. Sam had the same concerns about Nate. Like Brodie, he had no answers, only suspicions.

"Nate isn't saying much to anybody, Brodie. He stays to himself, does his job, then goes back to his room."

Taking a seat behind his desk, Brodie leaned forward, focusing his gaze on Sam. "Does he still have his room at the Gold Dust?"

"He does. Down the hall from mine." Standing, Sam walked to the window, watching the early morning traffic. "Nate usually meets me for breakfast. He hasn't shown up in several days. I haven't seen him in the dining room for supper, either." Turning back around, Sam's features were bleak. "I think he's sick. When I asked him about it last week, he became upset, left supper, and I've seen little of him since."

Brodie rubbed his chin, then stood. "I'm going over to the clinic. Maybe Doc Vickery knows something about Nate. I'd appreciate it if you'd stay around. If he comes back, tell him I want to talk."

Sam nodded. "I don't like it, Brodie." He shook his head, lowering himself into a chair. "Hope the doctor has some answers."

Chapter Twelve

"Do you mind finishing with the supply order while I go find Brodie?"

Camden stood in the general store, staring at the list Quinn and Caleb had prepared. "Nae, Quinn. As soon as the wagon is loaded, I'll come find you." After supper the night before, his uncle Ewan said he wanted Cam working with Caleb and Quinn at the new property. Even though he loved his older brothers, Colin and Blaine, he jumped at the chance to get away. He'd ridden up a few minutes before Quinn left for Conviction. "What about the additional men Uncle Ewan wants to hire for the new place?"

"That's one reason I want to speak with Brodie. He and his deputies keep track of most people coming into town. They may know of some men looking for work." Quinn didn't tell Cam the other reason for his visit with Brodie. He didn't think his cousin had confided to anyone else in the family about the conversation he had with August Fielder.

"I'll stop by Buckie's Castle. Most men new to town end up there."

Quinn's gaze narrowed on his cousin, his mouth twitching upward. "I don't want to come looking for you."

Cam held up his hands in mock surrender, a cocky grin enhancing his already handsome face. "I'll not be going upstairs in the saloon, if that's what you're thinking."

At nineteen, Cam stood well over six feet tall with caramel-colored hair and golden brown eyes, his muscles honed and skin tanned from years outside doing work some men couldn't imagine. Quinn had always been his mentor when it came to girls, and now women. And his cousin knew him as well as anyone.

"Be sure you don't." Quinn shook his head as he left, stepping out into the morning sun. Even though the air still held the crispness of winter, the trees and flowers indicated they were well into spring. He loved this time of year. To him, it indicated the beginning of new life and a view into the future, although it held little mystery to him.

Circle M would expand, his siblings and cousins would marry, another generation of MacLarens would enter the world, and the cycle of their clan would continue. Quinn had a hard time seeing where he fit in. When he closed his eyes, he didn't see more than a house set off from the others, a place to spend his nights and keep his possessions. Nights would be spent alone or with one of the women he visited in town. Women who would never be invited to a family gathering or holiday supper. Women who would never own a piece of his heart.

His step faltered when an image of Emma, laughing, her smile bright and sincere, flashed across his mind. He used to be able to brush the image aside. Not anymore. Ever since the first time he'd kissed her—the night in her barn with her parents so close they could've walked outside and caught them—he found it impossible to purge her from his memory. She haunted him day and night. The feel of her arms around him, her lips brushing across his, the way she moved against him, wanting to get closer.

Quinn groaned, then cursed as he tripped over a swelled board in the wooden walkway.

"Don't think I'm going to offer a hand if you fall."

He turned to see Brodie coming up behind him, chuckling.

"Eejit board should be fixed."

"Aye, Quinn. As should many things in this town. They all must wait their turn." Brodie studied him, seeing the tension in his expression, hearing the edge in his voice. "What's bothering you?"

"Nothing."

Brodie crossed his arms. "Aye. I can see by your expression everything is fine."

Quinn ignored the sarcasm. "I came to town for supplies and to talk to you."

The smirk on Brodie's face disappeared. "What is it? Is Ma all right? Someone hurt?"

"Nae. Your family is fine." Quinn glanced around, spotting the Gold Dust down the street. "If you've the time, I'll buy you coffee."

Brodie followed him, nodding to passersby, wondering what was so important Quinn had to make a trip to town in the middle of the week. Stepping inside the hotel restaurant, he scanned the room, hoping to see Nate.

Quinn glanced over his shoulder when Brodie stopped behind him. "Are you looking for someone?"

"Aye. Nate Hollis."

"Your deputy?"

Brodie nodded. "It's been a few days since I've seen him. Sam and Jack tell me he's been in the office, doing his usual rounds. It's just..." He pursed his lips, shaking his head. "Something doesn't seem right."

"Take a seat anywhere, gentlemen."

Quinn spotted a young woman he'd never seen before, nodding to her as they found a table near the window. "Is she new?"

Removing his hat, Brodie set it on the chair next to him, focusing on the girl for the first time. "Guess she is. I don't get in here much, what with

Maggie getting up early to fix breakfast. She says a man needs a full belly before starting work."

Quinn studied his cousin's face, seeing nothing but love when he spoke of his wife. He'd seen the same look on Colin's face when he mentioned Sarah. Quinn worried he might show the same expression when he spoke of Emma. He hoped not.

"You're lucky. She's been good for you."

Quinn watched the serving girl move toward them. Most days, he'd be attracted to the young woman, would engage her in conversation, learn enough to know if she were experienced or an innocent. He stayed away from the latter. Today, he had no interest in anything more than a cup of coffee and conversation with his cousin. They ordered, then settled back in their chairs.

Brodie looked at him. "You could have the same...with Emma."

Quinn cocked his head. "Emma's just another lass. A friend, nothing more."

Brodie blew across his cup of coffee, cooling the hot brew, then took a sip. Setting the cup down, he leaned forward. "You keep telling yourself that, lad, and someday you might believe it."

He didn't answer, afraid Brodie would detect more in his voice than Quinn wanted to reveal.

"You know, the only person you're fooling is yourself. Aunt Audrey thinks you've wasted enough time denying your feelings for Emma."

Quinn's eyes widened. "Ma said that?"

"Aye, she did. Maybe you should have a talk with your ma. She's a smart woman."

An uncomfortable tension surrounded Quinn, catching him by surprise. It squeezed his chest, making him feel light-headed, forcing him to confront the excuses he'd used to stay away from Emma.

"I'm not the type of man you or Colin are. Committing to one woman isn't important to me."

"I believe that's as much a lie as you making yourself believe you don't care for the lass."

Quinn opened his mouth to deny Brodie's words, then snapped it closed. Finishing the coffee, he signaled the girl for more. When she left, he leveled a hard stare at his cousin. "I don't need to explain my decisions to you, Ma, or anyone else."

Brodie waited a moment, then sighed. "All right. What do you want to talk about?"

"Uncle Ewan wants to hire more men. At least six, maybe more."

"That's a good number. Where does Pa want to use them?"

"Most will be working at the new property with me, Caleb, and Cam. Colin may keep a couple at Circle M. Cam brought word today when Uncle Ewan sent him over.”

Guilt surrounded Brodie as he thought of all the work with the expanded land. He still hadn’t made a decision, hoping to delay it as long as possible.

Quinn could see the lines of worry on Brodie’s face, the internal struggle in his expression.

“Brodie, even if you were at the ranch, the need is greater now. You being there wouldn’t replace the work of six additional men.” Quinn glanced around, then lowered his voice. “Don’t make a decision based on what Circle M needs. Do what’s best for you and Maggie.”

Brodie’s jaw worked. He hated letting his family down and wished he didn’t enjoy his work as sheriff so much. The decision would be easier if he’d taken the job strictly for the money.

Quinn cut into his thoughts. “Do you know of anyone who’s looking?”

“There are always men around the docks looking for work. Same with Buckie’s Castle or any of the saloons in town. A good number will be green, but you and the lads can teach them.”

“Aye, we can.”

“I’ll ask around, let Sam, Nate, and Jack know the ranch needs more men.” The mention of Nate had Brodie’s stomach tightening. He needed to talk to his deputy. First, he had to find him.

"There's something else. It's about Big Jim."

Brodie's expression grew serious. "Is he doing worse?"

"No worse and no better. It's his foreman, Boyd Doggett. Cam and I stopped by this morning. They're getting ready to take the herd to Sacramento."

"It's not unusual to move a herd this time of year."

"Nae, it isn't. I've this feeling, though..." Quinn couldn't explain to himself what about the man bothered him, making it hard to describe his sense of dread to Brodie. "There is something about him. When we spoke this morning, he kept glancing at a couple of the ranch hands, as if he were nervous or keeping a close watch on them. The man's actions bother me."

"Do you want me to check wanted posters for him?"

Quinn nodded, letting out a breath. "Aye. I think it would be wise." He stood, pulling money from his pocket and tossing it on the table.

As they walked outside, Brodie clasped a hand on Quinn's shoulder. "Be sure about Emma, lad. She's a fine lass."

Quinn sent him a warning glance.

"I'll say no more." Brodie dropped his hand, turning at the sound of shouting from down the street. "Is that Blaine?"

"Aye." They both started running toward their cousin, reaching him as he dismounted in front of the clinic. His panicked gaze landed on Quinn and Brodie.

"It's Sarah. The wee bairn is coming." Blaine didn't wait for a response before shoving past them and racing into the clinic. "Doc Vickery?"

"I'm coming." Jonathon Vickery rushed out of the back room, followed by Hugh Tilden. He looked at the three MacLaren men, an eyebrow lifting. "Has there been an accident?"

Blaine stepped forward. "You need to come right away. It's Sarah."

Circle M

"You need to sit down a moment, lad. You'll wear yourself out pacing back and forth." Ewan placed a hand on Colin's shoulder, encouraging him to take a seat. He remained there for a few seconds, then stood again.

"I can't sit, Uncle Ewan. Not while Sarah is in such pain."

"She's doing no worse than your ma or your aunts." Ian walked to the cabinet where his brother, Angus, always kept whiskey. "How about a drink?"

"It's noon, Ian," his wife, Gail, admonished as she passed around cups of coffee.

He cocked a brow at her. "Noon means nothing to me when one of ours is having a baby. Who is for whiskey?" All the men stepped up, taking a glass from the cabinet and holding it out. "Now that's more like it, lads." Like Ewan, Ian enjoyed his whiskey. Sometimes more than he should. Ian held up his glass. "Here's to a new addition to the MacLaren clan."

Quinn burst through the door as Blaine, Colin, Camden, Brodie, and Ian held the glasses to their lips. "Did I miss anything?"

"Nae, lad. We're helping Colin relax." Ian poured one more glass, handing it to Quinn.

As soon as Doc Vickery rode out of town with Blaine, Quinn had found Cam, letting him know about Sarah, while Brodie let Sam know he'd be headed to Circle M. Quinn wanted to ride with them, but someone needed to deliver the supplies. Climbing up on the wagon, he took the trail to the new property as fast as he could and unloaded the supplies, telling Caleb the news. Within a short time, Quinn was on Warrior, riding to the ranch.

Quinn downed the whiskey, studying Colin, who still held his full glass. Placing a hand on his shoulder, he leaned toward him. "Sarah will be fine."

Colin rolled the glass between his fingers, nodding.

"He's right, Colin." Brodie came up beside them. "Doc Vickery won't let anything happen to her or the baby. Drink up, lad. You'll be needing it."

Sarah's agonized cry had Colin's head shooting up, strong hands holding him back when he tried to dash up the stairs. "Nae. You can't go up there." Brodie's calm voice did little to soothe his cousin. "Take a breath and relax. It could be a long day."

Colin took a deep breath, raking a hand through his hair as he lowered himself to a chair. "I don't know what I'll do if..."

Quinn's gaze locked on Emma sitting at the dining table with Jinny and his mother. She glanced up, then looked away, not holding his stare. Hearing the anguish in Colin's voice, he crouched in front of his cousin.

"You must believe, Colin. You will *not* lose her." Quinn set his empty glass down. "Do you remember when your twin sisters, Chrissy and Alana, were born? You, Brodie, and me were about sixteen and thought Aunt Kyla was going to die." Quinn continued when Colin nodded. "And your da? He stood with his brothers, calm as you please, even through your ma's screams. A few hours later, the doctor yelled for your da. Uncle

Angus held up those twins as if they were a grand prize, then handed one to my ma and one to Aunt Lorna. He walked into his office, closed the door, and broke down."

Colin raised his head. "He stayed strong for my ma."

"Aye, he did. You must do the same for Sarah and the wee bairn." Quinn gripped his shoulder, then stood, turning his head toward Emma. He chuckled, noticing how she'd shifted her back to him. Walking over, he rested his hands on the back of her chair, looking at Aunt Lorna, who'd taken his mother's place next to Emma. "Ladies." Seeing her stiffen, he didn't remove his hands. "Would there be any more coffee?"

Jinny pushed back her chair. "I'll get you a cup. Lots of sugar and milk, right?"

"Black."

"Aye. That's right." She smiled, then grimaced when she heard Sarah's pained shout. "Ach. That laddie better be coming soon."

Quinn took a seat next to Emma, moving his chair close enough for their legs to touch. "Jinny thinks it will be a laddie?"

"Aye," her mother answered. "Jinny always thinks wee bairns will be laddies. It's her and Kenzie against four brothers, so she always expects to be outnumbered." Aunt Lorna stood. "I'm going to check on the food. It won't be long before the others will be coming in from their work." She started to walk away, then turned back. "Does Caleb know?"

"Aye." Quinn looked across the room at Cam, knowing they'd have to ride back to the hacienda as soon as possible. He didn't like leaving Caleb with so much work to accomplish, but he needed time alone with Emma. Shifting back toward her, he paused, feeling the tension between them.

She cleared her throat, her hands clasped in her lap. "Fletcher told me you've moved to the new place." He could hear the strain in her voice, the thread of disappointment.

"Aye. It's best if I'm over there."

"Away from me, you mean." She stood, sliding her chair back under the table.

"Emma..."

She straightened, crossing her arms, keeping her voice low and level. "No, Quinn. I understand. You didn't mean what you said. It was a mistake, nothing more." She turned away when she felt his hand grip her arm.

"Emma, let me explain."

Wrenching her arm free, she twisted away from him, her voice a trembling whisper. "I don't need any more of your excuses. You don't want me, don't love me. Well, I'll no longer bother you. All I ask is for you to stay away from me."

His jaw clenched as he watched her walk into the kitchen. Hearing the back door open and close, he stood, meaning to go after her. Before he could move, Jinny came out, eyes blazing.

"What did you say to her, Quinn?" She poked a finger into his chest.

"I didn't have a chance to say anything."

"Well, she's crying, and Emma never cries." She let out a frustrated breath, her face flushed with anger. "If you've hurt her again, I'll…" Her voice trailed off when she saw everyone staring at them.

He swallowed, pinching the bridge of his nose. "Again?"

"Don't you be daft with me, Quinn MacLaren." She stood several inches shorter than him, about Emma's height, and was four years younger, the same as Emma. Yet when Jinny got mad, no one wanted to be in her path.

"I'd better go find her."

She grabbed his arm. "Nae. Not if you're going to tell her how much you don't want her after telling her you loved her."

Quinn's eyes widened. "Emma told you?" *Of course she did,* he thought.

"Are all men such fools? Of course she told me. The worst is, she believed you." Jinny sucked in a breath. "Was it a lie?"

He closed his eyes, shaking his head, then looked at his cousin. "I'll go talk to her." He didn't give Jinny time for anything more before he stormed past her, stalked through the kitchen, and out the back door.

Jinny threw her hands up in the air on a loud groan. "Ach. That man is such an eejit."

Chapter Thirteen

Quinn spent a good amount of time searching for Emma behind the house, down the path leading to a small stream, then backtracking to the front of the house. Resting fisted hands on his hips, he looked around, trying to figure out where she'd go. *Moonshine.* He spun around, walking in the direction of Uncle Ewan's barn.

"You are such a good girl."

He heard her voice as he entered the barn, spotting Emma at Moonshine's stall, stroking the mare. His body responded as he watch her gentle strokes, heard her soft voice. Moving closer, he allowed himself to imagine he was the object of her attention, feeling his body harden even more. Groaning, he stopped walking when she whipped around, eyes filled with pain and anger spearing into his.

"What do you want?" Emma crossed her arms, her glare hostile and unyielding.

He swallowed the growing lump in his throat, searching for a plausible explanation for his actions. Whenever they were apart, he accepted what he thought was best for both of them. But when she was near, his heart and body responded, telling him Emma belonged to him and no one else. His actions when he took Emma in his arms and kissed her undermined every argument he had with himself. The line between what he should do and what he wanted to do blurred, resulting in uncertainty and pain for both of them.

"If you're just going to stand there and stare at me, I'd suggest you leave." She turned back to Moonshine, anger and humiliation flowing through her.

Clearing his throat, Quinn took a tentative step forward. "Emma..." He didn't know what he wanted to say. Feelings, emotions, and desire clashed with what he believed he should do. "Emma, I want..." Floundering, he raked a hand through his hair, shifting his weight from one foot to the other. He'd never been so tongue-tied, so befuddled around a woman. What he felt for Emma went well beyond the feelings he'd ever had for any other woman. All he understood was his need to protect her, the same as he felt for every female in his family, and the way his heart swelled whenever he saw her. He hadn't lied. He loved her...would always love her.

Continuing to move toward her, he wanted to ignore the voice in his head encouraging him to confess his feelings and hope for the best. He couldn't. Gently placing his hands on her shoulders, he felt Emma stiffen before she stepped away, whirling around to face him. He'd never seen her so angry or so beautiful.

"I asked you to leave me alone. It's all I've ever asked of you. Why can't you do it?"

He flinched at the plea in her voice. His body stilled when she took another step away. Slipping his hands into his pockets so as not to reach out and touch her, he shook his head.

"I can't."

For an instant, her eyes widened, then narrowed. "You can't what?"

"I'm sorry, lass. I can't promise to stay away from you."

She moistened her lips, trying to comprehend what he meant. "I don't understand. Why not?" Her voice had mellowed, her anger softening as they continued to stare at each other.

Breaking eye contact, Quinn let his gaze move over to Moonshine as he made the decision he knew would change his life forever. His heart beat a painful rhythm as he accepted what must be said. He reached out, stroking his hands down Emma's arms until he took her hands in his, feeling her flinch. Drawing her toward him, he searched her face

"I told you the truth the other night. I've loved you for years."

The air whooshed from her lungs. She shook her head, gripping his hands tighter, trying to calm her racing heart. "You moved to the new ranch to get away from me...because you lied about how you felt.”

“Nae, lass. It wasn’t a lie.”

“But...”

Quinn let go of one hand, bringing a finger up to cover her lips. “I’d never lie about something as important as loving you.”

Leaning down, he brushed his lips across hers, testing to see if she’d pull away. Her slight moan told him what she needed.

Wrapping his arms around her, he deepened the kiss as he cupped her neck, holding her in place. A low growl escaped his lips when she wrapped her arms around his neck, tugging him closer.

Desire pulsed through Emma as their bodies melded together. She could feel the pounding of his heart against her own, the sensations creating a fire, making her writhe against him. Clutching his shoulders, she moaned into his mouth, wanting something more, yet not knowing what.

She felt his hands move up and down her back, resting on her hips, exploring her curves as the kiss deepened. He explored her mouth as he did her body, growling when she arched into him. Tugging on his shirt, pulling it loose, she let her hands explore his back, heated skin to heated skin. Never had she felt anything like what Quinn's hard body did to her. She wanted to cry, scream, and moan as the tension built. The need in her increased, requiring a release she didn't know how to achieve.

Breaking the kiss, she buried her face in his neck, dragging her lips down to the hollow of his throat.

"Ach, lass. You don't know what you're doing to me." It took all his willpower not to take her right there in the barn. His lips brushed across her ear, settling on the sensitive skin below it. "We have to stop, Emma," he whispered, his voice full of regret.

She tightened her grip, her hands splaying across his back. "Please, Quinn…"

He pulled back, resting his forehead against hers. "You don't know what you're asking. Our first time should not be in my uncle's barn."

A smile curved her lips before she playfully nipped his lower lip, causing him to groan.

"Why not?"

Squeezing his eyes tight, he held her close, never wanting to let go. "We should wait until you're certain. Once I make love to you, there'll be no going back. You'll be mine, Emma…always mine."

"And you'll be mine?" she whispered as she continued to feather kisses along his jaw and down his neck.

His body throbbed, his need to be with her painful in its intensity. "Aye, lass. I'll always be yours."

"I don't want to stop. I don't care if we're in a barn, or on a hill overlooking the ranch, or in your bed. Make love to me, Quinn."

Sucking in a ragged breath, he cupped her face, forcing her to meet his gaze. "Are you sure, lass? You *must* be sure."

"I've wanted you forever, Quinn. Yes, I'm sure."

In one quick motion, Emma was in his arms, clutching his shoulders as his mouth captured hers. She could feel them moving, hear the sound of a stable gate open and close before he knelt, placing her on the straw floor.

Staring into her bright blue eyes, now moist with passion, he touched the back of his hand to her cheek, drawing it along the line of her jaw and down her neck. Brushing strands of hair from her forehead, he leaned down, kissing the tip of her nose.

"If you're sure this is what you want..."

"I want all of you. I want us to belong to each other. Please, Quinn."

"Then we'll wait no longer."

Wrapping his arms around her, he claimed her, taking the leap he never thought would be his right.

"I thought you said she left for our place?"

"She *did* leave, Fletcher. An hour ago, Emma ran through the kitchen and out the back door. I assumed she'd come back to the house." Jinny stayed close to her brother as they checked around their family's house. "I don't know where else she would go."

Their older brother, Brodie, and parents were still with Colin and the others, waiting for the baby's birth. After so long, Jinny became worried about Emma, sharing her concern with Fletcher. Stepping onto their front porch, he glanced around, then looked at her.

"You said Quinn went after her?"

"Yes. He..." Her voice faltered as her gaze landed on the barn. "Maybe she took Moonshine for a ride. There's still plenty of sunlight." She didn't wait for Fletcher's reply as she ran down the steps and toward the barn, hearing her brother running behind her. Slowing at the entrance, she felt his hand grip her arm.

"Wait, Jinny." He held her back, listening. A moment later, the sound of Quinn's deep laughter drifted from the barn, followed by the unmistakable sound of Emma giggling. Fletcher peered inside, then drew back, scrubbing a hand over his face. "Ah hell," he cursed, just loud enough for Jinny to hear.

"What is it?" She tried to pass by him, but Fletcher blocked her path, covering her mouth when she began to talk.

"Nae. You cannot go in there," he whispered. "It's Quinn and Emma. They're, uh…"

Her eyes widened before she nodded. When Fletcher dropped his hand, she licked her lips. "What do we do?"

Fletcher glanced around, seeing their ma on the front porch of Aunt Kyla's house. "It's Ma. We have to stop her from coming this way."

"I'll go. You do, well, whatever you need to do to warn them." Jinny took one more glance at the barn, then took off at a run to meet their mother.

Fletcher felt his chest tighten. Taking a deep breath, he took a few steps inside, then stopped.

"Quinn?"

"Oh no." Emma squirmed beside Quinn at the same time he let out a low curse. "What do we do?"

"It's Fletch. I'll talk to him while you get dressed."

Fear flashed across her face. "He'll know."

Quinn's features softened. "Aye." He planted a warm kiss on her mouth, then stood, picking up his shirt and slipping it on. He walked out of the stall as he secured the front buttons, his gaze landing on his cousin. "Fletch."

Turning to look behind him, he let out a breath before locking his gaze on Quinn. "Ma was on the way down here. Jinny went to stop her." Fletcher forced himself to focus on Quinn, not letting his attention be drawn to the stall where he knew Emma hid.

"Thank you."

"I'll go and leave you and Emma to, well...straighten up." The corners of his mouth curved upward. "I'll keep everyone away until you come out."

Quinn nodded. "Thanks, lad."

Fletcher turned to leave, then whipped back around. "You'll marry her?"

Quinn's eyes brightened, a broad smile crossing his face. "Aye."

Nodding, Fletcher left, dashing outside as Quinn returned to Emma.

"Are you all right?" Seeing her tremble, he moved to her, wrapping her in his arms, kissing her until she sighed. "Fletcher is going to make sure no one comes in here until I signal him."

Emma drew away, burying her face in her hands. "I'll never be able to face him."

"Or Jinny?"

She looked up. "Oh no. She was here, too?"

He chuckled at the horror on her face. "Aye, lass. She was." He ran a finger down her cheek. "I told Fletcher we would marry."

Nodding, she tried to relax. "I heard." Her voice held none of the excitement he anticipated.

"Isn't it what you want, Emma? To marry me?" His voice was strained, unsteady, afraid she'd changed her mind.

"I've never wanted anything more. It's just…"

Tilting her chin up with a finger, he forced her to meet his gaze. "What?"

She shook her head, smiled, then began to laugh. "Oh, Quinn. When you do something, it's all the way, isn't it?"

He chuckled. "Aye, lass. We do it all the way or we don't do it. Are you beside me on this?"

"Always."

Helping each other brush the straw and dirt from their clothes, they walked out of the barn, holding hands. No one stood on the porch of Aunt Kyla's house, and they saw no movement around the other houses or barns.

"I think we're safe." Quinn nudged her shoulder. He couldn't remember ever feeling so at peace, so contented as he did holding Emma's hand. The fear he thought would haunt him disappeared when he caught her bright smile.

She squeezed his hand. "I wonder if Sarah's had the baby."

"Nae. There'd be so much shouting, you'd have to cover your ears."

"How do you know?" She looked up at him, brows furrowing.

"You forget. Ten of the MacLarens were born after we came to America."

"Ah." Emma nodded. Being the youngest of two, she'd never been a part of a new baby entering the world. "It must be wonderful."

He cocked his head. "What?"

"Being part of such a large family. I mean, with Jimmy gone..." She shrugged.

Settling an arm around her shoulders, he pulled her close, placing a kiss on her forehead. "I know you still miss him. So do I. But I know he'd be happy for us. And you becoming a MacLaren means my family will always be yours."

Her eyes lit up. "Jinny and I will be related."

He shook his head. "Aye, and I can't imagine the trouble the two of you will stir up."

"Quinn, Emma, come quick. It's the wee bairn." Fletcher stood on the porch, motioning for them to hurry.

Breaking into a run, they dashed up the steps and through the front door, coming to a halt when all eyes turned to them. No one seemed to miss their joined hands.

"Quinn. Emma." Uncle Ewan's hard glare pierced them both, only softening when the loud cry of a baby had everyone turning to look up the stairs. "The bairn."

Quinn searched the room, then turned toward the others. "Where's Colin?"

Brodie came up beside him, nodding at Emma before glancing at the stairs. "He's with Sarah. We're waiting for him to bring the bairn out."

A moment later, the bedroom door opened and Colin walked to the top of the stairs. Holding the baby up, he almost choked on his words. "It's a laddie. We've named him Grant."

Emma watched as the men lifted fists into the air, then covered her ears at the MacLaren war cry.

"*Creag an Tuirc!*" the men shouted, then began slapping each other on the back.

Breaking away from Brodie and Blaine, Quinn grabbed Emma around the waist, kissing her as he whirled her around.

Laughing, Emma pushed at his shoulders. "Quinn. Put me down."

Sliding her to the floor, he saw his mother walk toward them, a hesitant smile on her face.

"Ma."

"Quinn. Emma," Audrey greeted them. "Does this mean we'll be planning another wedding?"

Taking a quick look at Emma, he pulled her close, never wanting to let go. "Aye, Ma. Emma and I will be getting married. We'd like to wait to tell the others. This is Colin and Sarah's day."

Audrey nodded, not trying to hide her smile or the solitary tear sliding down her cheek. "You've made a good choice." She gave Emma a quick kiss on the cheek. "Aye. A very good choice."

Quinn stared at his food, the prior night's stew they'd decided to eat for lunch. A couple days had passed since Grant's birth, and since Quinn had been with Emma. The fact he missed her so much stunned him. He'd never felt such craving for a woman, and now that he had her, he couldn't get Emma off his mind.

"Go on with you, Quinn. You're no use to us the way you are." Cam slapped him on the back on his way to fill his plate with more stew.

"I've no idea what you're talking about," Quinn grumbled as he hunkered over his food, forking some stew and stuffing it into his mouth.

"Cam's telling you it's all right to ride to Circle M, visit Emma, then come back in the morning." Caleb filled his own plate and sat down next to Cam. "You've been grumbling around, yelling at us and the men...and it's only noon. You might as well take your foul mood and leave."

"My mood isn't foul." The words were a lie and Quinn knew it.

"Fine. Leave anyway."

Quinn glared at Cam, then dropped the fork on his plate and stood up. "I need some air."

"Good idea. Look for it over at Circle M." Cam shot a smug grin at Caleb, who chuckled.

Stepping out into the glaring sun, he headed for the barn. The three of them and several ranch hands had been working on repairs to the buildings, sending a few men out to watch the herd. He hated the fact missing Emma made him feel weak, and that Cam and Caleb had noticed. In Quinn's mind, a man should be allowed a certain amount of dignity.

Glancing at the house, he shook his head in disgust, deciding to do what they suggested—and what he wanted. It didn't take long to saddle Warrior. He didn't look back when he rode away, heading straight toward Circle M. Quinn supposed they were right. An afternoon and evening with Emma would do him good.

Taking the trail as fast as possible, it wasn't long before he rounded the bend, Colin's home coming into view. Beyond it were Quinn's home, then Uncle Ewan's, then Uncle Ian's. To some, it seemed a strange sight. Four homes and four barns forming their own village. Having family close by always felt good...until he'd claimed Emma. Now he wanted nothing more than privacy.

"Quinn." He looked up to see Uncle Ewan coming down the steps of Colin's home. "Lorna is helping with Grant today. I came by to see how they're doing. What brings you over?"

Quinn's gaze met Ewan's, unsure of what to say, relieved when his uncle held up his hands.

"Aye. I'm sure you're here to see Emma. She's with Bram and Fletcher."

"I, uh...thought I'd take her for a ride."

Ewan worked to keep his face neutral. "Aye. A ride would be good. Maybe toward the hills to the east where the stream cuts across the trail."

Quinn knew the place. Quiet and secluded with an old, rundown cabin. Nodding, he reined toward the pasture where he knew they'd be, coming to a stop when Ewan raised his voice.

"You may want to take an extra blanket, lad."

Feeling his face heat, he kicked Warrior harder, anxious to get to Emma.

Chapter Fourteen

Quinn slid to the ground, tossed the reins over the fence, then climbed onto the bottom rung. Resting his arms on top, he watched Emma as she worked with Bram, who held Warrior's colt. He couldn't hear what they said, but he didn't miss the way her eyes lit up, her head bobbing in agreement with whatever Bram said. Feeling the fence shudder, he looked over to see Fletcher beside him.

"Wondered how long you could stay away." Fletch's voice held none of the teasing he expected. When Quinn didn't answer, he continued. "Emma's catching on. The lass watches everything, asks a lot of questions. Unless you convince her otherwise, my guess is she'll be an excellent breeder one day."

Quinn cocked his head, his brows furrowing. "I'd never ask her to give it up. Breeding horses is her dream. It's in her blood, the same as ranching is in mine."

"I thought so. She said Big Jim didn't like the idea."

"Big Jim knows cattle ranching. He saw no future in fine horse stock. Like you and Bram, Emma believes different. Now she has her chance to prove it." Quinn jumped down, opened the gate, and headed toward Emma.

"Want me to take care of Warrior?" Fletch yelled.

Glancing over his shoulder, his eyes sparked. "Nae, but you can saddle Moonshine." Quinn saw the smile on his cousin's face before Fletch headed to the barn. Turning back to Emma, he walked to within a few feet. "I think the lass needs a break, Bram."

"Quinn," Emma squealed, running to him, jumping into his arms.

"Ach, lass. You're going to knock me over." He tightened his arms around her, leaning down for a needed kiss. "I've missed you," he murmured next to her ear before setting her down.

"I've missed you, too."

Bram walked up beside them, nodding to the colt. "He's doing well. You're going to have a fine stallion in a few more years."

"If we're lucky, there will be many more like him." Quinn kept his arm around Emma's waist, unwilling to let her go.

"So you've come to take Emma for a ride?" Bram looked past them to where Fletcher led Moonshine toward Warrior.

"Aye, if you can spare her." He looked down at Emma, whose face brightened in surprise.

"Take her. Your lass asks so many questions, my head hurts." Bram winked at Emma, then strode off.

"Are you up for a ride, Emma?"

He didn't think he could be more in love with her, yet the smile she sent him sucked all the air from his lungs, causing his heart to pound in his chest.

"That would be wonderful. Where will we be going?"

"It's a surprise. You'll need a coat."

She ran to the house, emerging a few minutes later with a coat, gloves, and a bulging leather pouch. Holding it up as she drew closer, she grinned. "Food."

Moving along the trail Ewan suggested, Quinn couldn't help but wonder at the way his uncle openly encouraged him to be with Emma. As if he knew...

Quinn winced. Of course his uncle knew what he needed. It was easy to forget his uncles had been young once themselves, gone through much of what Colin, Brodie, and he had.

"Are you going the right way?"

Emma's question snapped him from his thoughts. "Aye. It won't be long now."

A mile later, they rode into a small clearing, a dilapidated cabin in the center.

"Here we are." Quinn swung a leg over Warrior's neck and dropped down. Reaching up, he settled his hands on Emma's waist, letting her slide to the ground in a long, slow motion. Pulling her close, he captured her lips. "I've thought of nothing but this for days," he whispered, then claimed her mouth again.

Several long minutes passed, their passion growing, hands moving over each other before he swept her into his arms. Carrying her inside, he set her down, his eyes widening.

"It, uh...needs some work."

Emma looked around and laughed. It couldn't be more than ten feet by ten feet with two wooden frames holding thin, hole-infested pallets. Dirt, at least an inch thick, covered the floor and every other surface. Spotting an old broom, she pushed past Quinn, grabbing it.

"Nae, lass. We've no time for that."

Quinn dashed outside, returning moments later with a blanket, their coats, and Emma's leather pouch. He shook out the blanket, laying it across one of the pallets, then stalked toward her. Taking the broom from her hands, he tossed it aside, ignoring the surprise on her face as he wrapped his arms around her and pulled her to him.

Not wasting time, he crushed his mouth to hers, his hands on her back, aligning their bodies.

When her lips parted, he took control, tasting her. He could feel her frantic hands everywhere...his neck, gripping his shoulders, running down his back. The passion was like nothing he'd ever felt or hoped to find. Pulling back, he searched her dazed eyes. Seeing them filled with so much desire made his chest squeeze.

"Emma..." His deep, ragged groan was all she needed to pull him down, kissing him with all the longing she felt.

"How much time do we have, Quinn?"

Lifting her into his arms, he walked to the pallet, laying her down, then kneeling beside her, loosening the buttons of her top. "A lifetime, which is not near enough."

Conviction

"I didn't expect to see you so soon after the announcement about you and Emma." Brodie walked around his desk, pulling Quinn into a hug. "You haven't changed your mind, have you?"

"Nae. I admit I was an eejit when it came to Emma. It took a bit of time, but I finally realized not having her in my life at all was worse than the possibility of losing her if we married. I'll not be changing my mind."

"Good. Your ma might disown you if you did. And Jinny would never forgive you." Brodie sat back down as Quinn took a chair on the other side of the desk.

Quinn nodded, taking a quick glance around, making sure they were alone. "It would be certain I'd have the entire MacLaren clan after me."

"Aye, lad. You would. So, what brings you to town?"

"Boyd Doggett."

Brodie shook his head. "I checked the posters and found nothing. This morning, I sent telegrams to the sheriffs in Sacramento and San Francisco. They've yet to get back to me. Tell me what's bothering you about the man."

Quinn steepled his fingers, resting his chin on the tips of them. "Wish I knew for certain. I stopped by again this morning to see Big Jim and Gertie, and talk with Doggett." He answered Brodie's question before being asked. "Big Jim's doing better, but he'll never be the same as before the shooting. Gertie says he doesn't sleep well and eats about half of what he used to. Even over her objections, the old man's determined to go on the cattle drive to Sacramento. Truth is, it might do him some good to get out with the men and do what he's done his entire life."

"What about Doggett?"

Quinn looked down, rubbing the back of his neck. "The man won't look me in the eyes. His gaze keeps darting around, watching the men, the horses. He talks in circles, never answers my questions. It's like he doesn't want to."

Brodie leaned forward, resting his arms on the desk. "What questions?"

"Nothing difficult. How many head are they taking to Sacramento? Does he have enough men? When are they leaving? Does he need help?" Quinn pursed his lips. "The only answers I got were he has enough men and doesn't need help. When Big Jim came up behind me, Doggett turned and left."

"Does Big Jim have concerns?"

"If he does, he didn't share them with me." He stared at a burn mark on the desk, his jaw tight. Looking up, he locked his gaze on Brodie. "I wish I could give you more. All I can say is there is something going on. I just don't know what."

Brodie sat back, his fingers thumping on top of his desk. "Do you want one of the Circle M men to ride along? We could talk to my da, tell him your concerns. Big Jim might do it if Da pushes him."

Quinn scrubbed a hand down his face, shaking his head. "Nae. I don't want to get Uncle Ewan or Uncle Ian involved. They have enough to worry about without adding Pearce ranch problems to the pile." Standing, he walked to the door. "I need to get a few more supplies, then head back."

Brodie walked up beside him, settling a hand on Quinn's shoulder. "Jinny says Emma is still staying with Ma and Da and you're over at the new place."

"Emma knows it's best—at least for now. I've work to do over there, and she's agreed to work with Blaine, Bram, and Fletcher. I'll go back on Saturday nights and stay until Monday morning." He glanced at Brodie, his mouth curving into a smile. "At *my* house, not your family's."

Brodie chuckled. "Long rides away from the ranch work pretty well for being alone."

"Aye. That's what Emma and I hope." Pulling the door open, he stepped outside. "It's odd. I never worried about Emma too much before a few days ago."

Cocking his head, Brodie lifted a brow. "What do you mean?"

"She's a good ranch hand, knows how to work with cattle and horses. I always knew she'd do what was right and be safe. Emma didn't belong to me...not until I asked her to marry me. Now I keep thinking about her getting hurt on the range, thrown from her horse, caught in a stampede..." Quinn rubbed his arm, then ripped off his hat, fingering the brim. "Hell, Brodie. I can't stop worrying about her."

Brodie leaned toward him, grabbed the hat from his hands, and slammed it down on Quinn's head. "You think you're any different from Colin or me? Nae, lad. He worries about Sarah, and I worry about Maggie. You may as well get used to worrying about Emma."

Quinn nodded, his face grim. "Aye. But I don't have to like it."

"Doggett." Leaning against the railing of the old cabin, Giles Delacroix tossed a cheroot out onto the dirt. Today, he'd come dressed in black slacks, boots, and white shirt. He'd left his vest at home.

"Delacroix." Doggett slid from his horse, tossing the reins over a post. "What did you want to talk about?" He didn't care if the frustration at changing his schedule for another meeting could be heard in his voice.

Giles narrowed his gaze, not liking the tension radiating from the man. "Is everything ready?"

"A few more details and we'll be set." He leaned against the cabin wall, then pushed away, crossing his arms.

"The drive starts tomorrow, correct?"

"At sunup. I've talked to the men and it's all agreed. An accident is the best way to stop Pearce from reaching Sacramento by the buyer's required date. Pearce loses money for every day they're late."

"How many are on our side?" Delacroix rested his heavy frame on the porch railing, keeping a close watch on Doggett. He had done all Giles had asked. Still, he had an uneasy feeling about the man, as if he held an important secret.

"Three." Giles cocked a brow at him. "It will be enough. The three are anxious for the money they'll get." Doggett chuckled. "Once they reach Sacramento, they'll get whatever Pearce promised them, plus the money we promised. If all goes right, Pearce won't have near enough left to pay off the loan. The bank will have to foreclose."

"The bank won't get the chance. Before that, my agent will be sitting down with Pearce and his wife, making them an offer they won't be able to refuse."

"Are you sure Big Jim doesn't know about the gold on his land? Seems to me he'd have discovered it long ago." Doggett grabbed a cheroot from his pocket and lit it, blowing the smoke out in a log stream. "It don't make sense he wouldn't know how much his land is worth."

Delacroix shook his head, his lips twisting into a cruel smile. "He's a rancher. The man knows cattle. I doubt it ever occurred to him to check for gold."

"What makes you think there's enough on the land to make what we're doing worthwhile? It could be a thin thread, play out on you in a few weeks."

"I'll be getting the land for well below what it's worth. The gold? It's a bonus for as long as the vein lasts. Once it plays out, I'll sell the land to the highest bidder."

"The MacLarens?" Doggett took another draw from his cigar, thinking about Delacroix's plan.

He shrugged. "The MacLarens, August Fielder, or one of the other ranchers who are ready to buy up whatever is available. There seems to be no limit to the number of people standing in line to buy up land at a good price. Perhaps I'll even sell while the mine is still active."

"Men as sharp as Fielder and the MacLarens aren't easy to fool. You'd be better off taking all the gold you can, keep the ranch running, then sell it all at a premium. From what I've heard, the Pearce land will bring a good price."

Pushing from the porch rail, Delacroix started down the steps, taking his time. His knees weren't what they used to be. He winced when he glanced at the horse he'd ridden, wishing he'd brought the wagon.

"All you have to worry about is holding up Pearce so he doesn't reach Sacramento until after the agreed date." Delacroix glanced over his shoulder, sending Doggett a hard glare. "There will be no room for error. I trust I'm making myself clear."

"There'll be no mistakes. You'll get your land and gold. Me and the men will get what we agreed." Doggett took the steps quickly, swinging up on his horse. "You make sure the money is ready. It'll take a few days to ride back from Sacramento. I expect payment to be waiting."

Delacroix heaved himself into the saddle, then sucked in a breath. Pulling a handkerchief from his pocket, he mopped his brow. "You'll get your money, Doggett. Then I'll expect you to ride off, exactly as we agreed."

"You don't have to worry about that. I'll have one last stop to make, then you'll never hear from me again."

Circle M

"Did you hear about Widow Jones selling out?" Blaine sat atop his stallion, Galath, watching the sun rise high in the sky. Colin sat next to him on Chieftain, every so often looking over his shoulder in the direction of the ranch house. Blaine knew he'd rather be with Sarah and the baby than riding miles away, chasing down strays.

"Aye. Uncle Ewan mentioned it before we rode out this morning. She told him the last few months have been hard, especially after she had to let two of the ranch hands go. The last one encouraged her to talk with a man who made an offer she couldn't refuse." Colin took off his hat, swiping an arm across his forehead. "The widow has three children, all under ten years old."

"They used to come to church before her husband died. I met him once." Blaine thought of Quinn and the reason for his reluctance to marry Emma. He feared losing her, and for good reason. Life expectancy wasn't very long for ranchers on the frontier. "Does Uncle Ewan know who bought the land?"

"A company from back east. He didn't have a name, but he thinks it's the same one who bought out those smaller ranchers on the other side of the Feather River. They were having financial problems like Widow Jones."

"I don't like it, Colin. These ranchers are being bought out before anyone else has a chance to make an offer. It's as if..." Blaine didn't like where his mind went.

"Aye. Someone knows what's going on before anyone else. They get the ranchers when their weak, vulnerable." He glanced at Blaine, his jaw working. "I've a need to ride into town tomorrow and speak with Brodie."

"Are you sure you want to leave the ranch right now?"

Colin blew out a breath. "You're right, Blaine. I need to stay close to Sarah and Grant."

"I'll start at first light. If Brodie's heard nothing, he'll know who to ask."

"Jinny, is that you?" Lorna wiped her hands down her well-used apron.

"No, Mrs. MacLaren. It's Emma."

"You and Bram are already done for the day?" She went back to kneading the dough for biscuits.

"He rode out to see how Fletcher and Sean are doing. Ian sent them down to the south border early this morning. I guess there are a number of steers missing." Emma washed her hands, drying them before grabbing an apron. "What can I do?"

"Ma! We have company." Jinny joined them in the kitchen, followed by Gertie Pearce.

Emma's eyes lit up as she wrapped her mother in a hug. "Mama. It's so good to see you. Is Papa here, too?" She glanced behind Gertie, hoping to see her father.

"No, sweetheart. I came by myself." She hugged Lorna. "I hope it's all right to come by."

Lorna grabbed her hand. "Of course it is, Gertie. You're always welcome here. Can you stay for supper?"

"Thank you, but I can't tonight. I came by to speak with Emma, then I need to get back."

"Of course. I'll make some coffee and the two of you can talk in Ewan's study."

Emma sat next to her mother on the leather sofa, seeing the lines of worry on her face. She hadn't gone back to the ranch since leaving a few weeks before, and the guilt she felt increased as she watched her strong mother struggle. Taking Gertie's hands in hers, she leaned toward her.

"Mama, what is it?"

"I'm sorry, Emma. I didn't want to come by, but your father has decided to ride with the men on the cattle drive to Sacramento. Doc Vickery advised against it, but you know your father. Once he's made up his mind, there's no reasoning with him."

Emma nodded. Her father's stubborn nature and pride had come between him and her mother many times in the past.

"Doesn't he trust the new foreman?"

Gertie let go of Emma's hands. Picking up the coffee cup, she cradled it, shaking her head. "I don't know. Big Jim seems to think he's the perfect man for the job. It still hasn't stopped him from deciding to ride along."

"Maybe it has to do with negotiating the price with the buyer. Except for you and Jimmy, Papa has never been comfortable letting others handle the money part of the ranch. It could be he needs to give the foreman more time."

"Perhaps. Time doesn't help the reality that he plans to ride out with the men early tomorrow." Gertie looked up at Emma, moisture in her eyes.

Emma's stomach clenched at the sight of her mother's rare tears. "Tell me what I can do?"

Gertie took a sip of coffee, her hands unsteady as she set the cup down. "I hate to ask. I know you want to continue here, learn about breeding horses."

"Mama. Please, tell me what I can do?"

Gertie lifted her face, meeting Emma's concerned gaze. "Ride with them."

Emma sat back, surprised. She'd gone on cattle drives many times over the years, always enjoying the experience, knowing the trips were a normal part of ranch life. For reasons she didn't understand this time, she hesitated.

"I don't know what I can do that the men can't."

"You can keep watch on him, make sure he lets the men do the dangerous work. Doggett and the men won't worry about him the way you will. He'll listen to you if you tell him to take it easy." Gertie eased back on the sofa. "I know it's a lot to ask…"

Emma shook her head. "No, Mama. It isn't."

She thought of Quinn and the promise she'd made to stay safe, not put herself in danger, and not leave the ranch alone. Cattle drives were one of the more dangerous activities on a ranch. Anything could happen. She knew of more than one ranch hand who'd lost his life when the cattle became spooked or rustlers tried to take the herd. Quinn would tell her not to go, that he or one of the other men would ride with her father. She couldn't ask that of any of the MacLarens. Their generosity had already exceeded what Emma expected, and she had no intention of asking them for more. Sucking in a breath, she touched her mother's arm.

"All right. I'll go. How do you want to do this?"

Chapter Fifteen

Emma couldn't calm the nerves she'd had since agreeing to her mother's request. They'd decided it would be best for her to join the drive a few miles past Conviction, telling her father she'd heard they were taking the cattle to Sacramento and decided to come along. If he became upset, she'd try to calm him, making it clear she intended to stay.

At the sound of the approaching herd, she twisted in her saddle. It wouldn't be long until she learned the extent of her father's anger at her showing up. Reining Moonshine around, she spotted the moving mass of cattle, her father and the chuckwagon at the back. Her mother used to drive the wagon, making the meals and coffee well before sunrise. Jimmy's death had changed so much, including her mother's desire to be a part of the drives.

Emma recognized the large frame and wide girth of the man they'd hired from town to take her place. He'd been on more than one drive with them, always doing well.

Sucking in a deep breath to calm her internal storm, Emma started down the hill where she'd been waiting, setting her pace to join her father at the back. The noise of the herd covered her approach until she reined up alongside him. He gave her a cursory glance before he realized who rode next to him. The shock on his face didn't surprise her.

"Hello, Papa."

"What are you doing here, girl? You're supposed to be at Circle M." His voice held a strong reprimand, even as his face softened as he looked at her.

"I told Ewan and Ian of my plans to ride with you to Sacramento."

His eyes widened before narrowing. "You aren't riding anywhere with us. I have all the hands I need for the drive, and not enough food for one more person."

"Then I guess I'll fend for myself." Emma reached behind her, patting the saddlebags. "Lorna made sure I left with plenty of food—in case you didn't have enough." She smiled, knowing the battle wasn't over.

"Doesn't matter. I don't need your help and neither does Boyd Doggett, the foreman. All the jobs are already doled out. You'd just be in the way." His gruff voice held a hint of hesitation, even as his stern features showed a finality in his decision.

"It's a pity you won't accept my help since I have no plans to leave until the cattle are in Sacramento." She kicked Moonshine, moving her into a slow gallop.

"You wait up, Emma."

She heard her father coming up behind her, but didn't slow her pace.

"I'm going to introduce myself to your foreman. Would you like to ride along?"

"Dagnabbit, Emma. I'm your father, and I say who rides with us and who doesn't."

Bringing Moonshine to a stop, she turned to face him when he halted beside her.

"Yes, you can decide who rides with you and who doesn't. What you can't do is stop me from coming along, even if I have to ride a quarter mile behind. It's your choice. You can either tell Doggett I'm riding with you or try to send me home, which will do you no good. I'll simply follow you."

Big Jim gaped at his daughter. He wasn't used to this side of her—hard, unwavering, and disobedient. She'd always been stubborn and determined, but never disobedient until the night she'd been told of his decision to hire a foreman. He hadn't seen her since she walked out the door to move in with the MacLarens.

He sat in his saddle, shaking his head. "You've changed, Emma."

"I've grown up, Papa. I'm no longer the young girl you remember." Sighing, she shifted her weight, then pushed her hat back from her forehead. "There are so many things you don't know about me, or have chosen to ignore."

"You've never hidden your desire to breed horses, Emma. Jimmy knew what it meant to you and tried to talk me into letting you try. Maybe I should've done what he said." His hand shook as he dragged it down his face. "I'm set in my ways...maybe too set."

Pushing down the lump in her throat, she nudged Moonshine until she was within a foot of him. Setting a hand on his arm, she squeezed.

"I love you, Papa, but I'm a grown woman, able to make my own decisions. You made the right one when you hired Doggett. I wasn't ready to be a foreman. I'm still not. What I want is to breed horses, develop the finest stock in this part of the country. Bram and Fletcher are willing to teach me all they know. I may not be their equal, but they treat me as if I am." She bit her lower lip, deciding to tell him the rest. "Quinn asked me to marry him. I said yes."

For the first time since she'd ridden up, her father smiled. "Well, I'll be. Took that boy long enough."

His complete approval surprised her. "You don't mind?"

"Emma, sweetheart, your mother and I love Quinn as if he were one of our own. As much as he tried, he's never been able to hide his love for you, and we've always known how much you love him. This is the best news I've heard in a long time. Wait until your mother hears the news."

Emma had no intention of telling him she'd told Gertie the evening before. Her mother had been just as thrilled.

"What can your mother and I do?"

Her eyes lit up, a mischievous smile curving the corners of her mouth. "Let me ride along with you. It may be the last time we'll be able to do this together."

Big Jim chuckled. "I do believe you have inherited your mother's skill at manipulating me."

"Does that mean you'll let me ride with you?"

"Do I have a choice?"

She shook her head. "Not really."

"Well, then, I suppose it's time for you to meet my foreman."

Boyd Doggett kept his thoughts to himself as he studied the young woman Big Jim introduced. From the comments the ranch hands had made, he knew the men liked her. He also knew none of them wanted to take orders from a woman. Although he didn't agree, he'd heard the same many times from Texas to Colorado to California.

"Emma will be riding with us to Sacramento. She's been on many drives and is anxious to help. Where would you like her to ride?"

Before Boyd could answer, Finn rode up, reining to a stop next to Emma.

"Miss Pearce." He touched the brim of his hat. "It's good to see you, and a bit of a surprise."

"Hello, Finn." She glanced at her father, smiling. "I heard about the drive and decided I couldn't stay away. I know Papa can always use the help."

"It's true. We can use help." Finn looked at Doggett. "If it's all right with you, she can ride with me."

Boyd thought a moment before nodding. "Are you comfortable riding near the front, Miss Pearce?"

Even though she didn't enjoy the dust riding in the back, Emma planned to stay near her father. She also needed to do what was best for the drive. "I've done it many times, Mr. Doggett. I'll do whatever you think best."

He'd heard she had much more experience than any of the other men, except maybe Holler Gibson. "Stick near Finn for today. I'll think on it more and let you know if tomorrow will be different."

Boyd thought of Jory's and the other two Irish ranch hands' lack of experience. She needed to stay separated from those three. He'd keep her near Finn at the front of the herd for now.

"You heard the man, Emma. I'll be riding near the back." Big Jim nodded at Doggett, then reined his horse around.

"Are you ready, Miss Pearce?"

"I am, Finn. Let's get moving." Emma watched her father ride off. He seemed a little unsettled in the saddle, as if he were in pain. She promised herself to ask him about it when they stopped for supper.

"Are you doing well, Miss Pearce?" Finn flashed her a cocky grin, the same one she'd seen numerous times when she still lived with her parents.

A tightness formed in her chest. It hurt to remember the argument, ending with her leaving to live with the MacLarens. Quinn's proposal meant she'd probably never live on her family's ranch again. They'd marry and either live with Quinn's mother and siblings or stay in one of the original cabins built when the MacLarens first arrived in Conviction. So much had changed...

"Miss Pearce?"

She shook her head, glancing over at Finn. "Sorry. What did you say? And, please, call me Emma."

"I asked if you're doing well...Emma."

"I'm doing well. The MacLarens keep me busy, whether it's learning about horse breeding from Bram and Fletcher or helping with the cattle." She hesitated a moment, moistening her lips. "Quinn asked me to marry him."

Finn came to an abrupt halt, intense astonishment on his face, too startled to respond right away. He stared at her, tongue-tied, before forcing a blank expression.

"Finn?"

"It's grand news, Emma. MacLaren is a good man." His words were sharp, an edge to them she'd never heard from him before. "We'd best keep moving." Kicking his horse, he moved into a gallop, leaving her to wonder what she'd said.

Doggett sat by himself on the other side of the fire from the men, eating slowly as his gaze moved over the others. Big Jim sat with Emma near the chuckwagon, Finn a few feet away with Holler. He'd kept watch on Jory and the other two Irishmen throughout the first day, making certain they didn't deviate from his instructions.

"Boyd."

Doggett looked up to see Big Jim motioning for him to join them. Mumbling to himself, he held his plate in one hand, picking up the dented tin cup filled with coffee in the other. He didn't want to spend time getting to know Emma or listening to inane banter about their family. His full concentration needed to be on what would happen tomorrow and where the men would ride. He was certain of one thing. Emma would continue riding near Finn.

"Find a place to sit." Big Jim motioned toward a log a couple feet away. "Emma was asking about you. I thought it best if you answered her directly."

Boyd nodded, settling himself down on the log. He placed his cup on the ground, then held his plate with both hands, his arms resting on his legs. He'd never been one for sharing much about himself or his family. The people he'd worked for in Colorado understood this. As long as he got the work done, they made sure he had his privacy.

"If I can." He didn't make eye contact as he scooped the last bite of food into his mouth, set down the plate, and picked up his coffee. "What do you want to know?"

His cold, distrustful tone sent shivers up Emma's spine. It hadn't escaped her how he stayed to himself during the day, engaging in conversation only to issue orders. The man and his manner were the opposite of the type of foreman she'd thought her parents would hire. The amount of freedom in his position bothered her more than a little, and not because she'd once wanted the job.

Emma leaned back, angling her body toward her father, away from Boyd. "I just wondered where you were from."

"As Big Jim knows, I last worked for a ranch in Colorado."

"Yes, he mentioned that. Is that where you're from?"

"No, ma'am."

She waited for him to continue, then sighed when she realized he'd given her all he intended.

"Where were you born?"

Boyd glanced at her, then Big Jim. "Texas."

"Ah...I thought I heard a slight drawl. Holler's also from Texas. Did you know each other before coming here?"

He chuckled, shaking his head. "It's a big state." He waited a moment, then stood, tossing his remaining coffee into nearby bush. "I need to speak to the men before they bunk down. Holler will watch the herd, then roust Jory after midnight to take his place." He nodded at Big Jim, then Emma. "Ma'am."

Big Jim waited until Doggett was well away before turning to Emma. "He doesn't talk much."

Emma bit her lip so as not to laugh. "No, he doesn't." She watched as he spoke with Jory, then grabbed a bedroll, shaking it out a good distance from everyone else. He took another glance at Jory and his two companions before lying down, setting his hat over his face.

"How old do you think he is, Papa?"

"Not as old as you think. At first, Gertie thought he might be close to forty. Now she believes he's in his early thirties. She thinks he's had a hard life, which shows on his face."

"Not married?"

"Not that he's ever mentioned. Why?" Big Jim shifted on the hard log, groaning as he tried to get comfortable.

Emma watched her father grimace, wishing she could ease his pain. "No reason."

She didn't want to confess her concerns about Doggett, which might cause her father more worry. Instead, she decided to watch him during the drive, try to alleviate her suspicions by getting to know him. Maybe by the time they reached Sacramento, her unease about him would disappear, along with the strange anxiety she felt around him.

Standing, she stretched her arms above her head, yawning. "I'm ready for bed. See you in the morning."

Big Jim had wanted her to sleep under the wagon. Emma declined, preferring to sleep in the open where her focus would be on the stars, not her guilt over leaving without telling Quinn. She knew he'd be furious when he learned she'd left the ranch, unaccompanied, to join her father's cattle drive. Emma didn't blame him. She'd feel the same if their situations were reversed.

Quinn worried about her, which gave Emma a certain amount of comfort. His instructions not to leave the ranch alone also rankled her. Laying out her bedroll, she climbed inside the blanket, settling on her back. Watching the sky, she wondered what Quinn was doing, if he might be thinking of her, and what he'd say when he discovered her gone.

At this point, there was no turning back. The decision had been made. If all went right, she'd be back at Circle M in less than two weeks. A short cattle drive by most standards, but a lifetime when she thought of being away from Quinn.

Closing her eyes, she let herself remember their time in the barn. They'd made love, then held each other, talking in soft voices, then laughing as they teased one another. Minutes before Fletcher had walked into the barn, Quinn had asked her to marry him. She'd felt like crying, not allowing him to see her tears as she nodded, whispering *yes* before he kissed her. If his cousin hadn't walked in, she had no doubt they would have made love again.

Turning onto her side, she brought the blanket up around her. She loved Quinn, had for years, and knew he felt the same. Ewan would

explain to him what happened, and she felt
confident Quinn would understand. He'd realize
she had no choice but to help her father. He might
not like it, but he'd wait for her return, welcoming
her home with a slight scolding and open arms.
Letting out a breath, her tension eased, muscles
relaxing as she drifted off to sleep.

Chapter Sixteen

Circle M

"What do you mean she isn't here?" Quinn glared at his uncle Ewan, his temper soaring. "You promised to watch over her, make sure she didn't do anything dangerous. Now you tell me she's been gone for two days?" He paced back and forth in Ewan's study, shoving fingers through his hair.

"Keep your voice down, lad, and give me a chance to explain."

"What's there to explain? A cattle drive isn't the same as checking the herd or branding." He stopped pacing, stark features turning his otherwise handsome face to an icy stare. "I don't trust Big Jim's foreman."

Ewan's senses sharpened, his back straightening. "What do you mean you don't trust him? This is the first I've heard of your concerns."

"Something about him isn't right," Quinn ground out, his hand resting on the butt of his gun, fingers stroking the hard metal.

Ewan's eyes flickered. "An instinct. You've no proof of anything he's done?"

Quinn shook his head, his jaw working. "Nae."

"Have you spoken to Brodie?"

He nodded. "Aye. He found nothing. Still...there is something about the man that isn't right."

Ewan had never been one to doubt the instincts of his family, and Quinn's were some of the sharpest. His internal warnings had saved them many times during their journey from Scotland, as members of the wagon train heading west, and on the ranch. Ewan's older brothers, Angus and Gillis, were big believers in following your intuition, no matter how much it went against common sense. Like them, Ewan would never discount such a warning without good reason. He lowered himself into an overstuffed leather chair, settling back.

"She's with Big Jim and the ranch hands. You've met them, Quinn. Would any of those men allow Emma to be harmed?"

Quinn thought a moment, shaking his head, then dropping into a chair next to his uncle. "Nae. They've no cause to hurt her. I don't know about Doggett. He doesn't know Emma. Anything could happen. It doesn't need to be intentional."

Ewan watched Quinn fidget, actions he never associated with his nephew. Whatever was going on inside the lad was serious, causing him great distress.

"All right. We will talk to Ian and Colin. You'll go after the cattle drive, but you'll take another man."

"I can go—"

Ewan held up a hand. "Aye, but you'll *not* go alone."

Quinn didn't like waiting for his family to decide who'd ride with him and when. He wanted to leave now, jump on Warrior, and ride fast and hard until he found her. Instead, he accepted his uncle's offer. Standing, he nodded, his right hand returning to settle on the cold metal of his gun.

"Now, let's go find Ian and Colin."

Conviction

Brodie sat behind his desk, reviewing the wanted posters once again, looking for anything that might tie Boyd Doggett to a crime. Studying them carefully, he set one after another aside, then stopped, his gaze narrowing as the door to his office burst open, the early morning sun almost blinding him. Raising an arm, he shielded his eyes.

"Sorry, Sheriff." Jack hurried inside, slamming the door. "I thought you'd want to know Nate is having breakfast at the Gold Dust."

Forgetting the posters, Brodie shuffled them back together, setting them inside a drawer. "Is he with Sam?"

"No siree. Nate's by himself."

Brodie grabbed his hat, opening the door. "Stay here until Sam comes by, then make your rounds. I shouldn't be long. Tell Sam I want him to stay until I get back."

"Absolutely. You can count on me, Sheriff."

Brodie shook his head in amusement, closing the door behind him. Someday he'd have to learn more about Jack. Besides being loyal and a crack shot, he knew little of the young man, not even where he grew up.

Pushing those thoughts aside, he stepped around wagons, between horses, and onto the boardwalk across the street. He needed to find Nate and learn what was going on with his newest deputy, get some answers to questions that had plagued him for weeks.

Pushing through the doors of the hotel, he spotted Nate sitting alone at a table in the darkest corner in the back. Walking up, he removed his hat, pulling out an empty chair.

"Good morning, Nate. Mind if I join you?"

Glancing up, he motioned toward the chair Brodie had already claimed.

"What can I get you, Sheriff?"

"Coffee, please." He looked at the same young woman who'd served Quinn and him a few weeks earlier. As she walked away, he looked at Nate. "She's been here a few weeks and I don't know her name."

Nate glanced up. "Rosie. She says it's short for Rosalyn." Ignoring Brodie, he went back to his breakfast, finishing his meal as Rosie delivered the coffee.

"Let me know if you need anything else, Sheriff."

"What about me?" Nate asked, setting down his fork.

Lifting a brow, she glanced at him. "Is there something you want, Deputy?"

Nate offered her a somber half-smile. "There is much I want, Rosie, although nothing you can provide."

That got Brodie's attention. Studying Nate, he wondered what had happened to the confident man who'd bested several men on the docks the day he arrived in Conviction—and with one arm hanging useless at his side. He looked years older, his eyes red and puffy, his skin sallow. At Christmas supper, Brodie had been certain Nate was on the verge of asking to court Sarah's sister, Geneen MacGregor. Geneen had thought the same, hiding her disappointment when Nate never came back around.

"Do you want to tell me why I haven't seen you in over a week?"

Nate leaned back in his chair, his gaze moving about the restaurant, doing all he could to avoid looking at Brodie. "I've been doing my job."

"I learned as much from Jack. I should have heard from you."

A sliver of guilt washed across Nate's face before he concealed it. Standing, he reached in his pocket, pulling out some coins.

"Put the money away and sit down, Nate. We need to talk."

Nate dropped the coins back in his pocket, settling fisted hands on his hips. He didn't want to open up to Brodie, yet knew he owed the man an explanation. "Not here."

Pushing from the table, Brodie left some money, motioning he'd follow Nate. "We'll go wherever you want."

"My room." Nate headed for the stairs, jerking to a stop at the sound of gunfire.

Brodie hurried to the windows. "Eejits," he muttered, drawing his gun, seeing Nate do the same. "Probably drunken ranch hands." A woman's scream had them dashing outside. The men doing the shooting continued down the main street, riding out of town and out of sight.

Nate muttered a curse, then nudged Brodie's shoulder. "Over there."

A crowd had already gathered around a man sprawled on the ground, a woman and several others crouched next to him.

"Get one of the doctors," Brodie ordered, then ran to where the man had fallen. "Let me see." He pushed through the crowd, seeing a shirt covered in blood, an unmoving body, a face devoid of life— the face of Bob Belford, a man he'd had in the jail several times for public drunkenness. His stomach clenched, knowing Belford was beyond help.

Ordering people to step aside, Doc Tilden joined him next to the man. It took less than a minute for Tilden to make a conclusion. Meeting Brodie's gaze, he shook his head, then looked at the woman on the other side of the man.

"Are you his wife?" Tilden asked.

Sobbing, she nodded.

"I'm sorry. There is nothing I can do for your husband."

"Where's Doc Vickery? We want to know what he says." The shout came from behind Brodie, followed by several others saying the same.

Glancing at Doc Tilden, he saw the man flinch at the obvious insult.

Standing, Brodie faced the crowd. "It'll do no good to find Doc Vickery. Doc Tilden did all any man could. Bob Belford is dead." He waited, letting the grumbling die down. "Go on about your business, allow Mrs. Belford some privacy."

Seeing Nate at the back of the crowd, Brodie motioned for him to join him on the boardwalk.

"I saw Jack. He's getting the undertaker."

"Thanks, Nate. Did you get a good look at the men who rode out?"

Nate shook his head. "Neither did Jack. I can start asking around, find out what happened."

Brodie blew out a frustrated breath, torn between identifying the shooters and finding out what was going on with Nate. He had no choice. Finding the killer had to come first.

"You take one end of the street and have Jack take the other. I'm going to find Sam. We'll need his help with this."

"Yes, sir." He turned to leave, rubbing his useless left arm with his right hand.

Brodie noticed the gesture, wondering how much pain it still caused him. "And Nate?" The man stopped, looking over his shoulder. "You still owe me that talk."

Nate's face flashed with an expression hovering between apprehension and pain. Brodie couldn't quite decide which.

"We'll talk. As soon as we find Bob's killer."

Brodie ignored the disquiet he'd been carrying for several weeks. He had to shove it aside until they tracked down the men who shot and killed one of his citizens. As soon as they did, he'd isolate

Nate in a locked room until they got a few things straightened out.

"Emma, you don't need to ride back here in all the dust." Big Jim repositioned his handkerchief across his face, lowering his hat on his forehead. The wind picked up as they drove the herd across open fields, unprotected by the rolling hills farther north.

"I know. Doggett said he wants me to stay close to Finn again today. As slow as they're driving the cattle, I don't see a reason I can't ride with you for a while."

Emma still hadn't formed a firm opinion about Doggett. He seemed competent enough, and the men worked well under him—as good as they had under Quinn. Doubts about him still nagged at her. No matter how she approached him, the way she worded her questions, he replied with little information about himself and his past.

And he seemed to pay special attention to Jory and the two other Irishmen. Emma told herself it was because they weren't as experienced as Holler and hadn't taken to the work as easily as Finn. If just two of the men stayed after the drive, she hoped it would be them.

"You and Quinn talk about a date for the wedding?"

She swiveled in the saddle, her eyes widening as she looked at her father. He wasn't one for small talk, especially about topics he considered more the territory of women than men.

"Not yet." Her mind went to their time together at the remote cabin. After the first, hectic round of lovemaking, they'd slowed down, taking their time, enjoying each other's company, and bodies, in a way she never dreamed existed.

Emma felt a shudder of guilt pass through her. She knew her parents would be disappointed in them for not waiting until after they were married. Few people spoke of what they did before they took their vows, and parents never spoke about it to their children, other than to warn them to wait. Emma found herself wondering if her mother and father had waited. Or had they given in to the temptation, the same as she and Quinn.

Emma hadn't mentioned how she learned about the cattle drive, or the fact her mother had ridden over to Circle M.

"Guess Doggett has come looking for you." Big Jim gestured to the foreman riding up to join them.

"I'd like to have you up with Finn, Miss Pearce. I've moved a couple of the men to the back. Holler is going to ride with Jory."

Emma thought over what Doggett said. He'd moved the least competent men to the back. She'd thought it the best place for them all along, but he'd been firm on keeping everyone in the same position each day. He must have seen or sensed something to make the change just two days before meeting the buyer.

"I'll catch up to Finn." Kicking Moonshine, she moved to the front, glancing around to spot anything Doggett would've considered a danger. The land spread out all around, flat with few trees and little opportunity for cover. She shook her head, telling herself not to create additional worries where none existed.

Pushing her concerns aside, Emma caught up to Finn, laughing when he flashed her his most charming smile.

"Doggett sent you here. I thought the man might let you ride with your father for a while."

"I thought so too. Do you know why he's changing the others around?" Glancing to her right, she saw Holler and Jory spaced out on the other side of the herd.

"I've no idea why he does what he does. The man is a mystery to me. I do think having Holler in the front is best, though." Finn slowed down, reining to his left to cut off a wayward steer.

He moved easy in the saddle with a natural grace some were born with. Quinn was the same, as were all the MacLarens. As had happened often since she left Circle M, a shiver ran through her, remembering how she felt in Quinn's arms. After all these years, all her days and nights of loving him without knowing how he felt, he'd asked her to marry him. She could hardly believe her good fortune. Many women settled for marrying out of convenience or need. Emma had been blessed with a man who loved her, who would do anything for her.

When her father had asked about a wedding date, she'd said they hadn't set one, which was true. She and Quinn *had* discussed marrying at Circle M in late summer, having a big celebration afterward.

She moistened her lips, a smile tilting up the corners of her mouth, her heart's rhythm increasing. By fall, she'd be Mrs. Quinn MacLaren, living permanently on the MacLaren ranch, spending every night with her husband.

A warm breeze blew across her face at the same time the herd began to move erratically, the cattle's mawwwing sound growing louder. Emma pushed her hat down, reining Moonshine to cut off several head moving away from the others. As she returned the strays to the herd, several more tried to break away. Emma's stomach clenched. The fact they hadn't grazed or had water in several hours made them more restless, ready to run if they sensed danger.

A faint whizzing sound split the air next to her. Reining Moonshine in the opposite direction, she heard Finn's frantic voice, but couldn't make out his words. Before she could turn to find him, at least sixty head started to run, heading straight ahead, the rest of the herd beginning to follow.

Breaking into a run, Emma yelled at Holler, using one hand to motion she planned to turn the herd to the right. She needed Holler and Jory to fall back, encouraging the cattle to mill into themselves.

"Turn them!"

She glanced over her shoulder to see Finn coming up fast behind her, both doing their best to change the herd's direction. Emma knew the land dropped off somewhere up ahead, a sharp cliff falling at least twenty feet into a ravine covered with rock. They had to get control before the panicked cattle ran right off the edge.

As the herd began to respond to her and Finn's efforts, several more shots flew past them, hitting the ground, sending the animals into a frenzy.

"Where's Doggett?" Emma yelled, pulling ahead of Finn, moving Moonshine as close to the stampeding herd as possible without getting in their path.

Finn shook his head in response, using his rope to get the herd's attention, noticing Holler ride up behind him.

"Drop off ahead!" Holler used his rope in the same manner as Finn, trying to push them right, while Emma fired her gun into the ground.

Dread filled her. She'd never been in a full stampede before, although her brother, Jimmy, had told her more than once about his experiences. They'd lost a man in one, his trampled body barely recognizable to his widow. In another, an experienced hand had broken both legs. He'd returned to work, but was never the same. If they didn't get control and turn the herd soon, Emma knew they'd lose some of their precious stock. Whatever happened, she prayed the men would come through unharmed.

Dropping their ropes, Finn and Holler pulled out their guns, shooting into the ground, the same as Emma. Slowly, the herd began to turn right, heading into themselves. Unfortunately, their movements weren't fast enough to avoid the gully.

The frenzied animals in the lead couldn't turn fast enough, their fear propelling them over the edge and onto the rocks below. Again, shots rang out, confusing the cattle, causing them to zigzag, sending more over the cliff. Their short turns and loud mawwwing made it hard for Emma and the others to gain the advantage.

"Emma, watch out!"

Finn's warning came too late for her to move Moonshine out of the way of a splinter herd coming up behind her.

Reining her horse to the left, she felt the instant Moonshine's front hoof slipped, her leg collapsing, thrusting Emma over the mare's neck, directly in the path of the raging cattle.

Chapter Seventeen

"Hold up, Blaine." Quinn reined Warrior to an abrupt stop. "Listen. Out there."

Blaine pulled alongside him, shifting his weight in the direction Quinn pointed. "I don't hear anything." A moment passed before the sound came again. He straightened in his saddle. "Cattle."

"And they're not happy."

Neither spoke as they rode toward the unmistakable sound of panicked cattle, stopping again when they heard gunfire.

"Ah, hell." Quinn kicked Warrior into a fast gallop, knowing Blaine would be right behind him.

Bent low over their saddles, neither slowed, pushing their horses faster as the noise of stampeding cattle and gunfire grew closer. Turning Warrior to the right, Quinn felt his heart pounding in his chest until he could barely breathe. Instincts raged within him, telling him Emma was in danger.

The rising cloud of dirt guided them, the sound of pounding hooves driving them on, even as their horses tired. As they drew closer, the flat ground provided an unobstructed view of the chaos a good distance away.

"Stampede," Quinn yelled. "They're running in the direction of the old river wash."

The MacLarens had driven herds south for years. He and Blaine knew every mile, each obstacle, and the best watering holes. They also knew the major hazards. The sheer drop into the rock-filled riverbed was the worst.

They pushed Warrior and Galath, knowing the stallions were giving all they had. A flash to the right drew their attention.

Blaine's shout carried above the noise of the cattle. "There's a shooter behind those trees. I'm heading that way. You get to Emma." He reined Galath around, riding to the spot where the sun reflected against metal, hearing the explosion of another shot.

So far, the shooter hadn't spotted them. Quinn almost wished he had, turning his aim away from Emma. He'd have to leave the killer to Blaine.

Quinn leaned forward, pushing Warrior to his limit. His stomach clenched at his inability to do anything except watch as Emma and the herd closed in on the deadly drop-off. Then his heart stopped when he saw Moonshine stumble, then fall, Emma flying over the horse's neck and into the path of the stampeding cattle.

Blaine circled behind the thick trunks and wide, glossy leaves of the stand of trees. The way the branches hung low provided perfect cover and a direct shot at the herd. Bringing Galath to a stop, he slid to the ground and drew his gun, stalking toward the man who appeared to be resting against the base of the tree. Aiming, he came to a halt a few paces away.

"Drop your gun and raise your hands."

The man didn't respond or move at Blaine's demand. Taking another step forward, he repeated his words, getting no response. Cocking his head to the side, he walked forward until he stood at the man's feet and kicked a boot. A low moan rumbled from the man's chest an instant before he toppled over, a revolver tumbling from his grip.

Blood dripped from a wound to his head and another on his arm. Blaine searched his face, seeing bruising and swelling. He'd never seen the man before.

Standing, Blaine looked around, spotting a horse in the distance. Looking down once more, he holstered his gun, then swung up on Galath. Ten minutes later, he returned with the man's horse. Although he stood a little over six feet tall and was muscled from years of ranch work, it took him longer than he wanted to lift the man and hoist him over the saddle, stomach down.

Blaine had tried to stop the bleeding, but couldn't find it within himself to hope the man lived.

"Where is she? Where's Emma?" Quinn jumped off Warrior, running to the circle of men. Pushing through, his heart lurched at the sight of the motionless body lying sprawled on the dirt, her hat gone, hair tangled. He shoved away the terror clamping around his chest, kneeling beside Big Jim. "Is she..."

Her father's voice broke. "She's alive. I don't know how badly she's hurt."

Quinn gripped Emma's hand, getting nothing in response. Leaning down, putting his fingers on her throat, he could feel a slight pulse, her soft breath fanning his cheek. Sliding his arms under her, Quinn lifted Emma, walking to Warrior.

"Finn, hold her while I mount." Placing her in Finn's arms, he swung into the saddle, then reached down to settle her in front of him. "Sacramento is closer. I'm riding there," he told Big Jim, who nodded. The man looked ten years older than the last time Quinn had seen him. Wrapping a strong arm around her, he whipped Warrior around, then stopped when he saw Blaine. "Who do you have?"

Blaine's concerned gaze took in Quinn holding Emma in his arms. "I'm pretty sure it's the shooter. Where are you taking her?"

"Sacramento."

"Not without me." Blaine tossed the reins of the second horse to one of the men. "He's injured. Make sure he stays alive. We'll wait for you in Sacramento."

Finn nodded. "You take care of her," he shouted as they rode away. Walking to the horse, he lifted the man's face, sucking in a breath. "Doggett." Holler helped him pull the man down, settling him in the dirt. "We'll keep you alive. At least long enough to see you hang."

Riding as fast as they dared, Quinn couldn't help whispering to Emma, telling her of his love and how he knew she'd be all right. He wouldn't allow himself to think otherwise. They slowed to traverse down a short trail.

"Let me take her for a while. Give yourself a rest."

Quinn's grip tightened, his eyes filled with pain. "Nae, lad. She's mine to take care of."

Blaine nodded. He'd expected Quinn's response. "Should I ride ahead, find a doctor and bring him back?"

Reaching the bottom of the trail, the land flattened out, allowing them to pick up their pace. Even so, they wouldn't reach Sacramento until well after the sun disappeared. He knew she needed a doctor, and the hard ride couldn't be helping.

Quinn slowed Warrior. "Aye. It would be best. See the hills over there?" He nodded to a spot off the trail in the distance with good cover. "We'll stay there tonight. If you ride hard..." He looked at Galath, knowing Blaine's horse was as tired as his.

"He's a strong lad. He'll take me to Sacramento and bring me back—with the doctor."

Quinn continued on as Blaine rode away, disappearing in the evening haze. The fog was a good indication of their location. It often appeared around the Feather River, which ran out of Sacramento, north to Conviction. With luck, Blaine would be back before midnight.

Reaching the place he wanted to settle for the night, Quinn slid to the ground, careful to hold Emma in place until he could take her in his arms. Setting her at the base of a tree, he dashed back to his horse, grabbing his saddlebags, water, and bedroll. It took minutes to wrap Emma in the blankets. Taking a shirt from his saddlebags, he dampened it with water, wiping the dirt and dried blood from her face.

To anyone else, she would appear to be asleep, not unconscious. He'd heard the men mumbling before he took Emma and left, learning a good deal about what happened.

If not for the quick action of Finn and Holler in redirecting the cattle, she'd be dead, trampled by the approaching herd. Instead, they'd managed to turn the animals away, putting themselves in more danger than they probably realized. He owed them a great deal. Unless she had massive injuries Quinn couldn't see, he had to believe she'd pull through.

Setting down the wet shirt, he stood, taking a look around. They'd need a fire. He didn't care about food as much as keeping her warm and comfortable.

"Quinn?"

His jaw dropped at hearing his name spoken in a soft whisper. Lowering himself next to Emma, he saw her eyes still closed as he brushed strands of hair from her forehead, letting his fingers linger.

"I'm here, Emma."

Her tongue darted out to moisten her lips before her eyes opened to slits. "Water?"

"Aye." He reached across her, picking up and opening the canteen. Bracing her head, he put it to her lips. "Just a little, lass." His breath caught as he saw her struggle to open her mouth. "That's the way, Emma."

Taking a meager swallow, her head fell back as she licked her lips. "Thank you."

Watching her eyes close, his breathing slowed. The fear that tortured him since seeing her sprawled on the ground began to recede. Shutting his eyes, he sent up a prayer, thanking God for getting them this far. All he needed now was the doctor to tell him she'd be all right.

"Quinn." Blaine shook his shoulder, trying not to wake Emma. "The doctor's here."

Quinn's eyes fluttered, then opened. Blinking several times, he pushed himself up and rubbed his eyes. "Ach. I must have fallen asleep." He glanced down, seeing Emma in the same position as when she'd dozed off again. He held out his hand. "Doctor. Thank you for coming."

The man's eyes narrowed on Quinn, then darted to Blaine. "Your friend here can be quite persuasive." His tone made it clear he hadn't come willingly.

Quinn looked at his cousin, lifting a brow.

Shrugging, Blaine's mouth tilted into a slight smile. "Well, I might have used a wee amount of encouragement on the good doctor."

"Yes. A gun pointed at my chest is quite persuasive, young man." The man knelt next to Emma, pulling the blanket away. After a minute, he glanced up. "There's no fever, no broken bones, and no swelling indicating internal injuries. He said she got thrown from a horse." The doctor looked at Blaine, then Quinn.

"Aye, Doctor. Over the mare's neck and to the ground." Quinn crossed his arms in an effort to keep calm. "She woke a couple hours ago asking for water. I gave her a small sip."

"Unless I'm mistaken, she came through this pretty well, considering what could've happened. Did she complain of a headache?"

"Nae. The lass wasn't awake long enough. After the water, she fell right back to sleep."

"Well, it's late. If you don't mind, I'll bunk down here tonight so I can keep watch on her. I'll ride back to Sacramento with you tomorrow."

Both Quinn and Blaine let out relieved sighs. "We'd appreciate it, Doctor..."

"Gillespie. And you are?"

"Quinn MacLaren. This is my cousin, Blaine."

"Ah...the MacLarens. Your family is no secret to those of us who've been around this area for a while. Neither is your history of protecting your family." He glanced at Blaine. "Next time, son, you might want to introduce yourself. The MacLaren name could prove to be more convincing than a gun."

Blaine's cheeks colored. "Aye, Doctor Gillespie. It's good advice."

Sacramento

"Where could they be?" Quinn muttered as he and Blaine stood near the stockyards.

They'd been in Sacramento two days with no sign of Big Jim or the herd.

"Remember, they lost some of the cattle and are down one drover." Blaine lifted a hand to scratch his forehead, then rub the back of his neck.

Quinn watched him go through the routine he'd seen many times. "Nervous, are you?"

Blaine's gaze snapped to him. "Nae. Why do you say that?"

Shaking his head, Quinn chuckled. "It's nothing, lad. It may be best to go ahead to Doc Gillespie's office. Maybe he'll let me take Emma back to the hotel today."

"You know she'll have to have her own room." Blaine snorted. "Big Jim will tear into you if he finds you sharing."

Quinn shoved his hands in his pockets, trying to hide a grin. "Aye, but she needs someone to watch over her until she's ready to ride back to Circle M."

"I can do it. Big Jim will know I'd never lay a hand on her." Although Blaine's tone was serious, Quinn could hear the slight snicker.

Coming to an abrupt stop, Quinn glared at him, his eyes blazing. "You'll not be alone with her in a room with a bed. Am I clear?"

Nodding, Blaine chuckled. "Aye. Quite clear. What kind of lad would I be if I didn't offer?"

Quinn closed his eyes, then glanced up at the sky, shaking his head. "You'd be a bright lad, which we both know you're not."

Stepping into Gillespie's clinic, they moved to the side in an effort to squeeze through the cramped space. At least ten people filled the waiting room, most glancing at them, then turning away.

"It appears we wait." Blaine leaned against a wall, crossing his arms.

Quinn took one more look around, then leaned toward Blaine. "I'm not waiting. I need to find Emma."

"But—"

"Not another word out of you." Quinn weaved through the people, avoiding several children as he walked to one of two doors. Opening it, he poked his head inside, seeing Gillespie bent over a table, a half-dressed man lying before him.

Moving to the second door, he repeated his motions, finding Emma sitting in a chair, her hands clasped in front of her.

"Quinn." She jumped up, running to him, wrapping her arms around his neck. "Have you come to take me out of here?" She placed kisses on his neck, jaw, cheek, and mouth. Laughing, Quinn held her away.

"Seems you're glad to see me, lass."

Crossing her arms, she looked around the small room. "You've no idea."

"How's your head? Does it still hurt? Are you dizzy?"

"It hurts a little, but please don't tell the doctor. I'll go mad if I have to stay here another day. Can't I get a room at the hotel?" She placed her hands on his shoulders, standing on her toes to stare into this eyes. "Or maybe I could share your room?" Biting her lip, she tried to hide a hopeful smile.

"Ach, your father would skin me alive if he found you in my room. Besides, I'm sharing with Blaine, and he'll not be seeing you the way I plan to."

Covering her mouth with a hand, she laughed, her eyes sparkling.

"I'll get you a room and keep watch until Big Jim arrives. It's the best we can do." Wrapping an arm around her, he pulled her tight, kissing her with eager lips. "I've missed you, lass."

"No more than I've missed you." She breathed in his scent, a shiver running through her at what she wanted to do, knowing how her body would respond to him.

The sound of the door opening, followed by a raspy voice, had them jumping apart.

"I see you've come for my patient, Mr. MacLaren."

Clearing his throat, Quinn winked at Emma before looking at Gillespie. "Aye, if you say the lass is ready to leave."

"I doubt I could hold her here any longer. She woke up this morning ready to leave." He took another look at Emma, placed a hand to her forehead, and looked into her eyes. "No pain in your head."

"Um... No, sir."

"No dizziness?"

She shook her head, not meeting the doctor's eyes as a jolt of pain ripped through her. "I feel good. Not that you haven't been wonderful, but I'd very much like to leave."

Gillespie laughed. "If you promise to find me if you start feeling worse."

"Oh, I will."

His narrowed gaze fixed on her. "I'm quite serious about this, Miss Pearce. You had a serious fall. Any pain, trouble breathing, or feeling faint, you have Mr. MacLaren fetch me right away." His hard stare moved from Emma to Quinn. "Do you understand me, young man?"

"Aye, Doctor. You can be sure we'll be back if she has problems."

"I'm going to hold you to that, Mr. MacLaren."

A sharp knock on the door woke Quinn. Unwilling to loosen his grip around Emma's warm, sleeping form, he ignored the sound and closed his eyes. A moment later, his peace was once again broken by more pounding. Harder and lasting longer this time.

"Up with you, Quinn. Big Jim is downstairs looking for Emma."

Quinn groaned, feathering kisses down Emma's neck and shoulder. "I've got to go, lass."

She mumbled something in her sleep, not stirring as he left the bed and dressed. He slid into his boots and grabbed his hat, then bent down, brushing hair from her face before kissing her once more.

"Hurry, Quinn. Big Jim's on his way up."

Stalking to the door, Quinn pulled it open to see his cousin's back. "Move, Blaine. I need to..."

His voice trailed off when he glanced over Blaine's shoulder to see Big Jim glaring at them.

"You just left my daughter's bedroom." The accusation came through gritted teeth.

"Aye, sir." Quinn stepped around Blaine, locking his gaze with Emma's father. "She's still sleeping."

"And you were in there all night?"

"The doctor wanted someone to stay with her. You weren't here, so…"

Big Jim continued to glare into Quinn's eyes, sizing him up. Nodding, he took a step away. "I want to see her."

Quinn reached behind him, turned the knob to Emma's door, and moved aside. When Big Jim pushed past, he grabbed the man's arm.

"She still has bruises and cuts on her face. Most of the swelling is gone, and Emma won't admit it, but I think she still has pain in her head." Quinn breathed in a slow breath. "Someone should be with her all the time, at least for a few more days."

"I think I can take care of my own daughter, MacLaren." Big Jim shook free of Quinn's grip, shutting the door behind him, standing still a moment to let his eyes adjust to the darkness. He let out a relieved sigh, seeing her quiet form under the blankets. Leaning against the door, he crossed his arms, happy to know she was safe.

Emma shifted restlessly, kicking at the covers. Turning, she reached an arm out, her hand grasping nothing but air.

"Quinn?"

Moving her arm back and forth, she still felt nothing. Sitting up, she rubbed her eyes, letting them grow accustomed to the semi-dark room.

"Quinn, are you still here?" Yawning, she dropped her hands, turned toward the door, and gasped.

"Hello, Emma. Quinn's waiting in the hall. I think we need to talk."

Chapter Eighteen

The strained mood between Big Jim, Emma, and Quinn continued throughout the day and into the evening. Whatever was said between father and daughter hadn't been mentioned outside her room. It didn't matter. Emma belonged to him. She'd always been his. When they returned to Circle M, Quinn would wait no longer to make it legal.

Eating supper in the hotel restaurant, Quinn glanced at Emma, then her father.

"It's good you got the price you wanted for the cattle." Quinn put another bit of steak in his mouth, his eyes on Emma as he talked to Big Jim.

"It'll do me little good. We lost a good number of head in the stampede. I needed every one to get what's needed to keep the place going."

Emma, Quinn, and Blaine all stopped eating to watch Big Jim, stunned at his confession.

"What do you mean, Papa? I thought the ranch was doing well." Emma set down her fork, fiddling with the napkin in her lap.

At first, her father didn't respond. Then he sat back in his chair, looking directly into her eyes. "Your mother and I have kept more than we should from you, Emma. We've always seen you as our little girl, the youngest, and in need of our protection." He cleared his throat. "When Jimmy died, we decided there was no reason to burden you with our problems."

She tilted her head, which had begun to throb. "What changed?"

He looked at Blaine, then Quinn, before returning his gaze to Emma. "The truth is, you're a woman. About to be a *married* woman, which makes me realize how grown up you are." Sucking in a deep breath, he continued. "The ranch has been in trouble for a while. I'm just a ranch hand who got lucky by buying land at the right time and in the right place. Jimmy had the brains, the head for numbers. He kept the ranch going, knew how to negotiate, how to make the most of what we had. Me? I took care of the cattle and hired the men, making sure they had what they needed. When Jimmy died, I realized how lost I was without him. A visit to the bank told me how well he'd handled the money. The savings account had grown. At the same time, he'd paid our loan down. Instead of figuring out how he'd done it, I bought a new buggy for your mother, added men, and acquired a new bull. We had some problems the first year, and instead of paying down the loan, I borrowed more, then some more. Before I accepted what I'd done, the loan had grown and the savings account was nearly gone. Until I got shot, your mother didn't know the extent of the debt. When I wasn't able to work, it became clear she had to know."

No one stirred as Big Jim shifted in the chair, then reached for his cup of coffee.

Breaking the silence, Emma leaned forward. "What are you saying, Papa? Are we going to lose the ranch?"

"I honestly don't know. We needed all the money we could get on this drive. Losing those cattle put us way behind what the bank expects."

"Surely August Fielder will work with you, Papa. You've known him for years."

Big Jim hung his head. "The loan I have is with Merchant Bank."

"The one from San Francisco?" Quinn knew his uncles had discussed the bank. They liked the manager, thought him a good man. With Uncle Ewan on the board at the Bank of Conviction, they'd decided it wise to keep their money in a place they knew. And they trusted August Fielder.

"Yes." Big Jim's voice had lowered to almost a whisper.

Quinn's brows knotted in question. "I thought you were on the board of the Bank of Conviction with Uncle Ewan."

"I am. It wasn't an easy decision. In the end, I didn't want your family or Fielder to know the extent of my debt. It was a mistake. One Jimmy wouldn't have made."

Emma's eyes moistened, her throat constricting at the pain in her father's voice. They had hidden their problems well. So well, she'd never suspected.

"Our uncles will help. When we get back, we'll sit down with them, explain your situation." Blaine had no doubt the MacLarens would do whatever they could, but it wasn't his decision to make.

"I appreciate the offer, Blaine. The truth is, I don't want anyone to know. I'm only telling you because I plan to sell. There's a man who's made an offer. It isn't good, but it will be enough to pay the bank and buy a small place in town."

"You'd sell the ranch, Papa? Please, *please* don't do this." She choked the words out, trying not to look at Quinn. "Talk to the MacLarens first. Let them help you." She swiped at a tear she hadn't been able to contain.

"I'm sorry, Emma. At this point, I have to do what's right for your mother. I'm getting older, and the gunshot wounds will never truly heal. My body is failing, along with the energy I once had." He shook his head, a weary smile on his face. "The decision has been made. I'll send word to the man once we're home." He nodded at the server, who filled his coffee cup, then moved on. "We have one other decision to make."

"Boyd Doggett." Blaine ground out the name of the man who'd caused the deaths of so many cattle and almost sent Emma to her grave. "Did you turn him in?"

"No. Holler and Finn are keeping him tied up a few miles outside of town. They helped bring in the herd, then hightailed it back."

"We'll take Doggett to Conviction. Brodie will keep him locked up until the judge gets to town, then we'll get our justice." Renewed anger ripped through Quinn when he thought of almost losing the woman he loved. Looking at Emma's face, her wounds still healing, he wanted to forget what he'd said about taking him to Brodie and deliver his own brand of justice instead.

"There's something else." Big Jim looked down at his hands, weathered and leathery with age. Pursing his lips, he looked at the others. "Doggett says he's innocent."

"That can't be," Quinn ground out.

Blaine shot out of his chair. "I caught him up on the hill where the shots came from."

"Sit down, Blaine." Big Jim waited until they calmed down. "You found a wounded man with a six-gun. The shots came from a rifle, which started before I saw Doggett take off toward the trees. It all happened so fast, and you left before we had a chance to talk to the man. Me and Doggett had a long conversation before we finished the drive. My mind's telling me he may not be the man who did it, but I can't be certain. That's why I had the boys tie him up and ride back out to keep watch on him."

Blaine shifted uncomfortably in his chair while Quinn dragged a hand down his face. Emma stayed silent, trying to figure out who else could've caused the stampede and why Doggett didn't stop him.

"If not Doggett, then who?"

"I don't know, Emma, but Boyd says he does."

"Of course he says he knows. He wants us to believe it's someone else." Blaine crossed his arms, leaning back in his chair. "I say take him to Brodie and let the judge decide."

Quinn looked at Blaine, feeling the same, but wanting to make sure they had the right man. "And you believe him, Big Jim?"

"Like I said, I don't know. Whoever shot at us, stampeded the herd, and caused Emma's injuries may still be out there. I want to find him."

"It could be Doggett and this other man are in it together," Quinn speculated.

"Then why leave Boyd behind? And what of his wounds?" Emma didn't want to believe Doggett was innocent. Condemning an innocent man didn't sit well with her either.

"There's no real choice." Quinn leaned forward, resting his arms on the table. "We must take him back to Conviction and let Brodie know what happened. If he's telling the truth, Brodie will figure it out." He glanced at Big Jim. "What about Jory and the others?"

"I fired them as soon as they got paid." Big Jim spit the words out, disgust on his face. "All three of them ran like cowards when the herd got spooked. They didn't do a thing to slow the stampede, just saving their own hides. I'll not have men like that anywhere near my ranch."

"What did Finn say? I thought Jory and Finn were cousins."

"They are, Emma. Seems Finn and Jory have been at odds for a while. He was glad to see Jory go."

Big Jim pushed himself up. "I'm tuckered out and we need take off at first light tomorrow. Will you see that Emma gets back to her room, Quinn?"

Standing, Quinn settled his hands on the back of Emma's chair, a slow smile drifting across his face. "Of course."

"Guess it's time for me to head up, too." Blaine picked up his hat. "I'll, uh...see you in the morning, Quinn." He made a slight bow to Emma, shot an amused look at his cousin, and left them alone.

Quinn sat back down, taking Emma's hands and leaning close. "How are you feeling? Your face is a little pale, lass."

"I, um..." She bit her lower lip, her brows furrowing in concentration. "Do you think Doggett caused the stampede?"

"I don't see how he could have. Not when your father says he was still with the herd when the first shots were fired. And the fact he didn't have a rifle with him makes me believe it was someone else. If Doggett had a partner, why'd the man leave him behind, wounded? Nae, Emma. It doesn't fit for me." He stood, pulling her up with him. "Come on, lass. Let's get you upstairs and into bed."

Emma leaned into him as they started up the stairs, her voice a whisper. "Will you be joining me?"

Quinn chuckled. "Can't get enough of me, lass?" Her face reddened as she tried to pull away. Not letting go, he leaned down. "I'll be staying with you tonight," he whispered so no one could hear. "From now on, Emma, it will be hard to get me away from your side."

She smiled, liking the sound of that, even as a wave of exhaustion wrapped around her.

"But I'll not be in your bed."

"Wha—"

He put a finger to her lips, then removed it to brush a kiss across her mouth. "You need your sleep, and I need to know you're ready for the long ride back."

"But…" Her next words turned into a giant yawn, her body sagging against his.

Chuckling, Quinn pushed open the door to her room, swept Emma into his arms, and carried her inside. Placing her on the bed, he shook out a blanket, letting it settle over her. A soft sigh escaped her lips an instant before her eyes closed.

The lump in his throat caught him unprepared. A possessive feeling unlike anything he'd ever known gripped him. In that instant, Quinn knew he'd do whatever was needed to keep her safe, never again letting anyone hurt her. Lowering himself to stretch out alongside her, he wrapped a large hand around hers. Emma was his, now and forever, and he'd never let her go.

Conviction

"I don't know what more I can learn from Doggett, but I'll do my best." Brodie hung the keys to the cell on a hook. "He doesn't seem inclined to talk much."

"The man's never been one to share his thoughts." Big Jim lowered himself into a chair, watching Quinn pace in front of the window, Blaine leaning against a wall.

They'd taken Emma to stay with Maggie, Brodie's wife. The journey from Sacramento had taken an extra day, a necessary delay due to the additional stops for Emma to rest.

"Tell me exactly what happened. And, Blaine, I want to know everything you saw when you found Doggett."

It took an hour before Brodie felt satisfied and stopped asking questions. He'd written it all down, rereading his notes as Quinn handed out a third round of coffee.

"I don't see how there's enough here to keep the man in a cell. Blaine finding him slumped over and injured tells me he surprised the real shooter, getting wounded for his efforts. If the estimated distance is correct, a shot from a revolver would never have traveled far enough. A rifle would've been needed." Brodie rubbed his brow, squinting at his notes. "You found rifle shells."

"Aye. Near the base of the tree where I found Doggett." Blaine leaned a hip against Brodie's desk, cradling the coffee cup in his hands.

"He'd left his rifle in the chuckwagon when he rode off in the direction of the gunfire. Right, Big Jim?" Brodie glanced up.

"That's right. The cook said he laid it down after cleaning it before breakfast, not grabbing it before we started moving the herd. When the shots started, he took off quick. I wasn't twenty feet from him when he went after whoever did this." Bracing his hands on the arms of the chair, Big Jim pushed himself up. "If it's not Doggett, we have to find who's responsible. Emma's at your house, Brodie, still recovering, and I want the man who hurt her."

"Doggett told you he knows who did it, right?" Quinn walked over so he could look into the cells, seeing Doggett stretched out on the bed, an arm resting over his face.

"That's right. After you and Blaine left with Emma." Big Jim walked to stand next to Quinn, his gaze moving to Doggett's prone form. "He refused to give me a name." His eyes widened for an instant, then he shot a look at Brodie. "He told me he'd be the one to take care of it."

Brodie rubbed his chin. "Then he must know where to find the man."

"Aye. That's my thought." Quinn's gaze locked on Brodie, a moment of understanding passing between them.

The door opening drew their attention. "Word is out that you boys brought someone in. What have I missed?" Sam closed the door behind him, shaking hands with those in the room.

It took no more than a couple minutes to explain about the stampede, the set of Sam's jaw and flash of anger in his eyes reflecting his thoughts. An image of Jinny entered his mind.

Although he'd never expressed his feelings about her, he knew he'd want to kill anyone who hurt her. "Emma's with Maggie?"

"Aye. We'll be taking her back to the ranch once we've finished here." Quinn wanted to leave now, except there were a few more decisions to make.

"What can I do?" Sam asked, walking to the back to take a look at the prisoner.

"I've just the job for you." For the first time since they brought Doggett in, Brodie smiled. "We know he's not the shooter. I believe it's time we let the man go."

Circle M

"I'm fine, Quinn. Please. I can't stay inside another day. I need to work with Bram and Fletcher." Emma paced to the front window, looking at the barn, wishing she were with the horses.

"Doc Tilden told us you should rest another few days, especially after the long ride from Sacramento." He walked up to her, cupping her face in both hands. "Two more days, Emma. It's not much to ask, is it?" Lowering his mouth to hers, he felt the warmth, the taste belonging only to Emma. When she melted into him, letting her arms wrap around his neck, he groaned.

"Excuse me."

Dropping their arms, they stepped apart. "Aunt Lorna. I didn't hear you come inside." Quinn glanced at Emma, his eyes still sparking with desire.

She smiled. "Aye, you didn't. I came in through the kitchen. Will you be staying with us for supper?"

"Not tonight, Aunt Lorna." Quinn shot a look at Emma, seeing her features fall. "And neither will Emma. Ma's invited us for supper."

"I can understand that. I'd have Brodie and Maggie here every night if he'd give up his job and return to the ranch."

He'd never heard Brodie's mother complain about him being gone. Uncle Ewan had voiced his displeasure at his son's choice many times, although always finishing with how he'd support Brodie's decision.

Quinn cleared his throat. "Aye. We'd all like to see them more often. Maybe he'll change his mind and return someday." He thought of their discussion, how Fielder had asked Brodie to consider returning to the ranch, possibly pass his job over to Sam. He still hadn't made a decision.

"After supper, I'll be riding back to town. Brodie, Blaine, and I are trying to find the man who caused Emma's injuries."

Emma crossed her arms, glaring at him. "I thought you were going to let Brodie and his deputies figure it out."

"Aye, they are. Sam's doing much of the work, but Brodie asked for our help."

"What's Sam working on?" Jinny joined them, her dress covered in dust, hair askew from the strong wind outside.

"We're trying to find the man responsible for the stampede. Big Jim lost a lot of cattle, and Emma could've been killed. Sam's using his skills to help identify the shooter. Blaine and I will be leaving after supper to find out Brodie's plan."

Jinny glanced outside, wishing she could go with them. It had been weeks since she'd seen him. "I heard Sam was leaving and returning home."

"Aye. He's talked about it with Brodie. For now, he's still in town and still a deputy." Quinn knew Jinny had feelings for Sam, suspecting he felt the same about her. It was too bad he planned to return to the east, possibly resuming his work for Allan Pinkerton. "We'll find whoever did this, then celebrate. Maybe I can convince Sam and Nate to ride out and join us."

Jinny nodded, her face devoid of expression. "It would be nice to see him once more before he leaves." She sucked in a breath, looking down at her clothes. "I'll clean up, then help you with supper, Ma."

Emma watched her closest friend walk up the stairs, shoulders slumped, feet heavy. She knew Jinny liked Sam, but hadn't realized how much until now. Her heart ached for her. Emma felt Quinn's strong arm settle on her shoulders.

"Come on, lass." He kissed her temple, inhaling the familiar scent. Stepping outside, they started toward Quinn's house. "It will work out for Jinny."

Emma glanced up at him, a smile curving her lips. "Another feeling you have?"

"Aye. I'm not often wrong."

"Does your *feeling* include Sam?" She bit her lip, holding her breath.

He chuckled, drawing her closer to his side. "Ah, lass. I'm no fortune teller."

She pulled away, mischief in her eyes. "I suppose not. It appears I'll just have to help Sam along."

Quinn shook his head as she moved away from him, laughing. "Now, lass..."

Turning, she sent him a bright smile. "Don't worry. Sam won't even know."

Chapter Nineteen

Pearce Ranch

"Are you certain we still have to sell, Jim?" Although her voice was strong, Gertie's hands shook around her coffee cup. The slices of pie she'd placed before each of them sat untouched. "Maybe we can ask Quinn to come back for a spell."

"No, Gertie. We have no right to ask the boy to disrupt his life and impose more of a burden on his family."

"But he'll be our family soon enough." She knew her thoughts were irrational. At this point, she'd consider anything to save her home. They'd married, had their children, and built a life on this land. Her only son was buried on the hill behind the house. She didn't know how she could ever leave.

Big Jim reached out, taking his wife's hand in his. "We have enough money to make it through another month, maybe two, with nothing left over to pay down the loan. The bank has done all it can." He squeezed her hand. "I'm sorry, sweetheart. If I could do anything different, you know I would."

Gertie knew the loss of their ranch devastated him as much as her, yet she couldn't help the resentment at him not coming to her sooner. She might be older, but she could still ride, knew how to work with cattle. Unlike some women, Gertie had never stayed inside the house for long. She'd ridden alongside her husband for years, doing the work of any other ranch hand.

"What do we do now?"

"I'll ride to town tomorrow, leave a message for the man who made the offer." He pinched the bridge of his nose, then let out a deep sigh. "The number he mentioned the first time we met would be enough to pay off the debt and the men, still having enough left over to buy a place in town."

"How will we live? We still have to eat." The worry in his wife's eyes cut through him.

"I've already spoken with Stein Tharaldson. He's offered me a job at his place. It would pay enough to meet our needs." Lowering his head, he fought to control the moisture building in his eyes. When he thought he'd won the battle, Gertie reached out and stroked a hand down the back of his head and neck. Her simple touch caused him to break. "I'm so sorry." He covered his face with his hands as a sense of absolute failure jolted through him.

Only one other time in her life had Gertie seen her husband this broken. The loss of their son had devastated them both, almost torn them apart. They'd survived. Standing, she wrapped her arms around him.

"We've made it through all kinds of trouble, including Jimmy's death. As long as we stay together, we'll make it through this as well."

Conviction

Brodie rummaged through one of the desk drawers, searching the wanted posters. Something he'd seen several days before stuck with him, but he couldn't remember what it was or why he wanted to find it now. The feeling it had to do with the stampede gnawed at him.

"Can I help you locate something?" Sam sat across from him, relaxed, giving the impression he had nothing better to do than wait around for Brodie to cut Doggett loose. They'd gone over the plan several times. Once they freed him, Sam and Quinn would follow. Sam didn't like it. He worked alone. Always had as a Pinkerton agent, and rarely with Nate or Jack while in Conviction. Besides the fact he hated to rely on anyone else, the freedom suited him.

Brodie shook his head, slamming the drawer closed. "Nae. It will come to me." He hoped.

"Morning, Sheriff, Sam." Jack walked in, pushing his hat off his forehead. "I saw Nate at the Gold Dust. Do you want me to get him?"

"Nae. Let the man finish his breakfast. He'll come over when he's done. Besides, Quinn and Blaine still need to arrive." Brodie didn't feel comfortable with how Nate explained away his behavior over the past few months. They'd met a few days before, Nate swearing he was fine, just tired and restless. Brodie knew there had to be more to it, but he wouldn't push any further. At least not until they'd arrested the man who'd fired the shots at Big Jim's herd.

Quinn stepped inside, followed by Blaine, both brushing trail dust from their shirts. "Seems like everyone is here."

"Except for Nate."

"I'm here." He followed Blaine inside, nodding to the others before closing the door. "Are we going to talk in here?" Nate nodded toward the cells in the back. Sound carried well in the jail, and they all knew Doggett would hear every word spoken.

Brodie's gaze traveled around the room. "Jack, why don't you take the prisoner outside so he can take care of his needs."

"Okay, Sheriff. Whatever you want."

Jack slid the key off the hook on the wall and headed to the back. A few minutes later, they watched as Jack led Doggett out the back door, shutting it behind them.

"All right. Let's go over what's going to happen as soon as I release Doggett."

"Aye, Brodie. We understood the plan after the second time." Quinn grinned, clasping his cousin on the shoulder.

Sam straightened, his eyes focusing on the back door. "What's taking Jack so long?" He glanced at Brodie, then Nate, understanding hitting them all at the same time.

Drawing their guns, they dashed to the back door, throwing it open to race outside. They found Jack thirty feet behind the jail, face down in the dirt.

Brodie let out a low curse, looking around, as Sam knelt down and rolled Jack over.

"Jack." Nate checked for a pulse. "He's got a lump the size of an egg on the side of his head. Other than that, I don't see anything."

"Sam, Nate and I will get him inside. See if you can find Doggett. He didn't have a horse, so he may still be on foot." Brodie holstered his gun, bending to pick his deputy up.

"We'll go with Sam." Quinn looked at Blaine, who nodded. "If we spread out, we might find him sooner."

"Remember, you want to follow him, not bring him back. He's the only one who knows the identity of the shooter."

"What's going on out here?" Big Jim asked. "Is that Jack?"

Brodie walked toward him, Jack in his arms. "Yes, sir. Doggett must have knocked him out, then took off."

"I'll go for the doctor, then stay with Jack. You fellas do what you need to do."

"Thanks, Big Jim." Brodie shook his head, disgusted at the change in plans. "You all know what to do."

"How long ago did he ride off?" Sam stood inside the new livery Stein Tharaldson built next to the feed lot, Quinn and Blaine by his side. They'd given up trying to track Doggett, deciding to ask about anyone interested in a horse.

"About an hour ago. Rode north and east, in the direction of your new land." Stein looked at Quinn and Blaine when he said the last. "Didn't even negotiate. Paid for the tack, saddled up, and took off."

"And you're sure he said his name was Boyd?"

"That's what he told me, Sam. Wish I could tell you more."

"You've provided us with excellent information, Stein. If he comes back, let Brodie or one of the other deputies know."

"I will, Sam." Stein shook his hand, turning to Quinn. "I hear you and Emma Pearce are getting married. Congratulations." He held out his hand, then pulled Quinn in for a hug. They'd known each other for years, spending many nights at Buckie's playing cards and toasting the ladies.

"I'll let you know when."

"You be sure and do that, Quinn. Hope you find Boyd."

"Would you mind sending someone to the jail to let Brodie know what you told us?"

"I'll do better than that, Sam. I'll go myself."

"Thanks, Stein." Sam scanned the horizon as they mounted their horses, glancing at Quinn. "He said Boyd rode out toward your new property. Is there any place someone could hide out in that direction?"

"You pass right by the Pearce ranch. He has at least one secluded old shack on the property. The old Estrada place has a couple areas. Hell, Sam. There are all kinds of places a man could hide out that way."

"I suppose the best we can do is get started and hope to find some tracks we can follow."

"You're sure you want to do that, Big Jim? Sell the ranch and move to town?" Brodie sat there, stunned at the news. He had no idea the Pearces were in trouble, and wondered if his father knew. "Have you talked to Da? I'm sure he and Uncle Ian will be glad to help."

Big Jim shook his head. "Nope. And I don't plan to. When I told Emma, Quinn, and Blaine, they said the same. I appreciate it, but it's my problem and I'll work it out in my own way."

"Aye, I understand. Have you spoken to anyone else?"

"Some fella came to me a few months ago when I was still laid up. He asked about buying it. I told him no. Then he came back a few weeks ago and gave me a price lower than I expected. This time, I told him I'd think on it. With the loss of so many head of cattle, I didn't leave Sacramento with as much as I needed. I've got no choice, Brodie."

"Aye, you do. Talk to Da and Uncle Ian. If you won't take a loan, talk to them about buying. You know they'll give you a fair price, probably letting you stay in the house as long as you want."

Big Jim tilted his head a little, his jaw working, mulling over what Brodie said. "I just might do that. First, I'm going to talk to the man who made the offer. Right now, all I want is what's best for

Gertie, and that woman sure would like to stay in the house."

"My ma would feel the same."

Big Jim nodded. "I'd better get moving. I told the man I'd leave a message for him at the Gold Dust. For all I know, he's given up and gone back to Frisco."

Brodie's eyes flickered at the last bit of information. "San Francisco?"

"That's what he said. Why?"

"You know Widow Jones and those two ranchers on the other side of the Feather River who sold their places?"

"Heard about them."

"The buyer for all three came here from Frisco." Brodie rubbed the back of his neck. "What does the man look like?"

"Short, thin as a fence post, with a face I'm not certain even a mother could love." Big Jim grimaced. "Has a scar on his right hand—jagged and angry. If it weren't for the city clothes, I'd think he was a hired gun."

"Did he give you a name?"

"Lyman Ziller. Told me he's an agent for the company in Frisco."

"Do you recall the company name?" Brodie jotted down notes, a bitter ball of suspicion building in his stomach.

"I don't recall he gave me the name. I'll make sure to get it when I meet with him." Big Jim stood at the same time the door opened.

"Good morning, Stein. What brings you in here?"

"Morning, Brodie, Big Jim. Sam asked me to bring you a message." He relayed the information about Boyd, and that Quinn, Blaine, and Sam were going after him. "It hasn't been that long. You could probably catch them."

"Nate's over at the clinic with Jack. Let me get him, then I'll get started."

"I'll do it, Brodie," Stein offered. "You go ahead and leave. If you ride fast, you should catch up with them in no time."

Circle M

"I don't understand why Quinn can't let Brodie take care of dealing with Doggett." Emma stopped grooming Moonshine to look at Jinny. "Your brother has three deputies to help him. Why would he need Quinn and Blaine?"

At the mention of Brodie's deputies, Jinny thought of Sam, wondering what she'd done to push him away. She'd been certain he felt the attraction between them, sending her the same secret looks she sent him. Whenever their eyes met, her body responded without thought, heart hammering at an almost painful pace.

"I don't know, Emma. It may be Quinn wants to be there when they find the person responsible for your injuries. He's protective of what's his, the same as all the MacLaren men." Jinny found herself wishing Sam felt the same about her. "If you're worried, don't be. Quinn knows how to protect himself, and he'll be with Brodie and Blaine, and probably Sam and Nate. They'll take care of each other."

Emma heard the disappointment in Jinny's voice, saw the dejected way her body moved, knowing it had nothing to do with Quinn. Tossing down the brush, she leaned against the stall.

"Geneen hasn't heard from Nate in months."

"I know. She and I have talked about Nate and Sam. Seems we're both eejits for thinking there was more to those men than we thought." Straightening her back, Jinny tucked an errant strand of hair behind her ear. Geneen, Sarah's younger sister, had traveled to Circle M when Colin, Quinn, and Brodie made the journey to Oregon to fetch Sarah. Her skills as a ranch hand matched Emma's, and she'd become a young woman the MacLarens could rely on. Like Jinny, she'd fallen hard for one of Brodie's deputies.

"I suppose it's time for me to give up my fantasy of a life with Sam and face the real world. He's not the only man out there." A pained smile crossed her face. "Too bad he's the only one I want."

Emma lowered herself to the ground, crossed her legs, then picked up a piece of straw. Twisting it between her fingers, she rested her head against the stall.

"I'm sorry I didn't know how much Sam meant to you. You've listened to me for hours going on and on about Quinn, yet you've never spoken of Sam."

Jinny settled herself next to Emma, grabbing her own piece of straw. "Your feelings for Quinn have been strong for years. You've always known how you felt, having the patience to wait for him to admit he loved you. Anyone who knows the two of you felt it was meant to be. Sam and I are different." A hint of frustration crossed her face. "I've known him for less than a year, and seen him a handful of times. Always with family around and Brodie nearby."

"Your brother being his boss may be one reason he hasn't made his feelings known."

Jinny snorted. "Nae. Sam is the type of man who'll go after what he wants, not worrying about what Brodie thought. He isn't interested in me, the same as Nate isn't interested in Geneen. I once

301

heard Camden say women were a diversion, a way for a man to spend his time without thinking of work or the dangers of what he did. I think it must be the same with lawmen. Their work is demanding. Women like Geneen and I are a way to get their minds off it—nothing more."

Emma glanced at her friend, resting a hand on her arm. "I don't believe that, and I don't think you do either. I've seen how Sam looks at you, and how Nate looks at Geneen. Both are still in Conviction, working for Brodie. Don't give up, Jinny." Emma gently shoved her shoulder. "Isn't that what you kept telling me, year after year, when Quinn ignored me?" When Jinny didn't respond, Emma squeezed her arm. "Well, isn't it?"

Jinny laughed, although it wasn't the robust, spontaneous sound Emma associated with her friend. "Aye, I suppose it is."

Pushing herself up, Emma held out a hand to Jinny. "All we have to do now is figure a way to get Sam to take action, and I think I have the perfect idea."

Chapter Twenty

"It took you long enough to get here." Giles Delacroix took measured steps toward Doggett, unmistakable displeasure on his face. "You should have been here long ago."

Doggett glanced around the inside of the ramshackle cabin. He'd grown to hate the man stalking toward him. He didn't like being ordered around, treated as if he were a fool, and shown little respect. Growing up, he had his fill of it. As the youngest son, with several cousins living in the same house, he wore the most tattered clothes, was given the worst jobs, and always scraped food from what was left in the serving dishes.

"I got held up." Doggett didn't elaborate. He didn't feel the need. "The job's done. The men have been paid, and now I want what you owe me."

"I already heard," Giles hissed. "Pearce left a message for Lyman that he wants to talk. I should have heard it from you."

Doggett crossed his arms, stopping himself from reaching out to grab Delacroix around the throat. "Give me my money and I'll be gone."

Lowering his bulky frame into a chair more suited for a woman of slight build, he reached into a pocket in his jacket, pulling out a pouch. Tossing it to Doggett, he sat back, a satisfied smirk on his face.

Opening the pouch, Doggett poured coins into his palm. "This isn't what we agreed to. Where's the rest?"

"Quite the contrary. As with the other ranches, the agreement was full payment when the property changed hands. I've given you half. The rest will come after Pearce signs over his property."

Doggett cursed, shoving the coins in his pocket. "And if he doesn't sell?" He took a menacing step forward. "I've done what we agreed and I expect payment whether he sells or not."

"My good man, if Pearce doesn't sell, then your efforts have been for naught. Be happy with what I've offered." He pushed himself up. "I wouldn't worry too much. Pearce contacted *us*, which means he's out of options. The ranch is as good as in my hands already."

Doggett fumed, although he kept his expression neutral. "If you try to cheat me out of the rest, you're as good as dead."

"I have no intention of cheating you. The rest will be ready as soon as Pearce signs. I'll contact you the usual way—unless you have plans to leave town."

He did, but he wouldn't admit it to Delacroix. Showing his face in Conviction wasn't a good idea.

Neither was riding away, leaving half his money with the man standing a few feet away. He'd have to find a place to hide until Pearce signed the papers.

"I have no plans, other than to get the rest of the money. Afterward…" Doggett shrugged.

"Lyman meets with Pearce tomorrow. With luck, the ranch will be in my possession within days."

Doggett wished he didn't need the money. What he wanted to do was end this with Delacroix, leave his body for the animals, and ride south. The man reminded him of the vultures in Texas who took advantage of ranchers at their weakest moment, stripping them of what they'd worked their entire lives to build. He wasn't proud of taking the job, but the money was too much to pass up.

Without another word, Doggett turned his back on Delacroix and stepped outside. He needed to clear his head and rid himself of the anger he felt at the man's deception. Sucking in a breath of fresh air, he grabbed the reins of his horse. Putting distance between himself and the man inside might be the only way for Delacroix to stay alive.

"He was here." Sam walked around the outside of the empty cabin, seeing signs of more than one horse. "And he wasn't alone."

Following Doggett hadn't been as hard as expected. Stein told him of the slight imperfection in one horseshoe and the uneven gate when the horse moved.

"He must have met the man we're after." Quinn took the steps up and into the cabin, grimacing at the filth. "It's sure no one has stayed here. The place isn't even fit for the men we're tracking."

Blaine glanced over Quinn's shoulder, then moved deeper into the cabin. "Sam, come look at this."

Brodie followed Sam inside, his hand resting on the butt of his gun. Taking a quick look around, he retreated to keep watch outside.

"What do you see, Blaine?" Sam knelt beside him.

"I think there are more than two pairs of boots."

Sam studied the imprints in the dirt-covered floor, then stood and looked around. "You may be right. I can see three different prints." A muscle in his jaw twitched, his gaze darting around the small space. "Let's take a look outside." It didn't take long to find what he expected in the soft ground. "Two of the men are about my weight. I'm guessing one is Doggett. The third man is much heavier." Sam pointed at the impression. "See how they sink into the ground and are wider than the others?"

"Sam, come over here." Brodie stood at the start of a narrow trail, studying the tracks at his feet.

"Two of them rode out this direction. North and east, toward your new property, Brodie." Sam looked behind him, turning in a circle, a slow smile spreading across his face. Walking to the other side of the clearing, he searched the ground, his eyes widening when he spotted what he wanted. "The bigger man rode out this direction. If I had to guess, I'd say it's another trail back to Conviction."

Quinn stepped next to him. "What are you thinking, Sam?"

"We could split up. Brodie and Blaine follow the trail to town. Quinn and I follow the other two." Removing his hat, he ran a hand through his hair. "If it were my decision, we'd all go after the two. I'd bet my life this is the trail Doggett took."

"Then that's what we'll do." Brodie looked at his cousins. "You heard Sam. Let's get moving."

Nate sat at a table next to the dirt-encrusted front window of Hong Wo's restaurant, trying to keep his focus. He'd finished evening rounds of the docks and Chinatown, doing his best to ignore the pain in his arm, the almost crippling need to seek relief.

Two days of feeling a hand that didn't exist, instead seeing the mangled stump of his left arm. The doctor he'd seen in Sacramento told Nate it was a phantom limb—the sensation of an arm or leg no longer there. In his case, amputated after a victorious encounter with Confederate troops.

The victory had been meaningless to him, more so each time his gaze locked on his missing arm. He woke up in a cold sweat several times every night, images better left forgotten crowding his mind, fighting for space. Whiskey had long ago lost its effectiveness, as had laudanum, the drug he blamed for his current plight.

Taking a small bite of the food Wo had set before him, he forced it down, knowing he needed the nourishment, but tasting nothing. Other than the texture, he'd been unable to distinguish between a well-cooked steak and a stale slice of bread for months.

Nate thought of Christmas supper at the MacLarens, Geneen MacGregor's emerald green eyes watching him the entire evening. She'd asked what he thought of the goose Colin's mother had prepared. He'd told her it was the best he'd ever eaten. In truth, he hadn't been able to taste it at all—nor the pie Geneen had made. It hadn't mattered. He would've told her anything to keep the smile on her face. The smile gave him hope he could someday move beyond the man he'd become and be worthy enough to court her. He choked on the memory, raising his eyes when Wo walked up.

"You no like?" Wo nodded at the almost full bowl, the smile slipping from his face.

"It's fine, Wo." Nate glanced out the window, hoping the man didn't say anything more or offer an alternative. The sun had begun to fade over the western hills, casting a reddish glow over the town.

His brows drew together when he spotted a man he'd seen more than once in Conviction, his fine clothes covered in dirt, hat askew, eyes darting around and then lowering, as if he didn't want to be recognized. His size and girth dwarfed the horse under him, its legs caked in dried mud.

Curiosity overtook him as the man reined the horse to a stop across the street and walked into a neighboring restaurant. In the weeks since he'd noticed the man in Conviction, he'd never seen him anywhere near Chinatown. A few minutes later, the man walked out, looked around, then slid several leather pouches into his saddlebags.

Mounting, he looked around again before moving down the street.

"You come in back with me. I have something you will like." Wo hovered over him, the smile Nate always considered sincere now filled with deception.

On a different day, he might have followed Wo into the kitchen. His body screamed for him to go, not overthink the reasons he shouldn't. Nate thought of Brodie, Sam, and Jack, the men he worked with and called friends. And Geneen, a woman he wanted to see again, get to know better.

As he started to stand, an intense pain ripped through his arm, then down his left side. Thinking he'd pass out, his face contorted as he grabbed his left arm with his right hand and squeezed. Sucking in a deep breath, he shut his eyes tight, expelling air through his mouth, beads of sweat covering his forehead.

Wo bent next to Nate's ear. "You come with me now."

Ignoring the nausea, he shook his head. "No."

"It best you come now." Wo kept a firm smile on his face.

Pain gripped him again, a light-headed feeling causing him to rock in his chair.

"I help you." Wo helped Nate stand. Taking slow steps toward the kitchen, the restaurant owner nodded at those he passed, his smile never wavering.

Nate knew he should shrug off Wo's help, somehow get himself outside and go straight to his hotel room—or Doc Vickery's clinic. But pain ruled his mind. Stepping through the curtains, he took one more glance behind him, seeing the questioning gazes of those trying not to look.

A stronger man could've dealt with this, handled the pain, not crumbled under the weight of the agony. Nate wasn't that man. Not today...maybe not ever.

Feeling someone on his other side, he let the person usher him behind the kitchen and into a small room, curtained off in sections. Within minutes, the cycle would start again, along with his self-loathing.

Circle M

"Oh, good. I'm glad I found you here." Kyla walked into the barn, watching as Emma finished measuring the young colt.

Quinn hadn't returned to the ranch the night before. Emma knew why he felt he had to help Brodie find the person responsible for stampeding the herd. Still, she'd rather have him at the ranch or with Cam and Caleb at the new place.

"What do you have there, Mrs. MacLaren?" Wiping her hands down the pants Quinn's younger brother, Thane, had offered her, her gaze landed on the covered dish in Kyla's hand.

"I made a pie for Caleb and Camden. I've also packed bread, fruit, and cold meat. Would you and Jinny mind taking it out to them? I'd ask one of the men, but they're all so busy..." She shrugged, knowing Emma understood. "If you leave soon, you'll have plenty of time to ride back before dark."

"Of course. I need to clean up a bit, then find Jinny—"

"She's with Geneen, doing the milking. They should be done soon."

"I will let her know. We'll come by your house, pack it all up, and go. Is there anything else you'd like us to take?"

"Nae, Emma. The food will be enough. I know they still have some supplies, but it's always better if someone else makes it. I'll take the pie back to the house and finish packing the rest."

"We shouldn't be long." Emma saddled Moonshine, then ran the short distance to where Jinny and Geneen would be doing the milking. So far, she'd missed out on this chore, for which she felt grateful. It had never been one of her favorites.

"Hey, Jinny. Kyla asked if we could ride to the new place, take some food to Caleb and Camden."

Geneen looked up from where she sat on the stool. She wore the same kind of pants as Emma. As Ewan was fond of saying, he had two additional ranch hands in Emma and Geneen, three if Heather ever returned from working at the Evanston ranch.

"If you two don't mind, I'd like to ride along." Geneen stood, placing the full milk bucket near the other two.

"We'd love it." Jinny finished, moving the last bucket aside, then put the stool away.

"I'll get Moonshine and meet you two at Kyla's."

Boyd needed to get moving. After he left the cabin yesterday, he could tell someone followed him. Assuming it were the sheriff and his deputies, Doggett followed the path until he felt certain he could find it again, then veered to the west. Changing directions several times, he finally made camp in a gully, settling in for the night.

Chewing on a biscuit he'd purchased from Stein, he kept watch on the trail, half expecting the sheriff and his men to ride up on him at any time.

He figured if that had been their plan, they would've arrested him last night.

Boyd had heard enough while in his cell to know Brodie MacLaren didn't believe he fired the shots causing the stampede. He didn't understand how the lawman figured it out, but the sheriff believed Boyd would eventually lead them to the real shooter. He didn't intend to lead them anywhere. The man he sought would be dead within minutes of Doggett finding him. Then he'd go after Giles. He didn't want any loose ends to clean up later.

Finishing his meager breakfast, Boyd mounted his horse, turning north, hoping to get away before the sheriff realized he'd left. He'd purposely ridden onto Pearce land yesterday. Working for Big Jim gave him time to learn the property, where to hide, where to bed down.

Spotting the sun peeking over the eastern hills, he pulled up his coat's collar, giving him more protection from the early morning chill. Boyd glanced over his shoulder, sensing someone behind him, seeing no one. Until he reached the top of a short rise ahead, he wouldn't change directions. He needed to reach his destination well ahead of the men tracking him.

Riding the easy grade to the top, Boyd leaned back in the saddle, allowing himself a few minutes to watch the sunrise. It had been too long since he'd given himself time to enjoy the simple pleasures. Ever since he left Colorado, his life hadn't been his. He'd been on a mission, his previous employer calling it a crusade. Boyd's total focus had been to do whatever needed to finish the task. He was close. Close enough he could almost taste it.

A few more miles, a little more deception, then he could put the past behind him forever.

Chapter Twenty-One

"I didn't see any sign of storm clouds when we started out." Emma pursed her lips at the change in the sky. Since they'd left Circle M, dark, threatening clouds had rolled in, now covering the entire sky.

"If we hurry, we might be able to get to the hacienda before they burst open." Jinny's words had barely left her mouth when the first drops of rain fell. "Maybe not."

Reaching behind them, all three grabbed their raincoats, hurrying to put them on.

"Caleb mentioned the property has some old casitas between Circle M and the hacienda." Geneen shifted in her saddle, looking around as the rain started to come down at a steady pace.

"Did he say where?" Emma asked, pulling the hood over her head, cringing as a bolt of lightning pierced the sky above them, followed by the loud crack of thunder a few seconds later.

"No. Let's head toward the trees. At least we'll have some cover." Geneen rode out, pushing her horse into a gallop, Jinny and Emma close behind. As they got closer to the trees, Geneen glanced over her shoulder and pointed. "Up there. I think I see something."

A few minutes later, they dismounted beside a dilapidated structure of adobe and rock. Untying their saddlebags, they rushed to the door and pushed.

"It must be stuck." Emma kicked at it. When it didn't budge, Jinny and Geneen joined her. "Gosh darn." Emma took a step back, then rammed into it with her shoulder, putting all her weight behind it. "Ugh," she groaned, then grinned when it moved. "Push."

The door couldn't hold up to the efforts of all three. A few seconds later, it opened enough for them to rush inside.

"It's so dark." Jinny shoved off her hood, then looked back through the open doorway, the other two women standing next to her. "We got in here just in time." Pushing the door closed, she shrugged out of the coat, shaking off the excess water.

"I'd say it would've been better if you'd moved on."

They whipped around at the deep voice, their eyes going wide at the sight of a rifle pointed at them, the silhouette of a man holding it.

"I'd tell you to turn around and ride off, but now that you've seen my face, I can't let you go."

Emma's heart pounded. Swallowing the bile rising in her throat, she took a step forward.

"Easy, missy. Stay where you are."

Emma froze, her body shaking. "Who are you?"

"Don't believe it matters. Truth is, I know who *you* are, Miss Pearce. My guess is these other two are MacLarens."

Jinny gasped, then straightened her spine, glaring at the man. "You're a coward, hiding in the shadows. I want to know who you are."

"Well, aren't you a feisty one." The man stood, walking toward them.

Emma stared at the face, his features somewhat familiar. The eyes, the set of his jaw, his build. Biting her lip, her eyes scrunched in concentration, trying to remember if she knew the man, had ever seen him.

"Get over in that corner and sit down." He pointed to the far corner at the back of the small casita. "Leave your saddlebags by the door."

Geneen crossed her arms, planting her feet. "No. Not until we know who you are and why you want to keep us here."

He took a menacing step forward, lowering the rifle. He pulled a six-gun from his holster, aiming at her chest. "You forget who's in charge here. I don't have to tell you anything." His voice hardened with each word. "Move to the corner, or there will be only two of you I have to deal with."

Grabbing Geneen's arm, Emma hauled her toward the corner, Jinny following.

Keeping his gun trained on them, he stepped forward. "That's better. Sit down with your backs to the wall." When they were settled, he walked to their saddlebags, rummaging through each one, a smile tugging at the corners of his mouth as he pulled out food, then chuckled. "Look what you brought me." Reaching inside, he drew out a six-gun, loaded, ready to fire. Doing the same with the other saddlebags, he was rewarded with more food and two more guns.

Emma leaned toward Jinny. "We have to get out of here." A gunshot hitting the floor at her feet had her jerking away, silencing further conversation.

"No talking." Keeping his gaze on them, he walked to his gear and pulled out his rope, cutting short lengths. "You." He pointed to Emma, tossing her two lengths. "Tie their hands behind their backs. And make 'em tight."

Emma's hand shook as she reached for the rope. "Why don't you just let us go? We don't know who you are and won't tell anyone what happened."

He didn't answer her question. "Do as I tell you."

Biting her lower lip, Emma tied Jinny's hands, then Geneen's, keeping the ropes as loose as she thought wise, hoping he didn't come over and test them. When finished, she turned toward him, lifting her chin.

"Come over here."

Glaring at him, Emma stood and walked over.

"Turn around." When she did, he tied her hands, then sent her back with the others. "Not a word out of any of you. We're miles away from another ranch, so don't waste your time screaming. If you try, I'll gag you." Holstering his gun, he stalked to the pile of food, ignoring the pie in favor of the cold meat and bread. Sitting with his back to the door, he dug in, never taking his eyes off them.

"How could we lose him? He's been right in front of us since sunup." Brodie stared at the spot where the tracks disappeared.

"The man is smart. He cut back and forth across the river, coming out here, then crossed once more on these rocks. He took advantage of them hiding his tracks." Sam lifted his field glasses, scanning the area beyond the rocks. "We need to scatter out, look for the spot he left the rocks and got back on soft ground."

The four fanned out, searching for close to an hour before Quinn shouted to the others. "I've found some tracks." He slid off Warrior.

Sam had never been trained in tracking. It wasn't a skill Allan Pinkerton required, and it wasn't needed on most cases. The one time he did need it, he had been fortunate to have a partner on the case, a man skilled in tracking. He'd been more than willing to share his knowledge with Sam.

"That's Doggett," Sam said, studying the tracks. "He's moving straight east of here."

This time, the four weren't subtle in their pursuit. His attempts to lose them meant Doggett knew they were behind him, and he had over an hour advantage.

Quinn kept watch, knowing the instant they crossed from Pearce land to the property the MacLarens owned with August Fielder. Dotted between here and the main hacienda were casitas used by the vaqueros and their families. The same was true heading east of the hacienda. Juan Estrada had been generous in erecting the structures. Some had been damaged by the occasional earthquake, but most were in good condition.

"There are numerous casitas on the property. Doggett could be hiding in any one of them." Quinn rode next to Brodie, Sam in the lead, and Blaine at the back.

"Aye. I've been thinking the same." Brodie kept his gaze roving back and forth, looking for signs of movement. "Except we're certain

Doggett's following someone, which means he could end up miles from here."

Sam turned in his saddle, looking at Quinn. "The hacienda is north of here, correct?"

"Aye. We're on the southern border of the property where it touches Circle M land. The main house is in the center of the ranch."

"The tracks keep moving east. Doggett isn't heading to the house, and neither is the man he's following."

"What do you mean, Sam?" Brodie kicked Hunter enough to catch up to him.

"I've been following two sets of tracks for a while, and they're both heading in that direction." Sam nodded toward the mountains leading into Nevada. "We'd better catch up to them soon or we may lose them both."

Emma shifted on the hard ground. She'd been picking at the rope, trying to free her hands. The man had tied hers tight, much tighter than she'd done with Jinny and Geneen.

"Don't any of you move." He walked to the door, yanking it open, then stepped outside.

The sound of horses caught the girls' attention. The structure had a window in front, one in each side wall, and none in the back.

Glancing through the small opening across from their position in the corner, they could see him leading their horses behind the casita.

"I wonder what he has planned." Jinny squirmed, working the rope. "My hands are almost free."

"Mine, too." Geneen huffed out a frustrated breath before flashing them a weak smile. "They're free. Emma, turn around and I'll—" She stopped, inching her back to the wall when the door slammed open.

He stepped inside, his narrowed gaze fastened on the three. Stalking toward them, he grabbed Geneen's left arm, yanking her up. Realizing the rope no longer held her hands, he ducked just in time to avoid her swinging right hand. Cursing, he slapped her across the face, then shoved her against the wall.

"Stop it!" Jinny screamed.

Ignoring her, his face contorted as he glared at Geneen. "That was stupid. Pick up the rope." She hesitated, still stunned by the blow to her face. Rubbing her reddened cheek, she bent down to scoop up the rope. "Turn around." This time, he made sure the rope was tight before shoving her to the ground. He looked at Jinny. "Stand up." He didn't wait for her to obey, reaching down and yanking her up. "Almost had yours off, too." Knotting the rope tight until Jinny whimpered in pain, he turned her around to look at him. "You try anything—and I mean anything at all—you'll regret it."

Storming away, he glanced over his shoulder to see Jinny slump to the ground. Picking up the guns he'd confiscated from the saddlebags, he stuffed one behind him in the waistband of his pants. He hid the other two in his saddlebags.

Picking up his gear, he shifted his stance to look at them, his jaw hard, face taut. After a minute, he walked to the door and disappeared outside.

"Is he leaving us?" Geneen's hopeful words whispered out as she again tried to loosen the rope binding her wrists.

Emma braced herself against the wall, using it as leverage to stand. Her gaze darted to the door, then out the windows as wobbly legs carried her to the other side of the room.

"Emma, get back over here. He'll hurt you, or worse, if he comes back and finds you're trying to spy on him." Jinny's soft plea didn't change Emma's course.

Emma had spent the time deriding herself for coming into the shelter without her gun, for wearing a dress instead of pants, and for her stupidity at not thinking they could be in danger. They were on MacLaren land, and few did anything to get on the wrong side of the family. A deluded sense of safety always seemed to wrap itself around her when she rode across their property, as if being on Circle M land would shield her from peril.

She knew better. Danger could be found anywhere, whether it be by people who seemed to pose no threat or complete strangers, such as the man who held them captive.

"He's tying the saddlebags to his horse. I can't see Moonshine or your horses anywhere."

"They must be in back, Emma. Surely he wouldn't turn them loose." Jinny spoke in a nervous whisper.

"Even if he does, they won't go far." Geneen's voice strengthened the longer the man stayed outside.

"She's right, Jinny. Moonshine might stray a few feet, but unless she's scared, she'll stay nearby." Emma turned to look back out the window, then jerked at the sound of gunfire. Dashing back to the others, she lowered herself to the ground, her back to Jinny. "We have to get free. See if you can loosen my rope."

They heard more shooting, the sound of a scream, then another few shots.

"Who do you think is out there?" Geneen pushed herself up while Jinny continued trying to loosen the ropes around Emma's wrists.

"Get down, Geneen," Emma hissed at the same time a stray bullet hit the wall of the casita close to the window where Geneen stood. Hunkering down, she hurried back to her spot, moving close to Jinny.

"I think I got it, Emma." Jinny looked over her shoulder, seeing Emma slip out of the rope. Turning, Emma settled on her knees, working on Jinny's rope. It took little time for Emma to release Jinny's hands, then move to Geneen's.

"Give up, Cliff. I know what you've done. You won't get away with it."

Emma's head snapped up. She recognized the deep, raspy sound. Jumping to her feet, she ran to the window, peering out.

"Emma!" Jinny came up beside her, tugging at her dress. "Get away from the window."

"I know that voice, Jinny." Emma couldn't see very far out of the small opening.

"Stay back, Boyd. You know I won't hesitate to shoot you." The angry voice of their captor had Emma ducking down as another round of gunfire split the air.

"There are men following me, Cliff. The sheriff and his men aren't that far behind."

"Brodie," Emma whispered. "Quinn and Blaine must be with him."

"And maybe Sam." Jinny's chest tightened, thinking Sam might ride right into danger, maybe death. "We have to warn them." She started for the door, stopping when Emma's hand clamped around her arm.

"No, Jinny. You have to stay inside where it's safe. The men will hear the gunfire."

"She's right, Jinny." Geneen scooted next to them. "It won't be long until they find us."

"Gunfire," Sam yelled, kicking his horse, knowing the others did the same.

The sound continued as the four men reined to a stop not far from a casita. Sam pulled out his field glasses, moving them from right to left, coming to a stop when he saw movement behind a cluster of rocks.

"Doggett is hiding behind those rocks. The other shooter is behind the casita."

"Just one, Sam?" Brodie asked, pulling out his six-gun.

"One is all I see." He continued looking, edging his horse to the left.

Quinn moved Warrior a few feet in front of the others, the reins in his left hand, one of his six-guns in his right. "It's time to end this, lads."

"Wait." Sam lowered the glasses, moving closer to the others. "There are three horses behind the casita."

"Let me see." Quinn reached out, taking the glasses from Sam. Focusing on the small structure, his breath caught. "Moonshine," he whispered, lowering the glasses.

"What?" Blaine took the glasses from Quinn's hand and looked through them. Lowering them, he glanced at Quinn, confirming what he'd seen. "It's Emma's horse." He looked at Brodie. "The others are Jinny's and Geneen's."

Brodie's jaw dropped, his features pinched in confusion. "What is my sister doing out here?"

"What are they *all* doing out here?" Quinn growled. "If those lasses are hurt..." He let the thought trail off. They all knew what would happen if any of the women were harmed.

Sam's chest squeezed at the thought of Jinny being inside. "They're smart. Assuming they're hiding in the casita, they'll stay down, away from windows. We surround the building and get the man Doggett's after." He took the glasses from Blaine, depositing them in his saddlebags before drawing his gun. He looked at Brodie and waited.

"He's right. Protecting our family means getting the man shooting at Doggett." Brodie glanced at each of them. "Ready?"

An instant later, they lined up, faces set, everything around them going still as they concentrated on what had to be done.

"Now." Brodie kicked Hunter into a gallop, Quinn on his right, Blaine and Sam on his left. All rode low over their saddles, guns aimed at the spot Sam had seen the shooter. No one spoke. No one had to as they raced ahead.

"Stay back, Boyd. I'll kill you the same as the others. It don't matter how long we've known each other."

"It doesn't have to end like this, Cliff. Give yourself up. I'll do what I can to help you."

He responded with a bitter laugh. "No thanks. I'll take my chances with you and everyone else."

Before Boyd could respond, a massive round of gunfire sounded, followed by a scream and shouting, then a low-pitched moan. One last shot rang out before everything went still, the wind passing through the trees the only sound.

The women waited, not knowing what to expect next. Sucking in a deep breath, Emma braced her hands on the floor and pushed up.

"We should go see—"

The door of the casita crashed open, followed by a gust of wind, then no sound at all.

Heart hammering in her chest, Emma took a tentative step forward, then another, her hands clenched at her sides. Scant feet from the door, she stopped, turning back to look at Jinny and Geneen.

Emma couldn't handle waiting any longer. She had to know what happened, who'd been shot. Biting her lower lip hard enough to draw blood, building up the courage to venture outside, she whipped back around, bouncing off the hard wall of flesh standing before her. Sucking in a shaky breath, she slowly raised her eyes.

"Quinn." A relieved cry broke from her lips.

Stepping up, he wrapped his arms around her. "Emma." Cupping her face with his hands, he tilted his head, lowering his mouth to hers.

"Well, I've seen enough." Jinny marched past them, placing a reassuring hand on Emma's back as she left, noticing they never broke their embrace. She hadn't made it two paces before coming face-to-face with Brodie.

"Ach, lass. What are you doing out here?" Her brother's voice was more scared than hard. She stepped into his open arms, sagging against him.

"I hate to admit it, but I was scared, Brodie."

"I know, lass." He pulled back, brushing a kiss across her forehead.

Jinny smiled up at Brodie, her eyes misting, then going wide when she spotted Sam behind him.

Clearing his throat, Sam took a couple steps toward her. "Jinny." His face broke into a relieved smile. "I'm glad you're all right."

They stared at each other, the air thick, neither allowing themselves to do more than look.

"Thank you, Sam," she whispered, her throat tightening.

"Now what?" Quinn's arm still held firm around Emma as they walked up behind Jinny, Geneen a few steps behind.

"I'm glad you were here."

They looked over to see Boyd Doggett walking toward them, his arms slack at his sides.

Brodie glared at him, fisted hands on his hips. "It would've been easier if you'd waited for me to release you from jail. We could've ridden out here together, rather than wasting time following you."

Boyd nodded. "I needed to do this myself. Track him down, see if he'd give himself up." He glanced at the motionless body as Blaine covered it with a blanket.

"Who is he?"

Boyd sucked in a heavy breath, his face crumbling into intense sorrow. "My cousin, Cliff Doggett."

Epilogue

Two weeks later...

"You seem quite happy, lass." Quinn leaned down, kissing his bride, feeling a sense of peace he hadn't expected. The decision to wed right away instead of waiting until August had been a good one.

After years of hoping, waiting, and loving this man, Emma couldn't contain her joy. Sending him a saucy smile, she laughed. "I believe I made a very wise decision in marrying you, Quinn MacLaren."

He laughed along with her, tugging Emma close to his side. "Aye, lass. I'll never argue the fact you're wise. More so than me."

"All right, you two. It's time to go inside and get ready for your trip."

Quinn wrapped his other arm around his mother. "Thank you, Ma. The wedding was perfect."

She brushed the compliment aside. "Ach. I've done no more than any another when her children marry." She swiped at a tear, her eyes sparkling. "Now, off with you."

They didn't need more encouragement before turning around and dashing inside.

The four elder MacLaren women, Kyla, Audrey, Lorna, and Gail, along with Emma's mother stood next to each other on the front porch of Audrey's home, each exhausted and happy. They'd worked together to make Quinn and Emma's wedding happen within the short time they'd been given.

After the scare with Cliff Doggett, the couple refused to be apart. Emma still shared a room with Jinny, but Quinn slept in Brodie's old room, unwilling to be the half mile away at his mother's house. Today, with the blessing of a good number of townspeople, they'd married at Quinn's home.

"Where are they, Ma?" Colin put an arm around his mother's shoulders, holding baby Grant in the other. "Certain, are you, they haven't started their honeymoon upstairs?" He laughed when Kyla swatted his chest.

"Ach, such language, and in front of your aunts. You still act as a brash young man, lad." She watched her grandson wiggle in Colin's arms, a sense of great contentment claiming her. "Give me the wee bairn while you go spend time with the other lads." She held out her welcoming arms, taking Grant, then turning toward the other women.

Shaking his head, Colin wasted no time finding Brodie, who stood with a group of other men, including Big Jim.

"Congratulations." Colin clasped him on the shoulder, then shook his hand.

"Thank you, Colin. Her mother and I knew we'd lose her someday. We just hadn't planned on it being so soon." Big Jim sipped his punch, more than pleased Blaine had added something to it.

"It was a good decision, working with Da and Uncle Ian to clear your debt." Brodie knew it had been hard for Big Jim to confess how he'd gotten into so much financial trouble. Ultimately, it had been the right choice.

"Having your family as partners is more than I could have hoped. After meeting with Lyman Ziller, hearing his offer, I'd have been a fool not to talk to Ewan and Ian. It was half of the first offer, which was far from fair. Now Gertie gets to stay in her home." He glanced at his wife, surrounded by her friends—their friends. "I know he did nothing illegal, offering an offensive price, but I can't help but think there's something crooked about what happened. If Cliff Doggett had lived, perhaps we would've found out if others were involved." Big Jim took a quick look at Boyd Doggett, who stood off to the side, watching the festivities, saying little. He'd been relieved when his foreman agreed to stay.

"Aye, but the man chose his own course. He could've dropped his gun, surrendered. Instead, he continued to shoot, giving us no choice. I promise you. I'll continue to ask questions, try to find someone who knew Ziller, maybe even who he works for.”

“I hear the man disappeared after Big Jim turned him down.” Colin kept watch on his ma, a grin spreading across his face at the joy she got showing off Grant.

“He did. And Sam hasn’t been able to find anything on the company he worked for. Allan Pinkerton is looking into it, too. I’m not giving up.” Between the disappearance of Ziller, no record of his company existing, and the strange conversation he had with Nate about a mystery man he’d seen in Chinatown, Brodie wouldn’t rest until he put all the pieces together. He didn’t want to see this happening to others in his town.

As if being summoned, Sam and Nate joined the men, making toasts and congratulating Big Jim.

“I understand Quinn and Emma will be riding into town, taking the morning steamboat south to Sacramento.” Sam stood next to Brodie, his eyes fastened on Jinny, who’d just stepped onto the porch.

“Aye. They’ll be staying at the Gold Dust tonight. Maggie and I will see them off tomorrow.” Brodie watched his wife join Jinny and Geneen. He still couldn’t quite believe his good fortune in marrying her.

Sam tilted his glass to his lips, casting another glance at Jinny. He didn't think he'd ever tire of looking at her, fantasizing about having her in his life. Not long after he joined Pinkerton's agency, he'd made a mistake with a young woman, telling himself lust was the same as love. They didn't marry, and the parting had been painful, a circumstance he never planned to repeat.

"She's a fine lass, Sam."

Sam's gaze shot to Brodie, seeing the amusement in his boss's eyes. "Jinny's an amazing young woman. More than most men deserve."

"Aye, she is. I have a feeling the lass may have an interest in one particular man."

Sam's response died on his lips when Quinn and Emma walked out of the house, holding hands, smiling at everyone. He'd been at Brodie's wedding, and now Quinn's. In his mind, the three MacLaren men who'd found the right women were fortunate beyond reason. They believed once you gave your heart, it was for life. Sam thought the same, also accepting he'd never be blessed with their good fortune.

Uncle Ewan wrapped Quinn in a hug, then kissed Emma on the cheek, turning them to the crowd.

"It is my pleasure to congratulate the newest MacLaren couple. Quinn and Emma." He hoisted his glass, yelling the MacLaren war cry in unison with the rest of his clan.

Brodie glanced over at Sam, seeing his friend's gaze still locked on Jinny. He wished the man would express his feelings, make his move, but Brodie would never push him. It had to be Sam's decision.

Sam cleared his throat. "I don't suppose you'd be interested in renegotiating our deal."

Cocking a brow, Brodie turned to him. "I'd be interested in what you have to say."

Nodding, Sam watched as Quinn kissed Emma, then helped her into their waiting carriage. His chest squeezed at the obvious love they shared.

"I might be willing to stay in Conviction a little longer. Given the right circumstances, of course."

Brodie chuckled. "Aye. The right circumstances are important. Would you care to share them with me?"

Sam nodded, swallowing the last drop of his punch, then laughed. "That I would, Sheriff. Yes. I very much would."

Thank you for taking the time to read Quinn's Honor. If you enjoyed it, please consider telling your friends or posting a short review. Word of mouth is an author's best friend and much appreciated.

Watch for book four, Sam's Legacy, in 2017.

Please join my reader's group to be notified of my New Releases at:
http://www.shirleendavies.com/contact-me.html

I care about quality, so if you find something in error, please contact me via email at
shirleen@shirleendavies.com

About the Author

Shirleen Davies writes romance—historical, contemporary, and romantic suspense. She grew up in Southern California, attended Oregon State University, and has degrees from San Diego State University and the University of Maryland. During the day she provides consulting services to small and mid-sized businesses. But her real passion is writing emotionally charged stories of flawed people who find redemption through love and acceptance. She now lives with her husband in a beautiful town in northern Arizona.

I love to hear from my readers.

Send me an email: shirleen@shirleendavies.com
Visit my Website: www.shirleendavies.com
Sign up to be notified of New Releases:
www.shirleendavies.com
Check out all of my Books:
http://www.shirleendavies.com/books.html
Comment on my Blog:
http://www.shirleendavies.com/blog.html
Follow me on Amazon:
http://www.amazon.com/author/shirleendavies
Follow my on BookBub:
https://www.bookbub.com/authors/shirleen-davies

Other ways to connect with me:

Facebook Author Page:
http://www.facebook.com/shirleendaviesauthor
Twitter: www.twitter.com/shirleendavies
Pinterest: http://pinterest.com/shirleendavies

Books by Shirleen Davies
Historical Western Romance Series
MacLarens of Fire Mountain

Tougher than the Rest, Book One
Faster than the Rest, Book Two
Harder than the Rest, Book Three
Stronger than the Rest, Book Four
Deadlier than the Rest, Book Five
Wilder than the Rest, Book Six

Redemption Mountain

Redemption's Edge, Book One
Wildfire Creek, Book Two
Sunrise Ridge, Book Three
Dixie Moon, Book Four
Survivor Pass, Book Five
Promise Trail, Book Six
Deep River, Book Seven, Releasing 2017

MacLarens of Boundary Mountain

Colin's Quest, Book One,
Brodie's Gamble, Book Two
Quinn's Honor, Book Three

Contemporary Romance Series

MacLarens of Fire Mountain

Second Summer, Book One
Hard Landing, Book Two
One More Day, Book Three
All Your Nights, Book Four
Always Love You, Book Five
Hearts Don't Lie, Book Six
No Getting Over You, Book Seven
'Til the Sun Comes Up, Book Eight, Releasing
2017

Peregrine Bay

Reclaiming Love, Book One
Our Kind of Love, Book Two

Find all my books at:

http://www.shirleendavies.com/books.html

Tougher than the Rest – Book One
MacLarens of Fire Mountain Historical Western Romance Series

"A passionate, fast-paced story set in the untamed western frontier by an exciting new voice in historical romance."

Niall MacLaren is the oldest of four brothers, and the undisputed leader of the family. A widower, and single father, his focus is on building the MacLaren ranch into the largest and most successful in northern Arizona. He is serious about two things—his responsibility to the family and his future marriage to the wealthy, well-connected widow who will secure his place in the territory's destiny.

Katherine is determined to live the life she's dreamed about. With a job waiting for her in the growing town of Los Angeles, California, the young teacher from Philadelphia begins a journey across the United States with only a couple of trunks and her spinster companion. Life is perfect for this adventurous, beautiful young woman, until an accident throws her into the arms of the one man who can destroy it all.

Fighting his growing attraction and strong desire for the beautiful stranger, Niall is more determined than ever to push emotions aside to focus on his goals of wealth and political gain. But looking into the clear, blue eyes of the woman who could ruin everything, Niall discovers he will have to harden his heart and be tougher than he's ever been in his life...Tougher than the Rest.

Faster than the Rest – Book Two

offering him another chance, or just another heartbreak?

As Jamie and Victoria struggle to uncover past secrets and come to grips with their shared passion, another danger arises. A life-altering danger that is out of their control and threatens to destroy any chance for a shared future.

Harder than the Rest – Book Three
MacLarens of Fire Mountain Historical Western Romance Series

"They are men you want on your side. Hard, confident, and loyal, the MacLarens of Fire Mountain will seize your attention from the first page."

Will MacLaren is a hardened, plain-speaking bounty hunter. His life centers on finding men guilty of horrendous crimes and making sure justice is done. There is no place in his world for the carefree attitude he carried years before when a tragic event destroyed his dreams.

Amanda is the daughter of a successful Colorado rancher. Determined and proud, she works hard to prove she is as capable as any man and worthy to be her father's heir. When a stranger arrives, her independent nature collides with the strong pull toward the handsome ranch hand. But is he what he seems and could his secrets endanger her as well as her family?

The last thing Will needs is to feel passion for another woman. But Amanda elicits feelings he thought were long buried. Can Will's desire for her change him? Or will the vengeance he seeks against the one man he wants to destroy—a dangerous opponent without a conscious—continue to control his life?

Stronger than the Rest – Book Four
MacLarens of Fire Mountain Historical Western Romance Series

"Smart, tough, and capable, the MacLarens protect their own no matter the odds. Set against America's rugged frontier, the stories of the men from Fire Mountain are complex, fast-paced, and a must read for anyone who enjoys non-stop action and romance."

Drew MacLaren is focused and strong. He has achieved all of his goals except one—to return to the MacLaren ranch and build the best horse breeding program in the west. His successful career as an attorney is about to give way to his ranching roots when a bullet changes everything.

Tess Taylor is the quiet, serious daughter of a Colorado ranch family with dreams of her own. Her shy nature keeps her from developing friendships outside of her close-knit family until Drew enters her life. Their relationship grows. Then a bullet, meant for another, leaves him paralyzed and determined to distance himself from the one woman he's come to love.

Convinced he is no longer the man Tess needs, Drew focuses on regaining the use of his legs and recapturing a life he thought lost. But danger of another kind threatens those he cares about—including Tess—forcing him to rethink his future.

Can Drew overcome the barriers that stand between him, the safety of his friends and family, and a life with the woman he loves? To do it all, he has to be strong. Stronger than the Rest.

Deadlier than the Rest – Book Five
MacLarens of Fire Mountain Historical Western Romance Series

"A passionate, heartwarming story of the iconic MacLarens of Fire Mountain. This captivating historical western romance grabs your attention from the start with an engrossing story encompassing two romances set against the rugged

Connor MacLaren's search has already stolen eight years of his life. Now he is close to finding what he seeks—Meggie, his missing sister. His quest leads him to the growing city of Salt Lake and an encounter with the most captivating woman he has ever met.

Grace is the third wife of a Mormon farmer, forced into a life far different from what she'd have chosen. Her independent spirit longs for choices governed only by her own heart and mind. To achieve her dreams, she must hide behind secrets and half-truths, even as her heart pulls her toward the ruggedly handsome Connor.

Known as cool and uncompromising, Connor MacLaren lives by a few, firm rules that have served him well and kept him alive. However, danger stalks Connor, even to the front range of the beautiful Wasatch Mountains, threatening those he cares about and impacting his ability to find his sister.

Can Connor protect himself from those who seek his death? Will his eight-year search lead him to his sister while unlocking the secrets he knows are held tight within Grace, the woman who has captured his heart?

Read this heartening story of duty, honor, passion, and love in book five of the MacLarens of Fire Mountain series.

Wilder than the Rest – Book Six
MacLarens of Fire Mountain Historical Western Romance Series

"A captivating historical western romance set in the burgeoning and treacherous city of San Francisco. Go along for the ride in this gripping story that seizes your attention from the very first page."

"If you're a reader who wants to discover an entire family of characters you can fall in love with, this is the series for you." – Authors to Watch

Pierce is a rough man, but happy in his new life as a Special Agent. Tasked with defending the rights of the federal government, Pierce is a cunning gunslinger always ready to tackle the next job. That is, until he finds out that his new job involves Mollie Jamison.

Mollie can be a lot to handle. Headstrong and independent, Mollie has chosen a life of danger and intrigue guaranteed to prove her liquor-loving father wrong. She will make something of herself, and no one, not even arrogant Pierce MacLaren, will stand in her way.

A secret mission brings them together, but will their attraction to each other prove deadly in their hunt for justice? The payoff for success is high, much higher than any assignment either has taken before. But will the damage to their hearts and souls be too much to bear? Can Pierce and Mollie find a way to overcome their misgivings and work together as one?

Second Summer – Book One
**MacLarens of Fire Mountain
Contemporary Romance Series**

"In this passionate Contemporary Romance, author Shirleen Davies introduces her readers to the modern day MacLarens starting with Heath MacLaren, the head of the family."

The Chairman of both the MacLaren Cattle Co. and MacLaren Land Development, Heath MacLaren is a success professionally—his personal life is another matter.

Following a divorce after a long, loveless marriage, Heath spends his time with women who are beautiful and passionate, yet unable to provide what he longs for . . .

Heath has never experienced love even though he witnesses it every day between his younger brother, Jace, and wife, Caroline. He wants what they have, yet spends his time with women too young to understand what drives him and too focused on themselves to be true companions.

It's been two years since Annie's husband died, leaving her to build a new life. He was her soul mate and confidante. She has no desire to find a replacement, yet longs for male friendship.

Annie's closest friend in Fire Mountain, Caroline MacLaren, is determined to see Annie come out of her shell after almost two years of mourning. A chance meeting with Heath turns into an offer to be a part of the MacLaren Foundation Board and an opportunity for a life outside her home sanctuary which has also become her prison. The platonic friendship that builds between Annie and Heath points to a future where each may rely on the other without the bonds a romance would entail.

the pilot training program are all she thought she wanted—until she discovered love with Trey MacLaren

Trey and Jesse's lives are filled with fast flying, friends, and the demands of their military careers. Lives each has settled into with a passion. At least until the day Trey receives a letter that could change his and Jesse's lives forever.

It's been over two years since Trey has seen the woman in Pensacola. Her unexpected letter stuns him and pushes Jesse into a tailspin from which she might not pull back.

Each must make a choice. Will the choice Trey makes cause him to lose Jesse forever? Will she follow her heart or her head as she fights for a chance to save the love she's found? Will their independent decisions collide, forcing them to give up on a life together?

One More Day – Book Three
MacLarens of Fire Mountain
Contemporary Romance Series

Cameron "Cam" Sinclair is smart, driven, and dedicated, with an easygoing temperament that belies his strong will and the personal ambitions he holds close. Besides his family, his job as head of IT at the MacLaren Cattle Company and his position as a Search and Rescue volunteer are all he needs to make him happy. At least that's what he thinks until he meets, and is instantly drawn to, fellow SAR volunteer, Lainey Devlin.

Lainey is compassionate, independent, and ready to break away from her manipulative and controlling fiancé. Just as her decision is made, she's called into a major search and rescue effort, where once again, her path crosses with the intriguing, and much too handsome, Cam Sinclair. But Lainey's plans are set. An opportunity to buy a flourishing preschool in northern Arizona is her chance to make a fresh start, and nothing, not even her fierce attraction to Cam Sinclair, will impede her plans.

As Lainey begins to settle into her new life, an unexpected danger arises —threats from an unknown assailant—someone who doesn't believe she belongs in Fire Mountain. The more

Lainey begins to love her new home, the greater the danger becomes. Can she accept the help and protection Cam offers while ignoring her consuming desire for him?

Even if Lainey accepts her attraction to Cam, will he ever be able to come to terms with his own driving ambition and allow himself to consider a different life than the one he's always pictured? A life with the one woman who offers more than he'd ever hoped to find?

All Your Nights – Book Four
**MacLarens of Fire Mountain
Contemporary Romance Series**

"Romance, adventure, cowboys, suspense—everything you want in a contemporary western romance novel."

Kade Taylor likes living on the edge. As an undercover agent for the DEA and a former Special Ops team member, his current assignment seems tame—keep tabs on a bookish Ph.D. candidate the agency believes is connected to a ruthless drug cartel.

Brooke Sinclair is weeks away from obtaining her goal of a doctoral degree. She spends time finalizing her presentation and relaxing with another student who seems to want nothing more than her friendship. That's fine with Brooke. Her last serious relationship ended in a broken engagement.

Her future is set, safe and peaceful, just as she's always planned—until Agent Taylor informs her she's under suspicion for illegal drug activities.

Kade and his DEA team obtain evidence which exonerates Brooke while placing her in danger from those who sought to use her. As Kade races to take down the drug cartel while protecting Brooke, he must also find common ground with the former suspect—a woman he desires with increasing intensity.

At odds with her better judgment, Brooke finds the more time she spends with Kade, the more she's attracted to the complex, multi-faceted agent. But Kade holds secrets he knows Brooke will never understand or accept.

Can Kade keep Brooke safe while coming to terms with his past, or will he stay silent, ruining any future with the woman his heart can't let go?

Always Love You— Book Five
MacLarens of Fire Mountain
Contemporary Romance Series

"Romance, adventure, motorcycles, cowboys, suspense—everything you want in a contemporary western romance novel."

Eric Sinclair loves his bachelor status. His work at MacLaren Enterprises leaves him with plenty of time to ride his horse as well as his Harley...and date beautiful women without a thought to commitment.

Amber Anderson is the new person at MacLaren Enterprises. Her passion for marketing landed her what she believes to be the perfect job—until she steps into her first meeting to find the man she left, but still loves, sitting at the management table—his disdain for her clear.

Eric won't allow the past to taint his professional behavior, nor will he repeat his mistakes with Amber, even though love for her pulses through him as strong as ever.

As they strive to mold a working relationship, unexpected danger confronts those close to them, pitting the MacLarens and Sinclairs against an evil who stalks one member but threatens them all.

Eric can't get the memories of their passionate past out of his mind, while Amber wrestles with feelings she thought long buried. Will they be able to put the past behind them to reclaim the love lost years before?

Hearts Don't Lie– Book Six
MacLarens of Fire Mountain
Contemporary Romance Series

Mitch MacLaren has reasons for avoiding relationships, and in his opinion, they're pretty darn good. As the new president of RTC Bucking Bulls, difficult challenges occur daily. He certainly doesn't need another one in the form of a fiery, blue-eyed, redhead.

Dana Ballard's new job forces her to work with the one MacLaren who can't seem to get over himself and lighten up. Their verbal sparring is second nature and entertaining until the night of Mitch's departure when he surprises her with a dare she doesn't refuse.

With his assignment in Fire Mountain over, Mitch is free to return to Montana and run the business his father helped start. The glitch in his enthusiasm has to do with one irreversible mistake—the dare Dana didn't ignore. Now, for reasons that confound him, he just can't let it go.

Working together is a circumstance neither wants, but both must accept. As their attraction grows, so do the accidents and strange illnesses of the animals RTC depends on to stay in business. Mitch's total focus should be on finding the reasons and people behind the incidents. Instead, he finds himself torn between his unwanted desire for Dana and the business which is his life.

In his mind, a simple proposition can solve one problem. Will Dana make the smart move and walk away? Or take the gamble and expose her heart?

No Getting Over You– Book Seven
**MacLarens of Fire Mountain
Contemporary Romance Series**

Cassie MacLaren has come a long way since being dumped by her long-time boyfriend, a man she believed to be her future. Successful in her job at MacLaren Enterprises, dreaming of one day leading one of the divisions, she's moved on to start a new relationship, having little time to dwell on past mistakes.

Matt Garner loves his job as rodeo representative for Double Ace Bucking Stock. Busy days and constant travel leave no time for anything more than the occasional short-term relationship—which is just the way he likes it. He's come to accept the regret of leaving the woman he loved for the pro rodeo circuit.

The future is set for both, until a chance meeting ignites long buried emotions neither is willing to face.

Forced to work together, their attraction grows, even as multiple arson fires threaten Cassie's new home of Cold Creek, Colorado. Although Cassie believes the danger from the fires is remote, she knows the danger Matt poses to her heart is real.

While fighting his renewed feelings for Cassie, Matt focuses on a new and unexpected opportunity offered by MacLaren Enterprises—an opportunity that will put him on a direct collision course with Cassie.

Will pride and self-preservation control their future? Or will one be strong enough to make the first move, risking everything, including their heart?

Redemption's Edge – Book One
Redemption Mountain – Historical Western Romance Series

"A heartwarming, passionate story of loss, forgiveness, and redemption set in the untamed frontier during the tumultuous years following the Civil War. Ms. Davies' engaging and complex characters draw you in from the start, creating an exciting introduction to this new historical western romance series."

"Redemption's Edge is a strong and engaging introduction to her new historical western romance series."

Dax Pelletier is ready for a new life, far away from the one he left behind in Savannah following the South's devastating defeat in the Civil War. The ex-Confederate general wants nothing more to do with commanding men and confronting the tough truths of leadership.

Rachel Davenport possesses skills unlike those of her Boston socialite peers—skills honed as a nurse in field hospitals during the Civil War. Eschewing her northeastern suitors and changed by the carnage she's seen, Rachel decides to accept her uncle's invitation to assist him at his clinic in the dangerous and wild frontier of Montana.

Now a Texas Ranger, a promise to a friend takes Dax and his brother, Luke, to the untamed territory of Montana. He'll fulfill his oath and return to Austin, at least that's what he believes.

The small town of Splendor is what Rachel needs after life in a large city. In a few short months, she's grown to love the people as well as the majestic beauty of the untamed frontier. She's settled into a life unlike any she has ever thought possible.

Thinking his battle days are over, he now faces dangers of a different kind—one by those from his past who seek vengeance, and another from Rachel, the woman who's captured his heart.

Wildfire Creek – Book Two
Redemption Mountain – Historical Western Romance Series

"A passionate story of rebuilding lives, working to find a place in the wild frontier, and building new lives in the years following the American Civil War. A rugged, heartwarming story of choices and love in the continuing saga of Redemption Mountain."

Luke Pelletier is settling into his new life as a rancher and occasional Pinkerton Agent, leaving his past as an ex-Confederate major and Texas

Ranger far behind. He wants nothing more than to work the ranch, charm the ladies, and live a life of carefree bachelorhood.

Ginny Sorensen has accepted her responsibility as the sole provider for herself and her younger sister. The desire to continue their journey to Oregon is crushed when the need for food and shelter keeps them in the growing frontier town of Splendor, Montana, forcing Ginny to accept work as a server in the local saloon.

Luke has never met a woman as lovely and unspoiled as Ginny. He longs to know her, yet fears his wild ways and unsettled nature aren't what she deserves. She's a girl you marry, but that is nowhere in Luke's plans.

Complicating their tenuous friendship, a twist in circumstances forces Ginny closer to the man she most wants to avoid—the man who can destroy her dreams, and who's captured her heart.

Believing his bachelor status firm, Luke moves from danger to adventure, never dreaming each step he takes brings him closer to his true destiny and a life much different from what he imagines.

Sunrise Ridge – Book Three
Redemption Mountain – Historical Western Romance Series

"The author has a talent for bringing the historical west to life, realistically and vividly, and doesn't shy away from some of the harder aspects of frontier life, even though it's fiction. Recommended to readers who like sweeping western historical romances that are grounded with memorable, likeable characters and a strong sense of place."

Noah Brandt is a successful blacksmith and businessman in Splendor, Montana, with few ties to his past as an ex-Union Army major and sharpshooter. Quiet and hardworking, his biggest challenge is controlling his strong desire for a woman he believes is beyond his reach.

Abigail Tolbert is tired of being under her father's thumb while at the same time, being pushed away by the one man she desires. Determined to build a new life outside the control of her wealthy father, she finds work and sets out to shape a life on her own terms.

Noah has made too many mistakes with Abby to have any hope of getting her back. Even with the changes in her life, including the distance she's built with her father, he can't keep himself from believing he'll never be good enough to claim her.

Unexpected dangers, including a twist of fate for Abby, change both their lives, making the tentative steps they've taken to build a relationship a distant hope. As Noah battles his past as well as the threats to Abby, she fights for a future with the only man she will ever love.

Dixie Moon – Book Four
Redemption Mountain – Historical Western Romance Series

Gabe Evans is a man of his word with strong convictions and steadfast loyalty. As the sheriff of Splendor, Montana, the ex-Union Colonel and oldest of four boys from an affluent family, Gabe understands the meaning of responsibility. The last thing he wants is another commitment— especially of the female variety.

Until he meets Lena Campanel...

Lena's past is one she intends to keep buried. Overcoming a childhood of setbacks and obstacles, she and her friend, Nick, have succeeded in creating a life of financial success and devout loyalty to one another.

When an unexpected death leaves Gabe the sole heir of a considerable estate, partnering with Nick and Lena is a lucrative decision...forcing Gabe and Lena to work together. As their desire grows, Lena refuses to let down her guard, vowing to keep her past hidden—even from a perfect man like Gabe.

But secrets never stay buried...

When revealed, Gabe realizes Lena's secrets are deeper than he ever imagined. For a man of his character, deception and lies of omission aren't negotiable. Will he be able to forgive the deceit? Or is the damage too great to ever repair?

Survivor Pass – Book Five
Redemption Mountain – Historical Western Romance Series

He thought he'd found a quiet life...

Cash Coulter settled into a life far removed from his days of fighting for the South and crossing the country as a bounty hunter. Now a deputy sheriff, Cash wants nothing more than to buy some land, raise cattle, and build a simple life in the frontier town of Splendor, Montana. But his whole world shifts when his gaze lands on the most captivating woman he's ever seen. And the feeling appears to be mutual.

But nothing is as it seems...

Alison McGrath moved from her home in Kentucky to the rugged mountains of Montana for one reason—to find the man responsible for murdering her brother. Despite using a false identity to avoid any tie to her brother's name, the citizens of Splendor have no intention of sharing their knowledge about the bank robbery which killed her only sibling. Alison knows her circle of lies can't end well, and her growing for Cash threatens to weaken the revenge which drives her.

And the troubles are mounting...

There is danger surrounding them both—men who seek vengeance as a way to silence the past...by any means necessary.

Promise Trail – Book Six
Redemption Mountain – Historical Western Romance Series

Bull Mason has built a life far away from his service in the Union Army and the ravages of the Civil War. He's achieved his dreams—loyal friends, work he enjoys, a home of his own, and a promise from the woman he loves to become his wife.

Lydia Rinehart can't believe how much her life has changed. Escaping captivity from a Crow village, she finds refuge and a home at the sprawling Redemption's Edge ranch...and love in the arms of Bull Mason, the ranch foreman. For the first time since her parents' death, she feels cherished and safe.

In an instant their dreams are crushed...

Bull is resolute in his determination to track down and rescue Lydia's brother, kidnapped during the celebration of their friend's wedding. He's made a promise—one he intends to keep. Picking the best men, they are ready to ride, until he's given an ultimatum.

Choices can seldom be undone...

As their journey continues, the trackers become the prey, finding their freedom and lives threatened.

And promises broken can rarely be reclaimed...

Can Bull and Lydia trust each other again and find their way to back to the dreams they once shared?

Reclaiming Love – Book One, A Novella
Peregrine Bay – Contemporary Romance Series

Adam Monroe has seen his share of setbacks. Now he's back in Peregrine Bay, looking for a new life and second chance.

Julia Kerrigan's life rebounded after the sudden betrayal of the one man she ever loved. As president of a success real estate company, she's built a new life and future, pushing the painful past behind her.

Adam's reason for accepting the job as the town's new Police Chief can be explained in one word— Julia. He wants her back and will do whatever is necessary to achieve his goal, even knowing his biggest hurdle is the woman he still loves.

As they begin to reconnect, a terrible scandal breaks loose with Julia and Adam at the center.

Will the threat to their lives and reputations destroy their fledgling romance? Can Adam identify and eliminate the danger to Julia before he's had a chance to reclaim her love?

369

Our Kind of Love – Book Two
Peregrine Bay – Contemporary Romance Series

Selena Kerrigan is content with a life filled with work and family, never feeling the need to take a chance on a relationship—until she steps into a social world inhabited by a man with dark hair and penetrating blue eyes. Eyes that are fixed on her.

Lincoln Caldwell is a man satisfied with his life. Transitioning from an enviable career as a Navy SEAL to becoming a successful entrepreneur, his days focus on growing his security firm, spending his nights with whomever he chooses. Committing to one woman isn't on the horizon— until a captivating woman with caramel eyes sends his personal life into a tailspin.

Believing her identity remains a secret, Selena returns to work, ready to forget about running away from the bed she never should have gone near. She's prepared to put the colossal error, as well as the man she'll never see again, behind her.

Too bad the object of her lapse in judgment doesn't feel the same.

Linc is good at tracking his targets, and Selena is now at the top of his list. It's amazing how a pair of sandals and only a first name can say so much.

As he pursues the woman he can't rid from his mind, a series of cyber-attacks hit his business, threatening its hard-won success. Worse, and unbeknownst to most, Linc harbors a secret—one with the potential to alter his life, along with those he's close to, in ways he could never imagine.

Our Kind of Love, Book Two in the Peregrine Bay Contemporary Romance series, is a full-length novel with an HEA and no cliffhanger.

Colin's Quest – Book One
MacLarens of Boundary Mountain – Historical Western Romance Series

For An Undying Love…

When Colin MacLaren headed west on a wagon train, he hoped to find adventure and perhaps a little danger in untamed California. He never expected to meet the girl he would love forever. He also never expected her to be the daughter of his family's age-old enemy, but Sarah was a MacGregor and the anger he anticipated soon became a reality. Her father would not be swayed, vehemently refusing to allow marriage to a MacLaren.

Time Has No Effect...

Forced apart for five years, Sarah never forgot Colin—nor did she give up on his promise to come for her. Carrying the brooch he gave her as proof of their secret betrothal, she scans the trail from California, waiting for Colin to claim her. Unfortunately, her father has other plans.

And Enemies Hold No Power.

Nothing can stop Colin from locating Sarah. Not outlaws, runaways, or miles of difficult trails. However, reuniting is only the beginning. Together they must find the courage to fight the men who would keep them apart—and conquer the challenge of uniting two independent hearts.

Brodie's Gamble – Book Two
MacLarens of Boundary Mountain – Historical Western Romance Series

Brodie MacLaren has a dream. He yearns to wear the star—bring the guilty to justice and protect those who are innocent. In his mind, guilty means guilty, even when it includes a beautiful woman who sets his body on edge.

Maggie King lives a nightmare, wanting nothing more than to survive each day and recapture the life stolen from her. Each day she wakes and prays for escape. Taking the one chance she may ever have, Maggie lashes out, unprepared for the rising panic as the man people believe to be her husband lies motionless at her feet.

Deciding innocence and guilt isn't his job.

Brodie's orderly, black and white world spins as her story of kidnapping and abuse unfold. The fact nothing adds up as well as his growing attraction to Maggie cause doubts the stoic lawman can't afford to embrace.

Can a lifetime of believing in absolute right and wrong change in a heartbeat?

Maggie has traded one form of captivity for another. Thoughts of escape consume her, even as feelings for the handsome, unyielding lawman grow.

As events unfold, Brodie must fight more than his attraction. Someone is after Maggie—a real threat who is out to silence her.

He's challenged on all fronts—until he takes a gamble that could change his life or destroy his heart.

Quinn's Honor – Book Three
MacLarens of Boundary Mountain – Historical Western Romance Series

Quinn MacLaren has one true love...Circle M, the family ranch. He makes it a habit of working hard and playing harder, spending time with experienced women who know he wants nothing more than their company. He buries the love he feels for one woman deep inside, knowing he'll never be the man she needs.

Emma Pearce is a true ranch woman, working long hours to help keep the family ranch thriving. Feisty, funny, and reliable, she's the girl all the single young men want—after they've sewn their wild oats. Few know Emma has her heart set on one man. A man who may never grow up enough to walk away from his wild ways and settle down.

When tragedy strikes, Quinn's right where he doesn't want to be—as temporary foreman of the Pearce ranch. Stepping in to fill Big Jim Pearce's shoes isn't easy. Neither is keeping his feelings for Emma hidden and his hands to himself. Honor-bound to do what is right, Quinn meets the challenge, losing Emma's friendship in the process.

Adding to Quinn's worries, something sinister is working its way through the thriving town of Conviction. Unforeseen forces are at work. Debt builds, families lose their ranches, and newcomers threaten to divide not only the land, but the people—including the Pearce family.

As events unfold, Quinn faces the difficult challenge of keeping his feelings for Emma hidden and his honor intact. Doing what he believes is right couldn't feel more wrong.

After all, what's a man without honor?

Find all of my books at:
http://www.shirleendavies.com/books.html